The Last Country

T0021299

THE
SEAGULL
LIBRARY OF
GERMAN
LITERATURE

The Last Country

SVENJA LEIBER

TRANSLATED BY NIKA KNIGHT

LONDON NEW YORK CALCUTTA

This publication was supported by a grant from
the Goethe-Institut, India.

Seagull Books, 2022

Originally published as Svenja Leiber, *Das Letzte Land*
© Suhrkamp Verlag, Berlin, 2014

All rights reserved and controlled through Suhrkamp Verlag, Berlin

First published in English by Seagull Books, 2017

English translation © Nika Knight, 2017

Published as part of the Seagull Library of German Literature, 2022

ISBN 978 1 8030 9 001 6

Typeset by Seagull Books, Calcutta, India
Printed and bound by WordsWorth India, New Delhi, India

For K.D.

Contents

I

1911–1917

The women harvest plums. Already another summer, sun like oil on canvas, laundry whitening. The women pluck and gather. They discuss Ruven, the younger son of the wainwright, Preuk. The boy has been standing between the field and the road since morning, and doesn't stir. 'Does God even know,' they say, 'what to do with such a child?'

Ruven Preuk stands apart from the village, on an August day in 1911, and listens. He counts the rhythm that the light and the poplars beat, light, dark, light. Everywhere the fields are blooming, German, Protestant, and muted by the heat. A lull in the ripened oats—and in this silence a *lala* and *lalay*, not quite audible, first distant, then closer and closer. Ruven tilts his head and closes his eyes. Then he twitches his fingers: the right ones follow the rhythm, the play between light and shadow, the left ones the song, *lala, lalay*. Now he raises his arms, he conducts. The women turn their backs and wipe the sweat from their faces. Just lying about and flailing doesn't lead to anything, they think, the basket won't be filled that way.

Two wooden carriages with tired draught animals approach the road. The first is driven with one hand by a man. He leans against the body of the wagon as if asleep. A woman in a skirt and red jacket drives the second; she's the one singing. A pack of teenagers from the village march behind it, one, two, one, two, they've also been lurking since morning, led by Fritz Dordel with his otter-face and too-short trousers. The caravan passes loudly by Ruven like a parade; the path is darkened by the figures as well as the woman's mocking songs, rage and triumph, she bares her teeth and cracks the whip to her side as well as at Fritz, who is now almost halfway onto her carriage. Hardly a hair on his face, he plainly fingers the hem of her skirt. Her bare foot kicks him off the prow and he falls backwards into the oats. Enraged, he picks himself up and follows the carriage into the village.

Ruven watches them go. Here they are, finally. He'd hoped that they were coming. Fritz wanted him to stay there on the lookout, as always, but this time he didn't want to. It's a special day, a day like this only happens once a year, and he'd like to follow them but his father arrives just then at the ford, squeezed closely on either side between the bushes. His father shouldn't catch him near the otter. Ruven steps behind the trunk of the nearest poplar. Well, old Preuk doesn't see him and drives his bay horses further through the soft sand. The reins rub the foam from their coats. The cartload clatters because the wagon must climb the slope. Nils Preuk dismounts and pushes from behind. At the top, he is riding along again and doesn't notice his boy jumping on. He only turns around because the clattering has quieted and he thinks that the load has fallen off, but there sits his son, his head as blond as cauliflower, saying, 'They're here again,' and then he's seated himself next to Nils.

'Who?'

'The fiddler and Sofie.'

'They were earlier last year,' says Nils and is quiet for a moment. 'This Sofie, always from farm to farm. Turning every head with her singsong. Even Röver. And those eyes! Double poison,' he says and stares intently ahead.

Farmer Röver's hand had gotten caught in the well's hand crank because of Sofie's songs. Four of his fingers were later brought to the pastor. But the pastor also hadn't known where to put them and so had pocketed and then forgotten them. In the afternoon, while discussing a baptism, he nearly fainted as his left hand suddenly grasped the cold fingers in his pocket and in the next moment realized what he was kneading—all while he spoke to the baptizand's mother, with a heavenward gaze and breathless voice, of the Lutheran afterlife. He then buried the four fingers in the young Röver's family plot. 'It's never gone too far for the woman,' he sang quietly as he did it, the schnapps he'd been handed for assistance pounding wildly through his veins.

The wainwright's workshop sits behind the village. The house isn't grand, but one could inherit less than a brick building with an acre and a well, all of it circled from morning to night by Wilder the ram. Wilder, because of his large testicles, considers himself the biggest around. He butts down anything standing upright: a short warm-up, a couple of leaps, and it's finished. Then he stands, silent, staring stupidly at his victim.

'He'll be castrated,' says Nils, grinding his teeth, whenever he's the one chased down, but he always lets him go. He lets the ram with his double-twisted horns into the pen and doesn't castrate him, as if by secret arrangement.

Now he unhitches the bay horses and unloads the cart. In the workshop it smells of tar. Nils scratches his beard. 'Yes, clear out,' he says to Ruven, who is standing before him with pleading eyes. 'But don't forget to deliver the pigeons to the Klunkenhöker woman.' The Klunkenhöker woman is the richest woman in the region, and she is always hungry for pigeons. Everyone in the village wants to sell her something, but for well-known reasons she prefers the pigeons of the little Preuk. The boy is beautiful, they say.

Ruven runs to the village square. He has just forgotten the Klükenhoker woman, or at least pushed thoughts of her aside, when he sees the two wooden carriages and remembers from last year how it smells in one of them.

Sweet and like a woman, thinks Ruven, although he understands nothing of such things. He had been on the other side of Sofie's door only once, because she had beckoned him over. And then she had only sat there and laughed and given him a piece of bread with jam and allowed him a single glimpse of her shin, while the boys from the village had piled against the window, Fritz Dordel at the forefront. But Ruven only thought, what do I do with a shin? And flushed almost as red as Sofie's jacket, which looked so shabby up close.

The carriages stand in shadows, slightly diagonal to each other, and Joseph, the old fiddler, has chased the otter away and fed the ponies. He leans now on the oak, where he keeps an ear out, smokes, and considers the square. His grey hair is bound in a braid and his sore eyes squint. It's widely believed that he comes from the Black Sea, perhaps also from Italy—from far away, in any case. Next to him stands Farmer Jacobs, here to represent the community and monitor everything with precision.

'If you don't cobble the street soon, I'm going to America,' says Joseph and spits out tobacco.

'If that's your stance,' says Jacobs as he pockets the money for the hay, 'we can also go on without you.' But with that, he grins, and Joseph grins, too, flashing a golden tooth as if he wants to dazzle Jacobs with it. But then he turns disdainfully to the ponies and mutters, they really need something decent, like oats, for example. At that, Jacobs hopes for an additional transaction, perhaps involving something like the gold on Joseph's tooth, but Joseph waves dismissively and says, 'This is fine, and if not, Satan will pull the wagon. You just have to cobble the street, then I can also hitch up a goat,' and he makes two horns with his index fingers. Then he suddenly notices a heartening sight. He has discovered the boy loitering close by, and waves him over. Ruven smiles cautiously. He comes to stroke the ponies and also to get a bit closer, and he carefully pats dust out of their hides.

'You want to see them?' asks Joseph, 'Come closer, quietly!' A small bow, and then Ruven is already blushing red again, thinking he will have to look at Sofie's shin once more. But Joseph is not that kind of man; he earned his gold tooth a different way. With his own talents he made people soft and pliable, they wanted nothing more than to shower him with money—in any case, this is how he tells it. He spins a key on a ribbon so that it whirs and beckons Ruven to follow him.

It's dim inside the carriage.

'Eyes closed,' says Joseph. He takes a top hat from the shelf on the wall. It is not actually a top hat but he calls it that when Sofie has to brush it out.

'What do you have there?' Asks Ruven and shuts his eyelids, or at least attempts to.

'What indeed,' whispers Joseph, and then: 'Eyes open!' Ruven can just barely detect something when the thing glistens red-gold and Joseph pulls it, with a small flourish, completely out of the hat: 'A violin!' He places it at his throat and begins fiddling. Then he holds the violin out to Ruven: 'Here, play!' But Ruven doesn't know how, two steps backwards and two forwards again, he'd actually like to, he thinks and takes the violin, the bow in his right hand, and scrapes quickly, once.

'You play like the cow shits,' says Farmer Jacobs, who is leaning on the window. Ruven spins around and glares at him.

'Hey!' Joseph gestures threateningly with the top hat and to Ruven he repeats, 'Play!' And then something like a screech comes out—at least it's better than mere cow shit— and the melody finally softens and becomes almost pretty.

'I say,' Joseph gazes at him softly. 'I see something in the distance.' Then he whispers, 'I see these notes, too!' He pulled Ruven tightly to him. 'Infernal brother, what are you doing to me. I see it blue and green and yellow, when I play! It rises up from the violin in front of me, like steam! And I think, you're delirious, Joseph, no one will believe it! You're fantasizing!' Thoughtfully, he strokes his hair down to the braid as he inspects Ruven.

'I believe you,' says Ruven quietly and with a shaking hand puts the violin back in the hat, which Joseph is now holding in front of his nose.

'Good,' he says, 'and now bye, bye, come back again tomorrow, I'm too tired today. I still have a whole evening in front of me.' He opens the carriage door. 'Now, disappear! And tell your father I need a new wheel. The last one didn't hold long.'

Ruven sets off. He walks along the field behind the farm, and just when he hopes to squeeze through the hedge the pigeons flutter from the rooftop, as if sensing the danger. 'I'm still bringing you to the Klunkenhöker woman,' murmured Ruven, 'She thinks the baron's pigeons are much better for her, anyhow, that they're of higher rank.' He enters the stable and holds his slingshot. 'I can wait a long time for you.' And what else but wait? The Klünkenhoker woman isn't doing anything either. No one knows where her money comes from. Perhaps it was a dragedukke—a fairy chest which always has a little money for a person to take—or another kind of spirit in a box, they say, as she always has money, and she buys and accepts deliveries, and that is why Mother Preuk sends her son over every two weeks with five pigeons. The money from that goes in the chest, and the mother hopes a little bit that at one point a thaler will be included onto which something invisible is attached, as she will then only have to close the top of the chest and not let the money spirit escape again.

Ruven has already gone a good portion of the way, he is walking so fast now. As he goes, he softly sings *da* and *dee* because he doesn't want to lose the notes. He must nab the pigeons before they go to sleep. They sit by the hundreds on the gables of the workers' houses on the estate, resting from their eternal around-and-around-in-a-circle, and Ruven has to go down through there, anyhow, when he goes to the Klünkenhoker woman. Five could easily be pulled off; it would be as smooth as plucking and it would be fast and silent. And if there happens to be too many men standing around who might wonder to themselves about the plucking of aristocratic pigeons, then he'll duck into the woods and fetch the wild ones from the linden trees.

'Bring me more of this kind next time,' says the Klünkenhoker woman, unsuspecting, when Ruven hands her the wild pigeons. 'The fat ones with the blue feet are especially good.' Then she always spends a long while taking him in, from top to bottom: beginning with his white-blonde hair, across his face, lingering in the two nearly translucent eyes and the black freckle above his mouth. The Klünkenhoker woman then breathes through her nose, whistling in and out, and her gaze wanders farther, across the slender boyish chest, over the short trousers and the stick-straight legs, all the way down to his naked feet. Then she crosses herself—the Klünkenhoker woman is Catholic—and sends Ruven home. The dead birds dangle head over heels beside her skirt.

Back at the house, Ruven squats outside below the window and listens in on the mood. Most of the time, the mood isn't good. Mother Preuk and Gesche, her ward, are rarely in agreement. Gesche is seventeen by now and she knows what she wants, as well as—above all else—what she doesn't.

'What are you always whining about? You're like a wrench looking for its bolt when you whine like that,' says the mother. 'Finish the stew and come here!' She removes her apron, pushes the ladle over to her husband and gives John, her eldest, a comforting nod, as she knows how attached he is to Gesche. But Gesche only goes on moaning and standing, and doesn't sit down.

Nils Preuk sets the ladle aside and rises so slowly and so threateningly that Mother Preuk has a lot of time to think.

'Gi-irl!' says Nils. At that, Gesche finally sits and bows her head, and keeps crying only because she'd wanted so badly to go with Werner the farmhand to hear the music in the village, and because now he surely thinks that she would perhaps have rather gone with someone else. Gesche's back shakes with sobs. Her braid shakes, too, heavy as a rope and so long that she can sit on it.

'You mustn't eavesdrop on Werner's thoughts,' says Mother Preuk, and then, 'Amen.' And Nils, too, silently sits back down on his chair and eats one serving, and then another.

'That Werner doesn't think,' he says, and later, 'Where's the boy?'

And although she's still sobbing, Gesche starts up again, 'He's with the musicians, you must pay attention to him or he'll run off with them.'

'Not him,' says Nils and stands up again, goes to the door, and looks a bit disquieted, despite himself, as he stands on the lookout for Ruven.

Mother Preuk shakes her head. 'How you always have to jump up. I'm eating like an animal and I still can't keep pace. You, Gesche, put something on to warm for the boy and bring Werner something in his room.'

'I won't bring anything to Werner,' says Gesche and clears the table, at which point Greta Preuk raises her hand but doesn't slam it down, since John looks so melancholy, and she herself is fond of Gesche, despite all the suffering, as Gesche has lived in the wainwright's home since she was small. Her father, the brick-maker, had suddenly died one day. 'It was the look,' said the villagers, always so much faster with their mouths than with their minds, 'that certain look'—and then silence, to give the sentence more weight.

The brick-maker, as far as they knew, had begun an affair with the magpie. They had named her that not only because she had black hair with two snow-white streaks above her brow. 'She steals,' people said, 'and she had, with her own father . . . well . . . ' and then demonstrated what they meant with their fingers.

The magpie lived with her father at the edge of the forest. They weren't from the area and also disappeared soon after what happened to the brick-maker. Everyone suspected her for a long time afterwards, just as they had from the beginning. They took hold of the mud just like a baker does his dough. That had almost helped. That had almost allowed a few of their own sins, the ones committed over the course of a lifetime, to be forgotten. The village had felt itself to be almost cleaner and more devout after the magpie was on her way, and everything would have turned out fine if the brick-maker's wife hadn't lost her mind because she believed that her husband had been with the magpie, each time, before he had been with her. In her pain, she had ripped the hair from her forehead in exactly the place where the magpie had her white.

'Leave the hair,' Mother Preuk had said, 'Truly, what could the hair have to do with it?' And then she had given the brick-maker's wife a harsh look, although she hadn't meant at all to be so harsh. But the poor one had simply kept tearing at her hair and didn't want to live any more until she finally climbed the village oak, higher and higher, just a bit more, and at last tried to fly. And that's when Gesche was left behind and went to Mother Preuk, and that was fine, if also a bit hard—just like Mother Preuk herself. 'It comes from the weather,' she says of herself. 'Summer is good, but the winter, too, has its way.' Now she lets a hand drop, because Ruven is coming through the kitchen door, and he silently lays the money from the Klunken-höker woman on the table.

'He is something special,' Greta Preuk whispered to her Nils one night. 'He must learn something proper; the cane said so.'

Greta Preuk has a wise cane that can be neither burnt nor destroyed, and at times she has to take it with her on certain secret journeys and learn many things that would otherwise stay hidden. But Nils only answered, 'He's going to primary school and then learning the wheel-making trade with John. And what your walking stick thinks about that doesn't interest me.' He then turned to the wall. He was, however, a little bit interested, as the next morning he'd seized Ruven by the neck and beaten him thoroughly, seeming almost detached, and Greta Preuk had seen it and knocked on the weatherglass, and then gone to the garden to take a deep breath.

'What do you actually want with our Werner?' she says now to Gesche, 'He can't dance at all, the way he is. Or can you do the laundry with one arm?' But she says this warmly, to help Gesche calm down. Perhaps Werner had ruined the arm for good. While soused one night he had stuck it in the forge, and the whole workshop had reeked like a tannery he was burnt so badly. And then they all thought, that's it, but that wasn't it; instead, it had begun to ooze. Mother Preuk had had Gesche pick comfrey and yarrow and then, murmuring, she spread it with a stick over Werner's arm, and it had given him the creeps to be so alone with her.

'He won't sneak around so easily today,' says Nils from the doorway, 'And if he runs off anyhow, he'll get the switch. The boy is needed here!'

'But the music is only here today, once in a year! And everyone is going,' says Gesche and starts to cry yet again.

'Then go with John or Ruven,' says Mother Preuk, thinking to herself that this won't work, and Ruven thinks it too: Not with Gesche, but I'd still like to go. A tiny violin is dancing in his mind's eye, and he shakes his head but nothing changes, the violin won't leave. It plunges into his thoughts like the bullet in Farmer Jacob's thigh, the bullet he collected during the battue in the year 1905.

'Do I look like a wild pig?' He had shrieked at the time, and shrieking is something Farmer Jacobs never does. But he took the matter of the wild pig to heart, despite himself, so that piggish stuff was almost the only stuff that came out of his mouth, especially when the wind came from the east and the bullet in his thigh had something to say.

'It roams,' says the pastor whenever he hears Jacob's maledictions, 'such things always roam, when you talk such filth! It travels to the heart, as if to a magnet, and then it gives up the ghost.'

Ruven sits down silently at the table and eats.

'And what's gotten into you?' asks the mother. But Ruven remains silent. Outside, something like a blackbird trills from the hedge and an answer comes from the roof, and amid the birdcalls they hear the ram at the gate. His driving bleats make Gesche blush, and she takes a plate and brings it to Werner in his room. And then despite everything she has a nice evening, if one without dance music. She even does a little waltz; at any rate it squeaks beautifully through the twilight, Werner has left the window ajar and everyone overhears.

Ruven has still said not a word. He taps the fork against his cup, closes his eyes—but it doesn't have anything to do with his eyes. It's more like he's seeing the colours with his ears. Until today, the clouds and shapes that arrange themselves in the air when he hears anything weren't something he would call colours at all. It was only when Joseph began to speak of them that Ruven began to realize that it isn't always like this, that there are also colourless notes and that one might have reason to be worried when such a colourful dance emerges when the milkmaids start to sing, or when he hears the blackbird, or even when his fork simply clinks against his cup. And how the dance goes, later, when the bats hunt thick above their heads and Ruven stands with John and their parents at the edge of the square while in the middle Joseph plays. Taut as his bow, the string player arches his back and flourishes the violin as if the music required it, as if he were about to throw himself onto his instrument. And the Sofie woman spins herself along with it with a hip- and a heel-step so that the men tilt their hats low across their faces and hide their eyes in shadow.

Nils Preuk turns around. 'It's jangling my nerves,' he says, 'I won't be able to sleep after this.'

Who wants to sleep now, thinks Ruven, and watches his father leave. I don't ever want to sleep again, if it means I can learn the violin.

It's cold the next morning when Ruven walks from the wainwright's to the village square. He had given Wilder a swat between his horns with a cane as the ram emerged from the elderberry bush. 'Get lost,' Ruven had said and then in the next moment felt ashamed, for Wilder was genuinely spoilt. From afar, he already spots the carriages, the doors are still closed, the windows covered. There is only a plume of smoke ascending from a stovepipe.

Joseph boils acorn coffee. Anyone who wants to make him happy gives him real coffee, but the farmers keep to themselves. They hate him, in fact, because he's not from here and because he does card tricks and conjures forth the future from his sleeves. And then there's that macabre shadow puppetry! On the other hand, he has stories to tell and buys hay and more, and he can make music, they'd heard that. Now Joseph brings the cup right under his nose and looks more or less pleased. He opens the drape with his left hand and sees the boy arrive.

'Do you want coffee?' He shouts out the door. Ruven shakes his head and pulls a flask of birch sap out from under his shirt. He had tapped it for days up in the trees, where no otter-face could see the bottles hanging. The birch sap is somewhat valuable. It is clear and very sweet. Joseph smiles, pleased. He pulls the flask towards him, turns it in his hands and nods: 'Ah, I understand. Well, get yourself in here!' He gestures behind himself to the shelf where the hat with the opening at the top is sitting. 'But don't maul any strings, or I'll send you off to where they'll fry your hands.' He hadn't needed to say it. In a hundred years, no one had handled a violin as gingerly as the boy's hands were doing now. 'Where did he get these hands, eh? Did you do it with a rabbit? Those are little paws,' Nils says from time to time. 'How is he supposed to swing a hammer? Or do you rub him with ointment in secret, with your soft mother's heart?' And then Greta laughs, her bosom quaking under her dress, for there was some truth to his words—she would have gladly done that, in any case.

'I'm listening,' says Joseph and cups a hand behind his ear. 'Now do it already, she'll show you where she wants your fingers!' Joseph leans back. He combs his fingers through his hair and chuckles to himself. 'Dirty joke,' he says, 'I'm showing my age. They shoot through my mind like a meteor shower in August. Even in prayer, Mary, even then! But you don't know anything about that, well, play!' Very quietly, Ruven attempts a stroke. It drags and sounds like the wind across the bottles that Mother Preuk had buried next to the vegetables to protect against moles. 'Don't be so frightened!' As you like, thinks Ruven, and presses a bit firmer as he pulls the bow more quickly back and forth.

'In a half-moon!' says Joseph, 'Always in a half-moon, otherwise the bow will fly over your shoulder when you quicken the tempo. A half-moon, I said!' Ruven attempts it. 'What's your name again?' asks Joseph.

'Ruven.'

'Ruven? Are you your father's first son?'

'The second.'

'What kind of name is that then, what was your father thinking? What is there to be said? Ruven is always the name of the first son! But play now, come on, I see you'll become good, boy. Not as good as I am, forget that, not as the second-born, but still good.' He looks out of the window. 'I'm growing old,' says Joseph. 'Every day I tell myself, Papa Joseph, you're growing old, nothing more. But do you think that makes it easier? It doesn't. Give me the little one, give it here! Do you hear the ponies outside?'

Ruven asks if he can feed them.

'You can. And bang on Sofie's carriage, you can do that too. The cat! She should get up. The leader of your townspeople promised me a late-season cherry tree. I'm allowed to pick one, even on Sundays, he said. Well, I'm sending my cat up the tree as long as she can manage it.'

The tree grows in the alleyway, just before the third bend. Ruven feeds the ponies quickly and follows the two at a slight distance. Sofie has tied up her skirt and climbs to the top of the giant cherry tree, almost uncannily, and throws the fruit to Joseph and his wide basket underneath. Some, she eats.

'Not too many,' mutters the old man as he also takes a few for himself from the basket. They spit the pits into the grass, and Ruven's mouth begins to water. Then Sofie leaps down from the tree. Her hair had been contained in a bun behind her neck, and now she undoes the ribbon and shakes her head so that the strands hang to the backs of her knees. 'The beauty of a woman lies in the length of her hair,' says Mother Preuk each Saturday and rubs egg and beer into Gesche's plait. However, what Sofie has hanging from her head here is much more than simply beautiful.

'Twelve o'clock and you're home,' the father had said. Ruven hears the church bells wailing from the neighbouring village, one, two, nine, ten, and he takes off. At twelve, he is already at the crossing, there he must dodge Peter, Röver's son, such a permanent fixture of the village, as he cries after him: 'Bye, bye . . . Pay attention that your eyes don't turn black, like all those foreigners'.'

At home, Nils Preuk is standing at the door. He turns his head once towards the front vestibule, looks at the clock—blue numerals on white enamel—and nods. He himself is always there shortly before the clock chimes. It's because of his birth; he was born shortly before the annexation of Prussia.

'Your mother needs water,' he says, as Ruven stands breathlessly before him. He walks into the courtyard, completely forgetting Wilder. After a prolonged approach, the ram leaps into ambush and knocks him so hard in the backs of his knees that Ruven lands beside the fountain. 'Oh, you'll suffer!' Ruven says, like an old man, then grabs a piece of wood from the pile and slams it against the ram's front leg. The powerful body buckles without a sound. The animal extends the unhurt leg, attempts to rear up, falls on his side so that his large balls are strikingly displayed, and rolls his marble eyes in bewilderment. Ruven stares at Wilder and says, 'Stand up!' But the ram doesn't stand up again.

'And I say once again, don't let him go to the string player any more, he won't make him any better. But he didn't want to hear that!' Farmer Jacobs sits with the others in the Heidkrug pub, at the large table with the window, and shakes his head. His Sunday haircut, like everyone else's here, is a mess. 'He goes too far! He's like a geyser, exploding like something has been cooking inside him for too long. I hadn't expected that.'

'If there's something to be expected, he's done it,' says Werner, who had run to the village extraordinarily fast, with his putrid arm, to bring help before the wainwright Preuk killed his son on a holy Sunday.

They had required three men, the rowdy otter running ahead of the others—no one knew why he hung onto Ruven like a wet nurse—three men to take the Preuk fellow off of his boy. They met soon after in the Heidkrug pub in order to recover from the fright.

'I'll drive your fiddling soul right out! he kept shouting,' says Werner, referring to Preuk, who had suddenly attacked his son like the north wind on the apple blossoms.

'And all of that, just because of an old ram! As if the ram meant more than his son.'

'Well, say something!' Nils Preuk sits on the footstool next to his boy's bed and wanders over the bedcovers with his rough fingers. He'd never done that before. Beside him stands his wife, hands up on her hips, with so much contempt in her eyes that it would have made him cold if he wasn't smouldering inside from shame.

'I'll go now and get the rope,' he says finally, after a silence broken only by sighs, and stands up.

'You'll get Düwel,' says the mother, 'you're going to go and get the pastor!'

But that wouldn't be necessary, as Nils has barely left the room when Ruven opens his eyes and looks for a long time at his mother. Then he stares for a longer while still at the wall opposite, as if his guardian angel himself was standing there, although nothing at all is standing there, but instead much more of a something is hanging there, and Ruven thinks he's dreaming, as Mother Preuk follows his gaze and nods: 'That Joseph fellow left it here for you. It's blessed, he said, you shouldn't break it.'

The mother takes the violin off the nail and lays it in front of Ruven on top of the blanket.

Without a look, he plucked the four strings: 'Good Dogs Always Eat.' He ran his fingers over the varnish. He traced over the scroll and the smooth neck.

'Papa says you may go to the cantor and study the violin, if you don't die today.' The mother wipes something from her cheek.

'What has death got to do with me?' Says Ruven quietly and smiles weakly, before he falls asleep again.

The mother goes to make the pastor coffee, because he'd otherwise be coming by in vain. He should, however, say something more to Nils and give him a bit of his mind, in a holy way, she thinks as she takes the heavy waffle iron and lays it in the oven to warm. She cracks seven eggs into the bowl; today will not be saved.

'My God, Nils,' says the Pastor later, and his bulging eyes look baffled. 'If it had at least been for the sake of the dear Lord, as Abraham was commanded, or at least for the lamb, but to do this for a kind of German ram! Why are you acting like your Wilder? You should be peaceful. Or do you believe that Charles the Great flogged the heathens here just for fun?' The pastor makes a pious face in which he purses his lips and thinks a bit about Charles the Great, before he spreads raspberry compote on his waffle, the jam spilling over on every side.

'He promised to allow the boy to go to the cantor, when he can get up again.' Mother Preuk seats herself across from the pastor. Her cheeks are always flushed because she has a mass of tiny veins.

'To the cantor? But he doesn't play the violin. But old Dordel, he plays the violin, send him over to Uwe. That should be good enough for his first lesson. And eventually he will have to go to the city, to a real teacher, in the event that he has talent.'

'He has,' says Nils, 'he has.' And it's not only his guilty conscience that is making him think it, but also the gleam in Joseph's eye as he held the violin out to him.

'I must be off,' the pastor wants to go. 'You both must not miss a single Sunday until Christmas, and bring Gesche and Werner and the two boys along with you, too. Then the Lord in his satiety . . .' confused, the pastor gazes at his empty plate, ' . . . and his mercy and so on.'

Nils nods, 'Yes, yes.'

As the pastor walks out the door, a swallow flies close to his head. 'Rain is coming,' he says, 'we could use it.'

'Yes,' says Mother Preuk, 'the cane also predicted it.'

'You shouldn't consult the cane,' the pastor says sternly. But the first heavy drops are already falling across the path. Mother Preuk reaches for an umbrella for the pastor. She smiles innocently.

It's half an hour by foot to Uwe Dordel's house. Ruven often walks there with the otter Fritz, who asks him this and that and steals sidelong glances at him and even carries the violin case that Ruven's father built for him, and which looks like a child's coffin. Ruven doesn't say much, but when he does say something Fritz repeats it, slowly, as if he would like to memorize it.

Sometimes Farmer Röver also gives Ruven a ride in his wagon. He takes the same path, although why he does isn't quite clear. Röver lives in the middle of the village. At times, though, he drives elsewhere, with his hair handsomely combed, and then he chauffeurs Ruven, because Röver with his six fingers has difficulty bringing the horses to a stop. They barely speak during the drive, and Ruven likes it that way, since his head is filled with notes anyhow. He has to learn everything now, keys and circle of fifths, without the proper education. Dordel bluffs a bit himself, and declares: 'Oh well, no one hears the end anyhow!' But Ruven wants to have it explained to him anyway, for the sake of professionalism.

Before the lesson, Ruven hands Ils Dordel the honey that Nils collects from the bees he keeps near the lilac bush. Or, for a change, he gives him two or three little pigeons— because Uwe Dordel is not the Klunkenhöker woman with her hungry eyes, Ruven is willing to sacrifice something for Dordel—even when it becomes difficult. The birds have now all known him since before they hatched from the egg, after all. He takes two at random, snaps their necks and sticks them in his linen sack, which Ils tactfully takes away to the kitchen. Then Ruven and Uwe Dordel clear off to the good parlour.

After six weeks, they're already playing duets. The Dordels' sheepdog puppy sits in front of the parlour door

and yowls with its snout raised, as if the notes mean something to him, too. And yet one day Dordel puts the violin
to his throat and doesn't play, but holds it in. 'You should
have been my son,' he says quietly. 'You'd be better for us
than Fritz, who is just such a rough child.' Ruven listens to
the ticking of the clock and the single dry flutter of the eye
of the peacock's feather; the bird had gotten lost and found
itself in the parlour, and it now exhausted itself against the
windowpane. Sympathy for Fritz rises in his throat,
although he dares not say anything, for Dordel still wants
to begin playing. 'Soon you won't be able to learn anything
more from me, though, if you keep practising like you
have been,' he continues and pulls the music stand close,
putting the violin to the side because his sight is so bad.
'Soon you'll need a new teacher.'

Uwe Dordel used to play at every village festival. But
then at one point he'd picked an argument with Hinrich
Werkzeugmacher because he'd been making such a din
with his accordion; it was as if he'd felt compelled to replace
a wind ensemble. It soon became too much for Dordel, and
he'd told Hinrich Werkzeugmacher that he should play a
bit more quietly. He continued, however, as if he'd never
heard, and perhaps he truly hadn't heard so well—in any
case, he had continued on in such a fashion that Dordel's
bow hand had slipped and caught Werkzeugmacher in
the eye before sticking a hole in the bellows. That had
made Hinrich go wild, and then a couple of farmers, a bit

overcome from drinking, joined him. At the end, they all lay under the remains of the festival decorations, and Dordel swore to himself: 'Not another single note for these pigs!' And he'd held fast to that. But he was still touched when Preuk had asked him whether he'd teach his Ruven a bit of this and that, particularly as his own son couldn't, for the life of him, find any fiddling in his fingers, no matter how much he tried. And now the teaching was nearly over, and that touched him as well. With his Fritz, there would be no music in this lifetime.

On the walk home, Ruven discovers Farmer Jacob's wife in front of him on the path. She's coming from the parsonage, where she tends to the garden, because in the previous winter the pastor's wife had—from pneumonia, and because he can't hoe the garden beds himself. Frau Jacobs is glad to do it. No one can dig as piously as she can.

'In such a well-heeled garden . . . ' she says ambiguously to her husband when she arrives home from her high station, and as she says it, she looks a bit puffed up. She knows something of books, is almost a little well read and a volunteer in all domains. That's why she's rummaging around the parsonage garden, too. Her own isn't small either, and also so clean that even the bees fly past it, as if Frau Jacobs had even cleaned out the pollen from the flowers.

'You with your excremental gossip,' she also likes to say to her husband when something reeking of bullshit escapes his lips, 'when will you ever improve!'

'I won't ever improve,' says Herr Jacobs, enunciating very clearly, 'because to improve something, someone needs to want it to be better. And just because you let your snobbish ways hang off you as if you were one of the twelve apostles, you, too, are still no saint.'

Now Frau Jacobs holds her breath and acts as if she were gazing at the weather. She adjusts her eyes to the sky, which swallows are crossing with a high buzzing sound. She wants Ruven to overtake her so that she can ask him something. And although he walks so slowly, as slowly as a person can without standing still, he is eventually next to her.

'Ah, and here we meet,' she says and attempts a smile. 'I heard that you practise very hard. Does that mean you're serious about the violin?'

Ruven shrugs. 'I like it is all.'

Frau Jacobs looks at him with disdain. 'Liking never amounts to anything! Or do you believe that just because Gesche likes that Werner boy that she'll soon be his wife?' She appears outright indignant. 'What do you think then, who's paying for your liking?' Ruven shrugs again and Frau Jacobs realizes that she won't get any further this way. They walk together in silence for a while. Frau Jacobs gives a little cough every so often and looks up to the sky again. If she could only disappear, thinks Ruven, and searches for a sentence that he might be able to say, but the longer the silence holds between them, the less his mind contains.

'I've forgotten something,' he finally says and turns around, then pretends to walk back in the direction of Dordel's farm. At one of the ponds on the way there he takes a different fork, wades through the reeds on the bank and squats down. It is still and damp. The day is quickly ending. The stalks quiver. Ruven opens his violin case. He pulls the small violin towards him and plays so quietly that no one can hear, and thinks about the king with the donkey's ears, the one Dordel told him about. The king's manservant had to whisper the secret of the long ears into a foxhole, so as not to burst from too much knowledge. Out of the hole grew the reed for the panpipes, whose sound whistled the king's secret throughout the world, and Ruven wonders to himself why it is that music should arise from the divulging of secrets.

Tired, he puts the violin back in its case. Fog already hangs over the pond, and Ruven starts off.

At the ford he meets Fritz, who is stabbing at frogs with a stick in the twilight. He has a young stork to feed, and doesn't see Ruven coming. When they're just a few steps away from each other, he looks up and his face clouds over.

'What's this?' Ruven stays standing where he is.

'We're not friends any more,' says Fritz.

'Why?' Ruven doesn't trust himself to look directly at the otter. He knows why, old Dordel had said it and Fritz had almost certainly eavesdropped. And in reality, Ruven had perhaps already long known, or at least had an idea, that there were paths that diverged. But so?

'Say why?' Ruven asks again.

'I'm saying nothing. I'm never saying anything to you again,' and with that, Fritz grabs his tin of frogs, stalks off and thinks: You watch. Next time, maybe I'll be spearing more than just frogs.

At the wainwright's, the mother had brought the bergamots into the kitchen. The scent of pear soup filled the house, floated into the workshop and tempted the men.

'So long as pears smell like this,' says the father, 'so long as my nose shows me this, I'll know that a loving God exists.'

'My ears show me things, too,' says Ruven quietly. The mother pets his light-coloured hair, hearing him. 'Uwe Dordel thinks I need a real teacher,' says Ruven a bit louder.

Father Nils looks at the soup as if he hasn't heard anything. Then he stands up, very slowly, and goes to the clock. He hoists the weights and clears his throat. One can hear the others' spoons tap against the bottoms of their plates. One can also hear that they're trying not to make a sound with their spoons, until Nils finally says, 'If Uwe Dordel thinks you need a real teacher, then I'll find you a real teacher.'

By late autumn, he had one: an old violinist for the theatre from the Jewish quarter.

'How did you sort that out, then?' Farmer Röver leans on the workshop door and rubs his chin with a finger stump.

'I turned six corners, and at the last one there was, as always, the pastor.' Nils reached his hand out to Röver. Everyone does that. Above all else, it is polite and beneath all else, it signals: you're missing something there. This comes from the fact that Röver, when he still had his best fingers, used them for so much swinishness, and everyone had been afraid of him—for on top of it, Röver is a handsome man. Perhaps they think a little bit, still, what a shame that it was only his fingers that were caught in the well crank. And that's why they must always hold the spot where he's missing something, even Nils, although he'd actually be out because of his age.

'And what does he want?' Röver puts his hand in his trouser pocket.

'Not much. He said that if the boy is ready, then he'll go with him to the city to audition. Something always comes around there.' Nils looks at his neighbour, looking a bit proud, in fact, he's about to burst with pride but he doesn't show it, he's holding such excesses in reserve. Röver sees through him anyway and grins. He knows Preuk. Budgeting his pride. Yet he has a weakness. And the weakness, thinks Röver, lies right beside him at night in bed, it's very possibly a question of manhood—while Röver rates Greta Preuk as entirely harmless, and he's also never been interested in her, that still doesn't matter in the least. A weakness is a weakness, and Röver leaves contently for his farm across the way, his six fingers deep in his pockets.

Some people were never afraid, thinks Ruven. He tries to quiet his breathing. Through the gateway to the side entrance of the municipal theatre blasts small flurries of the ice water of a November afternoon. Ruven holds the violin case protectively in the slipstream. It took him three hours to walk here; here a right, there a left, along the street. He had the feeling that he was being followed. At the canal, he'd briefly stood on the bridge and spat into the water, grey from the rain. In the city, he hadn't looked at anyone he was so ashamed by his village trousers and his village coat and his village face. Keeping his gaze low, he walked through the alleyways and, at one point, stood before a red brick wall—that path didn't go any farther, and as he looked up, the wall loomed almost into eternity. All the way up to God, thought Ruven, and stared up for a long time at the towers of St. Marien that seemed to never stop plunging into the cloudy sky.

Now he stands with a hammering heart in front of the municipal theatre, wanting to venture a prayer, when the tiny door edges open. A girl emerges, grey dress with a white collar, and a face so beautiful it's like none other he's ever seen, thinks Ruven, or he doesn't think anything at all because a person can't think in moments such as this, or because a person becomes a single thought in moments such as this—but then, the girl has already passed him. She walks a bit further down the street, as if she's looking for a place to cross over. She's tall and thin, and her limbs are delicate. Ruven is reminded of the poplars at home. The girl is carrying a bag on two leather straps slung over her shoulder. Suddenly she turns around and lets her gaze roam over the theatre's facade, lingering for a brief moment on Ruven. How she smiles at him, although she doesn't know him at all! Confused, he turns towards the side door from which the girl emerged at the same moment that a head pops out of the door with a profile as sharp as a paper silhouette: 'What are doing, standing out here in the wind? Come inside, boy, I've been waiting for you.'

The old man moves between constructed landscapes, cardboard clouds, and through portals. The light falls wanly through a dusty window, but Ruven has sharp eyes. In the air hangs a smell like a thousand years of sweat and stage make-up, and he shudders as he pulls the violin from its black case.

'And what's that, then?' Asks the old man and leans over precipitously, and Ruven would like nothing more than to leave again; he can't stand it when people lean over his violin as if it was a calf with two heads like the one born in Dordel's stable last year, where everyone had then gathered and gotten gooseflesh and thought there must be a reason for it, they'd find it in Dordel's family, look at what's come out of it!

But the old man, Goldbaum is his name, reaches towards the violin and Ruven soon relaxes when he sees how he does it: he takes it softly and strokes the well-worn lacquer as if it were the grey hair of an old girlfriend, and says, 'This will do. For the first one, it is fine.'

He then plays a few bars, tunes the strings, and Ruven hears exactly how well this Goldbaum knows the notes. He already wants to ask the old man about the colours, but then he leaves it alone and silently accepts the instrument from him.

'I've heard that you are gifted,' says Goldbaum. 'I hope that it is so. We'll try with this one; I'll join you soon, it's not difficult. But the music also needn't be difficult for us to recognize whether or not someone has a kinship with it.'

Ruven sees the sheet of music. His pupils grow very small. He goes rapidly through the first notes. Goldbaum is already nodding at him, with a look that brings the two of them to a point from which they can emerge, this looping path for the two parts alongside each other, and Ruven closes his eyes and sees it all and knows: this Goldbaum fellow is the right one.

Mother Preuk carries a hot stone in her apron. 'Don't tell me you're beginning and ending your music career in bed,' she says as she rolls the stone in linen and lays it on Ruven's feet. It was pitch dark when he'd arrived home last night, completely drenched, eyes already feverish, but in-between the dampness and the fever Mother Preuk saw a Ruven looking out who was new to her. It was a whole and entirely different Ruven than the one who had set out for the city that morning. And something had crept over her, she had to go quickly to the pantry and cover her face with her apron, because this enormous goodbye was knocking at the door, and that night as her eyes brimmed over again in bed, Nils lay next to her and looked at the blanket and then held her hand, as he hadn't done in years, and she said that it must be the worst part of motherhood, that after the birth there was nothing but goodbyes.

Ruven is also saying goodbye, but to what he still does-n't know, because at the age of nine, one only knows that something's coming and doesn't notice the going. With that, his mother is ahead of him. In each moment, he can forget, let go, make himself at home with something new, exactly as the fever is now making itself at home in Ruven, or the future. Perhaps the future lies in every fever. Like an altar boy, this fever circulates and smokes out every corner with its blazing incense. It drives Ruven into a dream that makes him shout aloud over and over, because he sees Joseph and Sofie disappear mutely behind their shadow-puppet screen, where they begin to play and dance, but so fast that they are hardly recognizable, and the audience begins to applaud to the beat and Ruven tries to meet the pauses with his claps but can't break through the rhythm of the others. That's when old Goldbaum also appears behind the shadow screen, and his silhouette holds itself completely still until a viewer cuts it out and everyone laughs, and he cuts Joseph and Sofie out, too, and sticks them to the wall.

Ruven awakes and sees the candles flickering, hanging in front of a brass disc in the candleholder on the wall: 'I had a bad dream.'

The mother lays her hand on his forehead.

'There was . . . ' says Ruven, and then he's already for-gotten, and neither of them say the word goodbye. Ruven turns towards the wall, tracing over the cool linen with this finger, back and forth, and with that he recalls the previous day, how Goldbaum, with a light bow, said, 'I'll take you. You'll be my last student, and so I will put you to work.'

Études, four hours, every day, for almost two years, how does a person do it. Five above, four below, half-step, five above . . . at some point going so fast that no one can sing along. Kreutzer, Sevcik, Kreutzer, technique, method. And pain that not only Ruven feels.

'Damn,' says Nils Preuk to his oldest, 'that is not beautiful.'

And John looks at him and says, 'I don't understand any of it.' His thin moustache makes him look younger than he is. It's not quite deliberate, which Gesche has already told a neighbour, and now it's spread among the girls in the village. As a joke, that girl Louise—Hans Werkzeugmacher's three-year-old—painted a moustache under her nose with coal, and when John saw it he'd hidden himself in the workshop, planning to only come out again when his beard was decently grown. For assurance, he rubs birch liquor and coffee into the skin before he goes to sleep, and if he's not mistaken, it's already worked and he's slowly catching up to Werner's beard. When it's grown, it will become clear whether Gesche truly desires the servant or perhaps might prefer the heir.

Nils Preuk notices none of it, but Gesche at some point discovers the thick strands in John's armpits, and from then on she brushes past him with her hip as if by accident when she serves the meals, and she also pulls her heavy braid to her front and toys with it. As she does it she smiles innocently to Ruven across the room, who closely observes her performance. 'Röver's hosting a slaughtering party tomorrow,' she says one day. 'You could play something for us, and we could all dance a bit,' Play for the slaughtering party? Ruven looks down at his plate, still so deep in other thoughts, in the midst of a short run-through of double stops and a position play that had refused to go smoothly for him all morning. 'No,' he says then, 'I'm not there yet.' In fact, he's already much farther. But to add music to dried sausage, blood sausage, liver sausage and mincemeat, that's too much, he thinks.

Gesche raises her chin: 'Are you already too good for it?'

'Shut your trap,' grumbles Nils, and then John must stand up, for better or for worse, as now is his chance.

'Don't be so rude, Papa,' he says. 'She's right, you know, why doesn't he want to play? He could fiddle us a little tune.'

'You shut your trap, too,' is all Nils says, and everyone is pained that John must sit down again. But something awakes then in Gesche, a delicate sympathy, which is not quite what John would have wanted, he'd rather have something closer to that stupid infatuation with Werner, that's all, but Gesche herself is growing confused, and only Ruven sees it in her gaze, and to put a stop to it all, for that reason alone, he now says, 'As you like. I'll play for all those sausages. Perhaps it will even save something of the evening if I play something clean for them.'

Mind you, he's saying that at the age of eleven, thinks the mother. Sometimes they say things at that age that sound closer to something the pastor might say with his forty-one years. Ruven looks his brother in the eyes. From now on, he owes him. At some point he'll pay, that's clear from his face. They eat in silence, until the wainwright rises and says, 'All right, then.'

Marble columns are painted on the walls of the front room of the Röver house. The rooms in-between display red stone tablets, also only painted, but still genteel enough that a person could develop a bit of a crick in his neck in there. And as the neighbourhood moves back and forth through the rooms the crowd looks entirely passable, scrubbed, combed and hungry. Luckily, there is no rye liquor in the fine front room; instead it's on the threshing floor, so that everything goes together nicely and a person can come back to life in the right ambience. In the midst of it all stands Ruven with his violin, wishing that the others were entirely different. Play, just play, he says to himself and closes his eyes to evade the endless, staring gaze of the otter, too, who leans on a post very close by and handles something in his jacket pocket. Play, well, perhaps to the honour of God alone.

R uven lifts his violin. In his head, he hears Goldbaum humming the prelude. He begins Fauré's Violin Sonata in A major. He roams through the notes. The colours climb up towards him from the violin, and so, he doesn't notice how still everything grows around him. With beer foam in their beards, Röver and the others stand still. Werner reaches for Gesche's hip, and Frau Jacobs flushes a deep red from excitement. Ruven stands where they placed him, in the corner by the brand new drive shaft for the threshing machine, and he plays the violin, legs set wide, perhaps with a bit of a swagger, but these hands— no one here has such hands! With such a wide grip, and with fingertips that seem made for the violin, or perhaps more made *of* the violin, or as though the violin were growing out of the boy. This borders on magic, thinks Frau Jacobs. Revolution! thinks the village schoolteacher, pulling a little notebook from his waistcoat and writing something down in tiny, frenzied letters. And Ruven plays his Fauré, who is so unknown here that it sounds to the ears of the village dwellers like a secret language. They'd reckoned there would be something more danceable and now this little guinea-pig buck—another little sip, no: an exotic!—is giving a concert, of the sort that was only ever allowed to happen in the capitol. It's applauded accordingly and the pride is so great that everyone's buttons nearly burst off their waistcoats, and Ruven gives a tiny smile and just nods instead of bowing, then goes out into the cold night and looks up to Orion, turns north to the great she-bear—she is scaling the high heavens because it will soon be Christmas.

Despite such applause, he's not happy. Too fast, thinks Ruven, I played too fast. It was as if someone was riding me who kept shouting: faster, Ruven! Faster! Then it'll be good! His shirt smelt a bit like sausage. No, not his shirt, it's the plate that someone is proffering him, and when he looks to the side, he spots Lene Lunten, the daughter of the estate steward, the girl with the light eyebrows. She says nothing, just looks at him and then up at the sky. Through the open door of the house climbs the steam of people, beer and aspic, and everyone is talking excitedly and much too loudly over one another because the concert was incredible, astounding! Ruven doesn't dare look at Lene. 'Thank you, but I'd rather not,' he says quietly and turns to go home. His father will pack up the violin. He doesn't trust it in there any more. He walks along the frozen path, between the paddock fences whose stakes jut from the icy soil like an army of the dead. When he notices that someone is following him, he starts to run. He knows immediately who is coming, and he also knows that it's just a threat this time, but he runs anyway.

John is sitting at the kitchen table, and a tower made of matchsticks is teetering on top of it. He hadn't gone; the way that Gesche eyes Werner is unbearable to him. And if he'd seen the way that Werner had taken her by the hip, thinks Ruven.

'And?' Asks John, 'How was it?

The new spring has brought so much rain to the region that the rotten fields must be planted yet again. The farmers don't ever stop shaking their heads. Nils Preuk has a lot to do as the carriages succumb to the mud and the rage of the drivers. The area in front of the wainwright's place is full of destruction. Ruven plays the violin at home so much that Nils' head begins to buzz, and he bellows all over the house because it's just too foreign, he can hardly breathe, this music sends him off rhythm. 'Can't you play something German? Does it always have to be so sweet and sour? I'll use your violin to mend the roof, if it goes on like this!' At that, the other room grows very still, and it pains Nils, and with a bad conscience he finishes slicing the plank of wood clamped in the vice. When he looks up, having felt eyes on him, Ruven is standing in the workshop. He looks at him steadily and says, 'It has to go on like this.' Nothing follows, because the father doesn't know how to answer his son, and so he unclamps the plank and puts another one in. He has slowly grown so far away from him, this boy. Ruven takes after neither Nils nor Greta, and yet he once took after them both. His shape was from him and his colouring from her. Now it looks as though he intends to become someone unrecognizable. At least, Röver said this recently, and when he did, he didn't look quite friendly. 'The bees recognize one another by smell,' says Nils. 'If one comes home and it smells different, it's chased away.'

For his next violin lesson, Ruven is ordered to Goldbaum's home. The Jewish quarter is somewhat similar to the village, and not so far away either. Ruven knocks and waits. The wind slams into his ear. Opposite, the mill turns its giant wheel, looking almost as though it's about collapse. The door opens without a sound, but old Goldbaum isn't standing in the entryway. Instead, it's the girl from the municipal theatre, in a grey dress, with a white collar and black hair that curls down over her forehead in a whorl. For a long moment the girl stares, surprised, at Ruven, then smiles and awkwardly clasps the pleats of her skirt in her left hand.

'I didn't know . . .' Ruven makes a half-bow.

'How would you?' The girl laughs. Then lets go of the door.

Goldbaum's granddaughter sits with them often after that. The old man puts a small chair by the oven for her. She loves to listen. When she does, her beautiful eyes are always moist, and once Ruven even thinks he sees a teardrop escape. The pea-sized shadows that appear on her grey silk blouse prove that he's not deceiving himself.

This spring, she cries more and more often when Ruven plays with Goldbaum.

'Rahel's heart,' whispers the old man once, 'it beats twice as much as other people's.' Ruven is frightened, as he doesn't know whether that's good luck or calamity. In any event, he must now look over at her every time he plays, which makes him think of Sofie and her shins, and then his heart, too, beats twice as fast, and he plays the wrong note twice as often, until Goldbaum shakes his head and says, 'Enough for today.'

On the way home, Ruven follows the edge of the forest, full of thoughts of Sofie and Rahel and, floating around between them, Lene. He searches for a spot with dry, thin forest grass and lays down in it. He'll lie this way until summer comes. He'll lie this way from now on, when too much is shinning around him. Words for all this, however, escape him.

'Come with me,' says Nils one day at home and waves Ruven over to the apiary, 'We're doing a death test.' In the tiny house he's entirely changed, he fingers the hives and says, 'They are so still, I don't like it.' He lightly taps the first hive and only a weak hum is audible; Nils shakes his head. 'They've lost their sun,' he says. 'You know, they don't live off the honey at all, the sun alone is what nurtures the bees.' Then he knocks on the second and the third hive and only the fourth answers with a fierce hum. 'This doesn't look good,' says Nils. 'It's not going well for the bees. We must pay attention to one another, my son, so that the sun doesn't go missing for us, too. Nothing has been shining for our country for a long time.'

The golden chain trees bloom with yellow poison. In the village, much is discussed but less explained. The men gather on every corner and grow louder and louder. In the evening, they strike at their wives, and the women laugh shrilly. And when the rats feast on Ruven's squabs before they're large enough to fly, he, too, believes that this time isn't a good one, and goes around the house with the pitchfork. He knows that the rats live under the stack of wooden boards. He builds a hurdle out of planks and stands in front of them, listening. He hears the rodents whimpering and raises the pile with a sudden jerk. Under the wood, the rat children are teeming, and Ruven pokes into the middle. The pitchfork has four prongs, of course, and he strings the small bodies along them, and doesn't notice how he, too, is yelling as he does it. Only when the last rat has stopped floundering does he slide the dead animals off onto one of the planks, before he runs into the house and throws himself, sweating, onto the bed. For a long time he thinks of nothing and then only: Well, so it is. And something flutters in front of his eyes, and he has a girl in his mind, a girl who sits on the edge of his bed, totally naked and with loose hair, her legs clasped together, hands crossed over her thighs so that her lap was hidden from view. She looks directly at him, with Rahel's eyes, until she suddenly dissolves into a shadow.

Later that day, the mother sends him to the grocer. The way there takes him past Röver's farm. Ruven hears Jacobs' voice, he can be so loud, and when the farm comes into view he sees the two of them: Röver with his good mare, an arm raised, and nearby the red-faced Jacobs stands with his stallion, whose mouth is wide open. When the men notice Ruven, they call out to him: 'Stop that nag!' they say and wave, and Ruven must run and take the halter, and Farmer Jacobs moves to handle the stallion.

'Come here with that leg,' he says and tackles the horse. More than half a metre, thinks Ruven, and Jacobs slides it into the mare so that her eyes roll back.

'Now she's livid,' says Röver, and the men grin toothily, while Ruven lowers his head.

'Hey,' says Jacobs. 'Are you another Düwel? That's how you make little foals.' The stallion pants and sweats, and

Ruven is close to letting go of the halter and running from the farm. The large animal throws itself on top of the other for the last time, and awkwardly moves backwards on its hind legs. Then the horses snort, as horses snort, the mare is led with a clattering across the farm to her paddock, Jacobs ties the stallion to one of the rings on the wall of the house, while Röver's wife carries out a bottle of schnapps and puts two glasses out on the tray of the milk truck.

'Bring another glass for our musician,' says Röver. 'He also helped.' Then they clinked glasses with Ruven and he found himself reasonably calmer, if only because he could think of nothing to say.

'Someday you'll be just like that,' says Jacobs and hits Ruven on the shoulder so that he almost chokes. And then they finally let him go, but at first he can't go to the grocer. He must go to the forest and lie in the grass, and then bring the groceries home late.

The air smells of blossoms. The gate smells of linden sap. In the kitchen everyone is sitting together. As Ruven gives his mother the mesh and seats himself at the table, his father just says, 'It's starting, my boy, the bees are setting off for battle. This house is too small for them. Men like Werner and John, they must join up. And then the bee-father must join up, too, and stay sharp. War is no pasture.'

It's not until September, though, that they actually set off. The wasps settle into the fallen fruit and writhe, dying, in the yard. The young spiders sail on their nets through the air and hang from people's hair. Werner and John argue through the nights and go, whistling and with deep rings under their eyes, to war.

Nils Preuk has been holding his Greta close in his sleep again, and when he leaves with the young men, Ruven and Gesche and Greta Preuk sit in the kitchen, watching through the window how Werner and John tread down the village road and don't turn back again to look at the wainwright's. Only Nils, he looks back at the window one more time. He's become very mellow in the past few days. He looks closely and sadly at Ruven. Then he turns, too, to the road, and they watch the three of them until they reach the bend. When they disappear around the bend, Gesche begins to scream as loud as she can. She raises her hands to her temples and shrieks, while the others sit, stiff and mute, beside her. Ruven sees the noise, a garish red, on the kitchen ceiling and on the walls, and Gesche screams and screams and screams.

'With your ears, you can read everything about the past of a person,' Goldbaum said once, as well as: 'No pair of ears in this world are the same.' With that, he'd smiled and eaten a ginger snap. 'Look, boy,' he said, 'When your ears are tired, go stand on a tightrope, or on a line you draw in the sand, for all I care. Or stand on one leg and close your eyes. You'll see, your ears will perk up again, they love balance, they need it.' Then the old man had looked in front of him, finished his tea and very carefully leant back in his chair, as if he feared that the furniture would give up and splinter into pieces.

Ruven doesn't go to Goldbaum often any more. Along with the rest of the youth in the village he is now wainwright, farmer and servant, all in one person. And none of the men had really had to go to war. 'But they wanted to, that's all. Like lemmings, as if there were something lacking here,' says his mother.

Despite everything, the harvest still has to be brought in. Ruven stands on the jolting thresher next to Röver on the threshing floor and shoves the sheaves into the wooden gullets and as he does it, he feels his bones as he's seldom felt them before. The machine ingests everything like an animal and jolts and shakes as if it wanted to gnaw on the harvest. It spits out the chaff and even sorts the seeds into three sizes in the sacks. It's loud up there, and Ruven knows he may not slide down. The machine can't take a life, to be sure, but it can take a foot or a hand, and again and again Ruven feels the force with which Fritz throws him the sheaves. As their eyes meet, a deeper red shades the otter's face, but it's impossible to tell whether it's from shame or rage.

Later, the helpers relax in the straw and drink. Across the way lies Lene in yellow, her head is hot, her hair sticks to her forehead and to her temples. Ruven looks at her and she laughs and is lovely and leans back, wipes the sweat from her face and squints past the village boys, who appear big and strong in her field of vision. What is she thinking, Ruven wonders, and doesn't at all want to know. He himself thinks about his father often, and imagines him looking back at the kitchen window. How he looked then! It was no age for foot marches.

And these foot marches are nothing for bee-fathers. That's another reason they stay abroad and don't come back. It makes no difference how long one waits. One waits for the fatherland and all in vain. In the end, one receives a fragment, but in the least of these bodies, there still dwells the original heart. The women accept what remains of them; the women were never consulted.

'What are you gobbling up like that, huh? You're even faster than your father . . .' Mother Preuk stops herself inwardly and looks down, ashamed, at her utensils, until she has a grip on herself again. She doesn't want to talk that way. She doesn't want to think at all. But she never thinks about anything but Nils, and on top of that today is Christmas, whether they like it or not, and it will be celebrated, if only half-heartedly, and also eaten well. The rest of the carp is already lying in bones on top of the watercress.

Only John has returned to this celebration in 1918, if it is actually John. He sits there, years after he set off down the village road like a confident gander, and now his eyes pop open wide and look up in fright whenever Gesche accidentally lets something fall, and he says, 'It's not all over yet, who on Earth believes in a cease-fire?' And he also says, 'Collect yourselves!' And: 'Stop that racket!' Until Mother Preuk prays and then still has to go on and cry. Ruven walks around the table and puts his hands on her shoulders; he is now nearly a man. He is almost as tall as the ceiling and as thin as everyone else, with hollow cheeks and a purple spot on his throat that everyone can't help looking at.

'Will you play us something?' John asks. Ruven picks up his violin. While he plays, John pulls a little box from his bag and holds it out to Gesche, and he gives a second to his mother. Gifts, still, despite it all. Gesche, her face flushed, sticks a brooch to her dress and isn't able to close the clasp, so that John must lend a hand, very close to her heart. Mother Preuk unpacks a piece of rose soap and smiles and leans down to smell it for a long time. They aren't listening to me, thinks Ruven, and why should they. He can play anyway, and it's the only opportunity to learn something, for there is no money in the house and certainly none at all for Goldbaum.

Mother Preuk stands and cleans up the rest of the carp. She leaves Gesche alone to admire her brooch and goes to take care of things in the kitchen. She serves the dessert, a puree of pears picked last summer that has been simmering for four hours, and fills five small bowls because the pastor is stopping by later.

The pastor has married Frau Jacobs, whose husband was felled in the first days of the war. She was hit hard by it because she had genuinely loved him, and his filthy mouth was something she had needed as a counterweight or for her own piety. And so, now that it's happened, now that she's finally married the pastor, astounding curses and impurities can be heard coming from the pastor's garden, which in turn causes the pastor to go around with his eyes turned heavenward because of holiness or holy despair, they say. And so on this Christmas evening, he gazes steadily up at the ceiling and has not much to say because this is the seventh dessert in today's round and because after the dessert, one or the other after-dinner drink will suffice, and besides, over the past several years, there have arisen in him a few questions in reference to the dear Lord and the clemency of heaven. If he doesn't pay attention, the pastor threatens to collapse entirely into himself, like a soufflé pulled by surprise from the oven.

Twelve nights later, on Three Kings' Day, there's a concert being given in the city. It could mean money. Ruven and Goldbaum go on foot, although the old man can't walk well any more. This morning, they are the only ones on the road. Ruven carries his violin until they reach the outskirts of the city. There, they play in front of snowy gardens. It doesn't bring much in, but what else did they expect, with snow? But at one of the largest mansions, a curtain in a side window is raised and shortly afterwards, the portal opens and a servant girl runs out, shivering, and gives them money. Ruven looks away. What they're doing here feels like begging.

In the pubs it's much easier, even when they are rewarded almost solely in drinks. Soon they also venture into the hotels, and Ruven grows hot and doesn't notice how tired Goldbaum is beside him, and how stooped and quiet he is, too. And then the second violin occasionally nearly disappears in Ruven's playing, which bleeds through more and more, and perhaps that's not at all a bad thing, for suddenly, a gentleman sitting alone and smoking at one of the tables in the back says, 'Young man, you are extraordinarily gifted! You shouldn't just go around to restaurants like this. Don't let your talent go to waste here!' At that, he gathers himself together and pays handsomely before he accepts a heavy fur coat and moves towards the doorway which opens into the ice-cold night. Ruven sees the money in his hand, and then looks at Goldbaum, who has to sit down.

'What's happening to you?' Ruven saves him at the last moment; the old man would have otherwise toppled from his chair.

'No strength,' he says, 'My blood isn't flowing fast enough. I'm too old for such things, my boy, I've gone and overestimated myself.'

Ruven orders Goldbaum potato soup. With a weak hand, he spoons the soup and says, 'That's it, my strength will come back again soon.' It doesn't come back, though, instead more and more of it leaves until he can just barely whisper the address of a former colleague from the orchestra, a trumpeter, they could perhaps spend the night there. 'It's not far from here.' And then Golbaum falls silent and grows very pale.

R uven waits for morning in a strange parlour room. He sits in a musty armchair and looks over at his teacher, who is lying feverishly on the chaise lounge, his head propped up by two cushions. Ruven doesn't know any more how the old man and the two violins were hauled over here.

'Just one night, Martin, we'll be gone tomorrow.' Those were the words that Goldbaum whispered. And Martin Rudolfsen had worriedly rubbed his trumpeter's cheeks and said, 'That doesn't look good.'

About seven in the morning, the door to the room quietly opens. The trumpeter nods with his eyebrows raised high and leans over the sleeping Goldbaum. 'A doctor is needed here,' he says in a half-whisper and turns his round head towards Ruven. He looks like an Ore Mountain angel from the heavenly orchestra whose wings have gone missing. He goes to the oven and begins to heat it. Goldbaum doesn't stir even slightly. He just lies there, his paper-silhouette face jutting into the air.

Rahel's eyes stare fixedly as she gropes behind her towards the kitchen table. The cab driver carried the old man into the house on his back, a horrible sight, and with his payment he's soon on his way again, while Ruven is still attempting to explain what's happened.

'You say it was his lungs, sir?' Rahel lowers her head. Her dress smells freshly cleaned.

Ruven sees the white grief in her voice and quietly says, 'Yes, or his heart, but please don't call me sir!' But she hasn't heard him, because Elias, her much-younger brother, is pulling at her dress and crying about a broken wooden donkey. Ruven kneels down next to him and says, 'Show me. I can paste that back together, just let me take it for a few days.'

'Yes, Elias, Herr Ruven is definitely a good donkey doctor,' says Rahel and attempts a smile. She stands, her fingers interlocked, in front of the grey kitchen wall. She has such a precise face, thinks Ruven, both halves entirely symmetrical. Two muscles in her throat twitch and a tear runs along her straight nose to her upper lip. Rahel takes no heed. She simply looks at Ruven, and in such a way that he quickly grows dizzy.

'What else can I do?' He finally asks, incapable of moving.

'Don't forget me, sir,' she says quietly.

Ruven reaches out to her. 'Of course not,' he says and feels her narrow, long fingers between his. She presses his hand briefly, but to Ruven it is as if something was being transferred from her to him. Then she pulls her hand back.

The little donkey is pasted back together as if it were a sliver from the holy cross. It stays in the workshop for another three days until Ruven decides to bring it to the Jewish quarter. He walks out of the house with a stiff collar under his winter coat, and his hair, too, is as hard as a helmet. He'd combed it from right to left and from left to right in front of the mirror while secretly smoking a cigar.

In front of him on the village road, he discovers Luise, Hinrich Werkzeugmacher's daughter, building a wall out of snow and looking entirely immersed in her task; she doesn't notice him greeting her. He goes a few steps further. The snow crunches softly. But Ruven hears something else, not exactly a sound, he thinks. But what then? Just then, John comes with his bay horse pulling his sleigh around the bend, and he shouts: 'Go! Go!' Behind him, the heavy blocks of ice are piled up. He shouts again: 'Go!' The bay horse is ancient and blind. But John is in a hurry—perhaps he's freezing—he drives and cracks the whip over the animal. The dog is standing and growling in the path to Röver's house. Suddenly, he leaps forwards and slams into the horse's leg. The bay horse shies, he can't see what's happened to him. He rips his large head in the air and tears along the road towards Ruven. 'To the side!' John pulls hard on the reins, but the snow is piled too high on the edge of the road and Ruven, still too dazed from the cigar, stands as if rooted, and the sleigh with all of its ice has much too much momentum.

'It must have been thirty kilos,' old Röver grumble and added: 'A real flat foot—I've never in my life seen a foot as flat as this one.' Röver stands beside the pastor, who feels very much like death today, and says, 'Perhaps you could include it in your prayer. My dog was involved there, too, and Ruven should be celebrated, but things don't always turn out the way they should.'

The pastor nods and claps his hand to his chest, near his heart: 'Yes, yes, Röver, I'll take care of myself.' His black robe dangles above the icy church floor in front of him because the pastor is so hunched over, standing there.

'And another thing,' says Röver, 'I know you don't like to do this, but I'll also be dancing cheek to cheek with death soon, and so I would like to be allowed to rid myself of a few things.'

'You want to confess?!' The pastor's eyes widen in shock. 'No,' he says and looks directly opposite; his expression turns dark: 'Even if I thought it was necessary, I don't want to hear it, Röver, it will send me once and for all to the grave.' And with that, he leaves Röver standing and disappears into the vestry, and Röver reckons he can hear how he quietly turns the key in the lock.

The little donkey, then, is staying in the village for the moment, until finally Ruven writes a letter. In the end, there's only a short bit written in the most beautiful Sütterlin script on the page. Ruven reads the lines again and again, trying to imagine how it would read to someone else. Then he copies it out one more time, lending the *l* and the *r* a delicate loop, and finally folds the letter, wraps it along with the little donkey in brown paper and posts it the following Tuesday. He slowly limps home through the snow from the post office. Halfway there, the otter-Fritz drives past him. He has the tame stork sitting next to him in the carriage. The stork no longer wishes to return to his own kind and carries itself like a somewhat thinner human, looking right and left from the coach-box, far too lazy to fly. Fritz reins in his mare and directs her a few steps towards Ruven. At first, he doesn't say a word, and Ruven, too, can't think of anything to say. He just looks at the stork and would have actually liked to reach out and pet him. But then, without warning, Fritz says, 'You are nothing but a coward, Preuk!' And they both know what he means by it, and he slaps the reins against the horse's back so that it takes a tremendous leap forwards, which nearly unbalances the stork, and the coach disappears behind the next bend.

Half an hour later, Ruven is home, too. His foot hurts more often than it doesn't. He thinks about fighting the otter one day. He'll receive a letter from Rahel, and then he'll show Fritz how cowardly or brave he is. In his room, Ruven takes up the violin and tries to play. He plays seated, his foot propped on a stool. He sent off the letter only today but he's already waiting for a reply.

He waits a whole year. Because the post, of course, delivers the letter to the correct address but there's no longer a Goldbaum living in that house in the Jewish quarter across from the mill, and his two grandchildren have moved somewhere unknown.

Well, a year. An étude. He plays four or five hours of suites each day, as if he could cure his foot and himself by playing dances. Courante, saraband, otherwise he sits at the table over notes, books, scores, and thinks: When the music is over, perhaps I'll be over, too. He also imagines the notes as if they were running on and on, without fading away, as if they had a place somewhere in the universe where they would never stop. And he thinks: *Please don't forget me.* He sets it in eighths and on the open D-string: *Please-don't-for-get-me-please-don't-for-get-me.* He limps back and forth in his room. *Please-don't-for-get-me.*

The suit hasn't grown with him, a part of his leg is visible as he walks along the road, violin case on his back, foot still a bit iffy, hair parted in the middle, not quite the optimal style for his face but meant to look neat, meant as: Today parts the one side from the other. Today it will go this way or that.

Because instead of praying for Ruven's foot, the pastor had rather written a letter to a professor in the city and then quickly received a reply with an invitation for Ruven to present himself here and there, now and again, with his violin. And so now he's heading to the city. With an uneven gait, he walks down the road.

He hadn't slept the night before, only dreamt. He dreamt in A major, never in a minor key, but always in circles and in an excruciating way because a note was always missing, a single note that he should have been able to sweep away if only it hadn't been a part of the adagio. And so he'd woken up with this gap in the adagio and had set out with Schumann's Von fremden Ländern und Menschen in his head, just like Hinrich Werkzeugmacher always played it on his accordion; he walked until he reached the city. He whispered a prayer in a Henry the Lion cathedral while someone practised a toccata on the organ in D minor, making the candelabras shake. Finally, he arrived at Professor Bernhard's. He introduced himself and shook his hand, his sleeves riding up almost to his elbows.

Half of the professor's face droops. His right eye is almost entirely shut. He strokes his moustache and doesn't appear very interested. As Corelli is played, he even looks out the window and begins to walk slowly back and forth, a red cat always at his feet with her tail raised, rubbing her head on his leg.

Of course, this bothers Ruven. He is entirely stiff, believing so strongly that the professor isn't listening to him. But he is.

'And besides that?' The professor makes a kissing noise at the cat and lifts her up towards him. What? Ruven thinks and asks if he's allowed to remove his suit jacket. The professor nods and seats himself at the grand piano: 'Beethoven, A major.' The cat leaps away as if she knows what's coming. Ruven stands next to the professor, a curtain behind him billowing with the first gust of wind, and then it thunders outside and the cathedral bells ring out six o'clock, and the professor plays, but not in the normal way, instead he plays with his hands crossed over each other! The lame right hand, with the ungainliness of a bear paw, grinds through the bass part, but what emerges is so powerful that Ruven thinks, I must leave, what was I thinking? I can't practise any more. If he can play like this with a hand like that, he must think I'm nothing but laughable.

'What sort of funds are you in a position to procure?' The professor asks in the middle of the second movement.

'What do you mean?' Ruven surfaces from his thoughts with difficulty. What can I procure? Honey, he thinks, sausage, pigeons, wagon wheels. Nothing. He names a small amount, and the professor simply raises his left eyebrow. 'You would need a new instrument,' he murmurs then and says he'll think about it; perhaps it would be worth the attempt.

He has already walked the longest portion of the road when the rain sets in. Ruven runs. The violin case isn't thick. He pulls it in front of him and tugs his coat over it as well as he can. In the next copse, he seeks out a fir tree and lies down flat underneath it in the circle of bright needles, to wait out the storm. The wind calms down eventually but the old, toneless hissing fills the evening and won't be over as quickly.

Ruven watches the rain and thinks about his father. He never resisted leaving, he thinks. If the rain, the road and the fir trees were also to leave so easily—everything that was taken for granted, and what was more taken for granted than a father? It isn't possible to be in the world and to have no father. It is unthinkable. One had to go insane because one goes on living even though he who keeps on living, he who has been there since long before one's own existence, and he who once cared for everything, no longer is. And the love one had for one's father is now running on and on for ever into the dark as if one had a leak somewhere. And you, Mother? Where are you leaking? You are growing thinner and thinner, like everyone here. Do you still know how Nils the Grump loved you? Do you know that still? How he brought you a dress and said, sit down in front of the lilac bush and be as beautiful as you like until I've built an arbour for you. You didn't know at all what he meant by that because you were always so modest. And now the arbour is still there, but the father is rotting somewhere in Flanders, and for a whole portion of time we've gone on living.

When it becomes still and only scattered drops fall on the sorrel that sprawls nearby, Ruven stands up. He has a long way still to go before he reaches home. When he arrives, he knows he won't be able to accept the professor's offer. He doesn't want to be given anything without paying; he has his pride, and from now on, he'll use it to organize the beehives and take up honey collection and try to forget the violin.

Gesche harvests the lilies-of-the-valley behind the garden and comes with bright clouds into the kitchen and says, because she doesn't know better: 'You should perform something for another professor.' She is all smiles. 'You're looking so gloomy,' she says and scatters a handful of oats for the chicks under the oven. The chicks pick eagerly at the grains. Ruven bends down low over the centrifuge. He turns the crank with his bow hand, his knuckles white.

Two days a week, he brings honey to the district capital to sell, and also to avoid John, the glowing John, who has been so plumped up by the impending wedding that Ruven can't bear to look at him. All the more so because Mother Preuk believes that the father hadn't gone off to war for no reason; he hadn't at all had to do it but she believes he'd deliberately stayed there with Werner so that Gesche was finally given the push to marry John and live here. 'She hasn't needed a push for a long time, Mother,' Ruven had once countered, knowing that his mother doesn't examine things closely any more. She'd simply quit it with close examinations because the truth, as she means it, doesn't live in this world but rather in the one where the father is now. And she hurries to seek him out there, she curls her back into a hunch so that Death doesn't overlook her, because she's actually not yet very old and she consults her cane every evening. But the cane only counts off other names and Death overlooks her still. Death is forever loping past her house and snatching the most peculiar cases, such as that of little Luise, who had nothing worse than a cold. He strikes here and there and doesn't appear to be looking for reasons, doesn't trouble himself for a Spanish flu but, rather, helps himself to everyone, with the sole exception of Mother Preuk.

No, Gesche doesn't need a push. She simply opened her heart and allowed the broken John in and then closed her heart again, so that he almost grows too hot inside it.

They are married in August of 1920, with tall cakes, marzipan and coffee, and a dance floor which clatters and clangs. Ruven stands with his violin in the farthest corner, and beside him, on a chair, Uwe Dordel, and on the other side Hinrich Werkzeugmacher with the accordion, without a single glance for Dordel, but still quieter than he used to be, perhaps because of Ruven, perhaps out of general good will, for this is the first wedding since the war.

On the other side of the dance floor, a gramophone has been set up under the walnut tree and it broadcasts a bit of America. All the village children loiter around along with the rest of the wedding guests. They wipe a finger off on their trousers before they handle the device and all day Gesche laughs so loud that each time the pigeons flutter up and fly off in a harried circle above the wainwright's. When everyone looks up, John clasps the nape of Gesche's neck, pulls her to him and kisses her, bending his head down low, even almost genuflecting. The white dress glows past midnight amid the colours of the guests, who seek out the edges of the dance floor with careful steps so that they don't, with their inebriated brains, stumble into the garden beds. Two children, with tired eyes from staying awake too long, gather piles of crumbs on the abandoned dishes and quickly push them into their open mouths before they are remembered by their mothers and sent off to bed.

Ruven dances with Lene three times. He holds her by her waist and it is already so dark that he follows her into the lilac arbour. He has never rebuffed anyone—there hasn't yet been an opportunity.

The seventh and eighth week of cherries. They come and go. The violin is on the table in front of Ruven. The air in the room stands still. The sweet smell of the bedclothes next to him nearly sedates him. In the sunspots on the roof, flies bathe. The terrible noise they make, when they copulate in a bright buzzing, shoots through him each time.

Ruven holds a letter in front of his face. The sender's name is missing, there's only the address and his own name. Unfortunately, it wasn't written by a woman, the letters are small and jagged. This was someone who has a lot of power. It is the second invitation: *Don't wait until autumn!* writes Professor Bernhard, and Ruven looks outside and sees how dry and brittle the leaves have become, when he received the letter everything was still green and full. And instead of writing a letter in reply, he goes to the return address himself the next day. He hums the whole way and thinks, Now it goes from C to G, that's the way someone from the village modulates himself in the city. He's happy that the journey is long.

'Come in, come in!' The professor nods, 'Go ahead.' In the music room, it smells like wax. 'Have you been working since I saw you last? Listen, I'll sit here. Set yourself up there, OK?' He leans his head on his hand. 'Pardon me. I tire quickly, the twisted musculature, you know. A stroke. It was a few years ago, you'd have surely noticed it already. Ah well, I'll be all right. In a sense I'll be better than before, but I'll discuss that later. What are you thinking? Haydn? B-flat major? Good. I'll listen, and then we'll talk.'

He's closed his eyes already, allowing Ruven to tune his instrument.

'Yes, what is that pitch, actually?' The Professor raises his head again. 'Has the human ear always known when the notes agree? Ask yourself that,' he says, at which point Ruven asks himself nothing at all.

'Now, perhaps. But do you know Terpandros, seventh century BC? He arranged all the notes into ladders, each with seven rungs. His ear told him that there exists a form that coincides with that which is beyond form.' The professor noticed Ruven's uncertain look. 'Enough of that, play!'

And Ruven plays. The professor almost forgets him as well as his own words. Ruven doesn't let him hear a mistake, the music just lacks real force, perhaps, but the fault for that lies with the tiny violin, for which he gives himself a small rebuke.

And the old man agrees: 'You will begin again, even though you've got far. But it must happen from the ground up. And you will have to learn to take the notes seriously. One has the feeling that you're falling asleep when you play. And this simpering *wee-wee*, you're not a professional mourner! At every note, you must get to the point and stay awake! We'll begin with this: Think of a short series of notes, every day. Let nothing distract you, everything else should be silent.' The professor stops himself and looks at Ruven mutely for a while. 'And now let's work together, I'd like to see where we can find an instrument for you. For now, I'll loan you one. Look here, it's not especially valuable, but it will do for practice and allow you more runthroughs. Try it!' He holds a dark brown violin out to Ruven.

'Take it with you,' says the professor, chuckling. 'Go back there to where you're undisturbed and where no one can hear you. We'll see each other in three weeks, then.'

With two violins on his back, Ruven walks back through the Jewish quarter. He is still lost in a daze from everything the professor said. He stops and stands when he reaches the mill, looks across the road to the small house on the other side, finally crosses the lane and knocks on the door. A stranger opens the door. She is so stooped over that Ruven stares at the parting in her hair.

'The Goldbaums?' She asks hoarsely. 'But they left long ago! Ages ago, now. To Hamburg, supposedly, but who knows. The violinist passed away, he was unimaginably ill.

And the little grandson, Elias! His sister went with him to an uncle's, but I don't know the details exactly,' she says. And then the door is closed again, and Ruven hasn't once actually seen the woman's eyes.

And really, what had he wanted? Nothing, in fact. Perhaps just to say something. But it hadn't happened, and so now he is walking alone along the edge of the woods: one, two, one, two, he keeps practising the steps and suddenly loses his way and goes through the undergrowth to the old grassy spot where he used to always lie down. He takes out the professor's violin and begins to play.

The acoustics and isolation are a challenge in the forest and playing the violin doesn't improve things. But suddenly, as if the instrument had lured him out, a person leaps into the copse; they call him the badger. He wears his coat with the opening at the back, a very old story. There was a time when this badger was still called Klas Ankermann: back then, he had a house and home, and a sound faith and mind, a hat for work and a hat for holidays, and of course, he also had a very sound wife who kept everything in its place, who wore clogs and only went to church in leather shoes and even her thriftiness was kept in exactly the right place so that Klas Ankermann could only ever be happy. And so he was, until one day he went out to mow the hay.

Half of the field had been quickly taken care of when he heard a breath at his side that wasn't his own. He stood still and looked around and thought he saw two leather shoes poking unnaturally and on a workday out of the grass, and even more unnatural was the white backside that somehow shone out from between them. And perhaps everyone could have still gone mildly if Klas Ankermann, in those confusing moments, had found a couple of suitable words. But nothing came to his mind at the right moment. A terrible muteness descended upon him as soon as he was surprised by life. And so he only had his hands, those enormous shovels that he had once used to pull out one or two of his wife's teeth. And now the scythe stuck to these hands, and the question was posed, what applied more: *Thou shalt not covet thy neighbour's wife* or *Thou shalt not kill?* It was fast and easy, separating that slowly grown flesh from man and woman. Much easier than making it disappear. But who was at all surprised by Klas Ankermann driving his pigs to the swampy part of his hayfield on a May afternoon? It was only the way that he went crazy from grief and began to eat beetles because his wife and his farmhand had departed this world; no one bought that. They didn't take themselves for idiots.

'You can confess it, you can also be silent,' they said. And he'd decided in favour of silence and went on as though he'd lost his mind. Today, he was the badger who had arrived at his own verdict and punishment.

'You play the violin,' says the badger now to Ruven, '*As the apple tree among the trees of the wood.*' He comes closer and nods. 'You play the violin.' It sounded as though something was caught in his throat.

'Yes,' Ruven hid his unease.

The badger went over to the small violin in the black case. 'What's wrong with this one?'

'It's still mine.'

'Good,' the badger examines his face closely and says, 'Good.' He lets out a horrible laugh and then: 'And where is your father, now?' He laughs again.

Ruven tunes the strings. 'Go away,' he says, 'That's none of your business.'

'Only a little,' says the other man, and: 'You, too, will end up like me. To love something very much is to become dangerous.' Klas Ankermann says that, not the badger, and that frightens Ruven even more. And then, yet again: *I will sing unto the Lord, for he hath triumphed gloriously: the horse and his rider hath he thrown into the sea. The Lord is my strength and song, and he is become my salvation; ta-da-dee, ta-da-day, tan-der-a-day.*' He spins in a circle and lets his coat billow around him. '*The enemy said, I will pursue, I will overtake, I will divide the spoil; my lust shall be satisfied upon them. Ta-da-dee. Thou didst blow with thy wind, the sea covered them: they sank as lead in the mighty waters. Ta-da-day.*'

'Be quiet,' says Ruven, 'I can't play with all this.' And the badger is quiet and still and everything goes well, and Ruven is at the wainwright's in time for dinner, and everyone has carefully arranged expressions, for today it's official, Ruven is studying the violin. With a professor who is much talked-about. In the relevant circles, in any case. And a little bit of information about the pastor is also leaked to the village, as a result. The conversation sways in hips old and young, from house to house. It can do this in the quiet of winter. Whoever has a topic of conversation finds the winter only fair. Ruven, too, submits to the stillness outside. He establishes himself under the sky that looms high above the frozen fields at night. He plays and practices his new freedom, and his fingers hurt like the unwrapped feet of Chinese women. Ruven plays on against the pain. And he reflects on the badger and Klas Ankermann, on what he said: To love something very much is to become dangerous.

Sometimes Ruven plays in church on Sundays, on the mornings that the trombone choir blasts its collective foul breath in the air above the mangled bedclothes instead of into the plated gold of Protestantism, sleeping off last night's intoxication. On those days, the farmers slip in the pews and don't sing along quite right. They don't like it, his violin playing, it sounds too much like that Southerner's playing, the old fiddler, and if it's not that, then it owes too much to the city, and in-between it somehow comes to nothing. They also say that the new pastor, who recently took over the post because the old one decided to devote himself entirely to the salvation of the cussing Frau Jacobs, has nothing in-between and nothing behind but otherwise he has too much of something, only it's not yet clear exactly what. He's very young, in any case, and strict. He chews tobacco every fifteen minutes and speaks his sermons in a flat voice, so fast, like his housekeeper's sewing machine's chatters; she uses it all night long because she likes to walk around the village—it's a simple pleasure for her, to sport something decent. She also keeps the pastor's household in all its finery. It is not unattractive and it makes the pastor hot and tight under his robe, even though the housekeeper isn't so young any more. Reading books and writing sermons sometimes seems very dull to him, and with every paradise-greedy theological insight that reaches towards him in his study from on high, a trapdoor opens underneath him, and he would happily come to an understanding with his housekeeper about it but her only vice is her addiction to cleaning, nothing else. Well, the pastor chews tobacco more and more and asks Ruven to play quickly, he understands, and above all else, to finish quickly. The pastor watches Ruven out of yellow eyes as he plays and says, 'Tempo, Preuk, tempo!' But Ruven only thinks, there's nothing here for the violin, all the mould and the cold will ruin the sound. Lene Lunten also sits there and somehow he's no longer able rid himself of thoughts of her, perhaps because Röver's son is often hovering around her, as if he were tethered somewhere. On the way home, Röver's son even holds his arm out to Lene and she hooks hers around his and glances quickly down at the pleats in her skirt, and as she does so, her gaze sweeps over Ruven, and it is highly controlled: a pinch of a glimpse, where had she learnt that? There was, besides the schoolteacher, only one other person in the region who could have taught her that: the nurse Emma Braren. And she loves to fill her house with girls. They join her for tea, they say. But Ruven has seen how their necks and cheeks glow when they walk home from the nurse's house and it seems that she teaches the girls things that others are ashamed to teach, or things that one refrains from teaching for tactical reasons—such unappetizing things, perhaps, as the self-determination of a woman when it comes to her own fertility and her own desire, who knows.

The nurse studied in Hamburg and is only here for love, they say, without saying whom or what she loves. In any event, she assisted the doctor for a few years until he went in the direction of the Battle of Verdun, out of the belief that he would be able to sew up the surviving lemmings, who had gone over the cliff at the sound of stirring poetry, from all that remained of them. He carried on this new handicraft for a few months, always hoping that he'd be a stitch ahead of Death, and the nurse vomited every time behind the hospital tent and afterwards, with a bad taste in her mouth, tossed the useless human rags into a pit, until the day came when the doctor accidentally saved himself by falling into too deep a sleep, because the human rags from the fields of glory had perhaps overwhelmed him, too. Emma Braren requested furlough then, and came back home to the village, and since then she's been the only person in the area well versed in medicine and midwifery, even more well versed than the doctor and ragtailor had ever been, for she is more awake, in every sense, than he was.

Emma Braren is in possession of all mental and spiritual faculties and even goes each week to workers' assemblies in Hamburg and the district capitol. She commands listeners' attention, and when she speaks, her strong chin sometimes wrinkles and her eyes shine with compassion when she says, 'It's a problem, with our women, it is so and so, and it should not be so and so. They are not healthy, our women, and they should be healthy. And it is a problem with this century, and I say to all of you, the social has a mouth, a heart, and hands. It is not just an idea.' And when one of the men retorts, 'The subject here is politics and the worker,' the nurse retorts with a smile, 'Yes and no.' She even once, surprisingly, had said to Ruven, 'Go to the assemblies, everything is addressed there —even you, you guinea-pig buck!' And then she had laughed. But Mother Preuk knew well to prohibit such visits because she found these workers' assemblies suspect. 'Playing the violin is enough,' she said, 'Really, that is more than enough for the future! Not politics, too!' And: 'Not yet another problem!' She went on like this and banged her pots and plans.

But he is in an entirely different place with his thoughts. He is where politics is the farthest distance away, in a place that some here still call love. There are two possible reasons for it: first, Rahel is gone, or second, the young Peter Röver is there. It's the only way to put it. And the more Peter Röver walks with Lene up and down the village street, the more beautiful and attractive Lene seems to grow. But there is yet more to it. The way she moves, even when Peter isn't around. That is what had caught Ruven's attention at first. He had been sitting at the table in the front room, a mirror hanging on the wall behind him, and at the same moment that Ruven looked up to observe the street through the mirror's reflection, Lene walked through the picture, and suddenly Ruven wasn't sure whether she was walking into or out of the village. He had been so taken with her then. She didn't necessarily belong here in the village. She would, perhaps, someday walk away.

In the parlour, Ruven stretches his bow and rubs it with resin. Beside him, his mother sighs. The walls are thin and crumbling. When John and Gesche argue, too. And when he shags her, the walls seem even thinner. Ruven holds his breath when the time comes. It can be during the day or night, and it has its course. It will be still for a long moment and then grow stiller and stiller, Ruven will see the hairs on his lower arms stand up, and then the furniture will begin very gently to quiver and shake, and the parlour wall will, too. Ruven sees the dry clay flake from the seams and thinks: Now they'll be furious, that's how you make little foals. And then, he blushes and tries to play the violin.

Afterwards, Gesche insists on looking in on him, acting as though there were something in there to sweep, and carries all the smell and the warmth with her into the room. She is finally round and full and in her fifth month. And she is beautiful. But insatiable, too. Or perhaps John doesn't really know his own business. She slinks around Ruven like a cat, very round and glowing: 'It really is from John, anyhow—there will never be anything to prove, with us.' And they both listen to the blows coming from the workshop, until Ruven shakes his head and Gesche tosses hers back. 'Well, then,' is all she says, and leaves.

How is he supposed to play the violin now? He walks out into the fields with his coat open, stomping across the frozen acres. It hasn't snowed yet this year. My God, Gesche with her character! And he'd really like to be pious and still.

Gesche grows larger and larger, at least it looks that way from the outside; in reality she's becoming smaller and smaller and making space for a tiny person. Spring comes, the lilies-of-the-valley rise out of the dark leaves, and then Gesche only wants to quickly drive the sheep into the meadow and so she walks barefoot across the farm and past the water pump on the slimy planks—she should have thought better of that, for she slips, the world tilts in her field of vision and disappears, only very briefly, in a red fog, and for a long moment she lies motionless on her back, before she grips her stomach and tries to scream aloud in pain. But she can't scream. She only utters, quietly, 'Mother . . . ' But Mother Preuk is sitting in her room and sighing, and doesn't hear her. It is sheer coincidence that Ruven has already raged at his sheet of music and is running outside to the farmyard in order to hold his head under the pump.

The both of them have to carry Gesche into the house, John at the front and Ruven at her feet. Mother Preuk has already run for the nurse, her skirt flapping.

'You two boil water!' Shouts Emma Braren as she arrives, and then she's already in Gesche's room. The brothers obey, although John flutters his hands so much that nothing stays in them.

'Sit down,' Ruven says quietly, 'I'll do it.' And he tries not to listen to the way that Gesche is suffering. They both feel ashamed for being men. Finally, the door to Gesche's room opens quietly and the nurse enters the kitchen.

'A coffee,' she says, 'as black as possible.' And: 'Please.' And she drinks and braces her left hand on her hip as she sits, puts the cup down and looks straight at John. 'It's bad,' she says. 'There's nothing to be done. Perhaps we'll be able to save your Gesche.'

In the bedroom, there lies a stranger. She stares at the blanket and can't hear any more. A person who doesn't decide anything any more because she is so undecided between life and death. 'Hold on,' is all the nurse says. And then, 'None of you look up again until I've left!' Then she prays, the nurse of all people! She folds her bloodied fingers and prays for forgiveness.

Ruven stares at the wardrobe the whole time, but he can't avoid listening, partly because he has to hold Gesche with both hands. There are quiet and horrible noises, for what hasn't gone must, however, go. Piece by piece.

In 1922, Gesche's lilies-of-the-valley wither on the stem, while some other things begin to sprout poisonously. Not only here but elsewhere, too, in Northern Italy, Königsberg, Berlin, here and there. Hard to see where it's going but it's going towards something, and no Law for the Protection of the Republic will help.

'You should have picked the lilies-of-the-valley,' Mother Preuk says to Gesche. 'None of us have had any now.' At that, Gesche went to the middle of the field and lay down flat, like she is again now, and sniffed and hoped that she, too, would die.

Ruven must play through it all. But until July he only plays the easiest and happiest pieces in the forest. Sometimes the badger is there. Sometimes wild rabbits, too.

Then, finally, Ruven has his first real concert in the city. His teeth hurt, his whole jaw, and his head has been feeling dull since the morning. I won't think of anything to say, he thinks. He has tried to remember all of the professor's words and to read the newspaper very closely, so that the city-dwellers, whose language flows so perfectly from their mouths, don't dismiss him a total dullard.

The professor's wife, Helene Bernhard, accompanies him on the piano. She is a rotund, caring woman with stubby fingers that scamper like mice across the keys. She plays Dvořák, ballad in D minor, and a few of Paganini's capriccios. A hall on an upper floor in a bourgeois house on the water—the hostess, Irene Jensen, has a rare beauty for this city and is never at a loss for an apt sentence; she was someone for whom intelligence didn't destroy grace, quite the contrary, here skin and hair flourish again on a second, in a sense more sophisticated level, that's how the new pastor would perhaps have put it but he's not here because he lacks the contacts, and the old pastor is doing his damnedest to mediate nothing for his successor. He

gave up his mediation duties on the same day as his eccle-
siastical post. Ruven was his last candidate. Ruven still
has to honour what is expected of him and that is a lot. Ever
since the divine began withdrawing from the world, people
have been bearing down on those whose fingers are capable
of more than moneymaking, and so they sit in neat rows
and hope almost religiously for the as-yet untested violinist
from the village with his ill-fitting suit and the stiff
demeanour, at which it's hard not to laugh. But at least the
stiffness has equilibrium, it distantly reminds one of a
ship's mast, and it could be the start of something.

The whole thing is over much faster than Ruven had
expected, mostly because he played faster than was to be
expected. He played so quickly that the polyp-plagued
page-turner at the piano had nearly slipped up even though
she was listening and watching closely and counting one,
two, three, four. At last, applause, slightly delayed because
the audience hasn't all caught up, and handshakes later, the
precious rings and stones clearly visible, everything that
could be preserved from the crises of the young century,
which demand more frugality with fabric, too, than was
called for a mere few years ago. The dresses are slim, the
shoulders free and the necklines low, everyone half-
naked—it's very foreign to Ruven. The whole fuss. The
awestruck semicircle of genuflecting people surrounding
the senator, who keeps repeating lines from his father-in-
law, a wealthy marmalade magnate, and his scowling wife;

the three gaunt officials, whose necks protruded vulture-like from their suits, their sad long faces swivelling hopefully back and forth as though they were waiting to be promoted here; the few meaningless aristocrats, cold and with underdeveloped lower jaws, visibly annoyed by the noise of the fully-bearded, cognac-swilling building tycoons standing next to them with their voluptuous wives—this is not his world. Ruven clamps the violin under his arm just as the professor nods to him and says as he walks past, 'Keep going. That had soul.' Ruven smiles absently. He'd been thinking about the page-turner while he played. She has the same hair as Rahel Goldbaum.

A lady keeps glancing over and then approaches the professor. He nods and smiles his half-smile, waves Ruven over and introduces the two to each other. Frau Marie Linde holds his gaze and says, 'Who is caring for you in these hard times?'

'I care for myself,' says Ruven. 'And the professor is here, too.'

'Yes, Professor. You are there, too,' Marie Linde laughs and reaches her hand out to Ruven to say goodbye, the other hand is already being held by a man Ruven's age, probably her son, their eyebrows are the same shape, and Ruven lowers his face to the woman's hand and feigns a kiss, he'd practised doing it this way with Gesche until she wouldn't be roused from her sighing any more, and Frau

Linde and the young man leave, the professor accompanying them both.

My first solo concert evening, thinks Ruven and steps out onto a wide terrace. Some men are smoking cigars and right away Ruven feels his foot. They're not discussing the music any more. They're bargaining, thinking about sacks of pepper and corn, chests of coffee and tea, new constructions and diversifications, increases and reserves, but surely not about him and his violin. The night is warm, the cigars are becoming more and more expensive, the heavy scent of linden trees and flowering freshwater draw near.

'Are you leaving tonight? Or may I invite you to be our guest?' Helene Bernhard is suddenly standing very close to Ruven, already wearing her hat.

'No, I'm leaving, I have a bicycle. But thank you very much for the invitation.' Ruven takes her hand. His tongue lies dull and heavy in his mouth. It's not his mouth, any more.

'But it's already so late and such a long way for you to go,' says the lady professor.

'It feels fine to me, and the night is lovely.' How I said that! he thinks. I'm already trying to sound like these people.

She hesitates, as if she wanted to say something more, or just to breathe the air. Then she smiles and leaves.

The bicycle belongs to John. It rides well but it rattles. It startles a herd of cows. They leap sideways and run in a heavy gallop farther into the pasture, where they turn around, panting. Ruven stops and stands close to the fence and holds the violin from the back. He plays. The animals hold still and watch him. Their eyes glint in the darkness.

You poor cattle can only do what you can, thinks Ruven. And we kill you in passing, with the same hand that we use to make music. Ruven lets the bow sink. He sits in the grass which is wet with dew, forgets the cows and everything else. From the village, the cocks crow across the canal that runs in a straight line behind the field and through this region. Further south is the next lock. Everything is still asleep; it is four in the morning at the latest.

Everything goes on. In the officer's association, in the church, in the ratskeller, in the historical society; two weddings, a baptism. Apart from that village music, Saturdays, with old Dordel, eyes shut and one two, one two, and some money in the hand and beer in the throat and then home and door shut, deep breath and shake off the simple fiddling and stand at attention and say no. And no means practise more. At the same time, he's already exhausted from the idea that he must keep playing and practising to prevent a violin player's finger from turning back into a wainwright's son's finger. Because that is it, yes, he thinks, we're going beyond nature by going beyond that which is simply there, such as the rock or the cow, for example, but all that which isn't nature any more we must think and obtain ourselves because no one else thinks and obtains. A person could go mad over it. Over this self-made solitude. Suicidal, he thinks, and for strength, he hangs the vice admiral's letter on the wall.

Dearest Herr Preuk!

On behalf of the German Officer's Association, please allow me to express the most heartfelt thanks for the beauty   you provided through your art to our evening social benefitting the Ruhrhilfe.

The applause of our members and guests demonstrated to you the great enjoyment you brought to all of us. Your selfless sacrifice is to be thanked for making the evening such a tremendous success, and for allowing 70,000 marks to be sent off to the Ruhrhilfe.

With the hope that now and again I'll once more have the pleasure of listening to you, and with the best wishes for your future success,

I remain yours,

Vice Admiral Veit Kröner

'Psh,' goes Gesche. 'I thought an admiral's letter would be snappier. And what is it doing on the wall?' Mother Preuk says nothing, but writes something down from the catechism and hangs it on the opposite wall.

Ruven takes down both pieces of paper and says at the table, 'Mother, I'm twenty.'

'That is nothing compared to the age of the world!'

Mother Preuk is falling deeper and deeper into her beliefs, as well as her superstitions. She's already preaching more than the new pastor, whom she also won't acknowledge. She has the second sight, whenever she casts her gaze up or down and consults her cane. And as she is no longer steady on her legs, she always walks with her cane, so that she is flooded with images and visions. At the millpond in the neighbouring village, for example, she sees a woman in a white dress with a skull; she sees the snow, which falls on the church roof in July as a sign from heaven; she sees and sees and doesn't discriminate any more. Instead, she packs everything into a single sentence, together with her latest recipe and a 'good day', and then immediately afterwards she asks Ruven, 'When will you finally get married, boy?'

Ruven puts his cup down and looks at her, smiling: 'Soon, Mother. But to whom?'

The question is justified, for Lene has recently begun sewing a dark red P and R in every napkin, and the

Röver-son Peter ploughs and harrows and sows so that the dirt puffs up and billows all around him. No one knows why she wants the Röver boy, whose chin gets lost between his lower lip and his throat, when she obviously likes Ruven, too, whose chin sits at just the right place. And perhaps the P doesn't stand for a first name at all and the R not for a surname either, but no one thinks about that, as the order of things is the order of things. So, whom should he marry? Ruven rides his bike to the train station, and then he takes a train to Hamburg. He rides to the synagogue at Bornplatz, perhaps someone there knows Rahel, he asks around. 'Goldbaum? Rahel Goldbaum?'

A Rahel Goldbaum lives on the Alster, comes the answer. Over there. No one knows the house number. And finally Ruven is standing in front of a large and silent mansion on Fontenay Street. A girl in a black dress with a white pinafore opens the door and bends into a quick bow and disappears into the background. Then a woman appears who has very dark hair. And the eternal song in Ruven's head is suspended for a few bars, and all other functions, too, are for a moment interrupted.

'Ruven Preuk!' And although her expression has something fundamentally sad in it, for a moment Rahel beams so openly at him that Ruven entirely forgets to say anything. 'Please come in, sir,' says Rahel and leads him into the small hall with a fireplace.

Leave the 'sir', Rahel, thinks Ruven, already sitting in a blue parlour. The cup rattles against the saucer as she holds it out to him. These white hands! This smell! Ruven doesn't stir so that he can drink in every breeze her movements make, which waft a bit of her fragrance towards him.

The girl brings biscuits. Rahel's eyelids rarely rise, but when they do, he is nearly knocked from his seat. He sits there, deadly serious, inwardly tumultuous. Incapable of conversation. Incapable, even, of humour. And while she talks about this and that, Ruven's gaze falls upon the armchair's expensive upholstery and then on the worn material of his sleeve. This is, he thinks, an unbridgeable gap. He should not be so happy to have found her.

'I'm so happy to see you,' says Rahel. 'You can see that I've been lucky. Lucky and unlucky. Elias . . . my brother . . . and our grandfather, ah, anyhow . . .'

'I'm so very sorry,' says Ruven.

At that, she smiles valiantly. 'When will we hear you here in Hamburg? You know, my uncle loves concerts as much as I do. We feed ourselves at the concert hall.' She laughs and puts a hand on Ruven's arm: 'Play me something on Grandfather's violin, please!' She stands up lightly and disappears into the next room.

'What shall I play?' he asks when she returns.

'Play Grieg for me! The G major sonata! I've just been practising it on the piano. Perhaps we could even do it together? The second movement? I love that one especially!'

The tea grows cold, the biscuits remain in the little porcelain bowl and it is dark when Ruven runs along Fontenay Street and shouts like a maniac into the night: 'Visit me again!'

Three crimson visits later Ruven writes, against his better judgement, a letter:

> *Dearest honourable Doctor Jakub Hermann Goldbaum!*
> *I am well aware of the obstacles standing in the way of a union between your niece and myself, but please allow me to nevertheless request her hand in marriage!*
>> *Hoping for a joyful reply,*
>> *Yours faithfully —*
>> *Ruven Preuk*

And it is not even two weeks later before he has his answer.

> *Dear Herr Preuk,*
> *The obstacles you've mentioned appear to me to be insurmountable.*
>> *I remain sincerely yours,*
>> *Dr Jakub Hermann Goldbaum*

Mother Preuk cuts flowers with the knife, puts them in front of Ruven and is finally, for once, still. She knows that it hurts. At night, the owls hoot. Ruven listens and doesn't sleep.

'Close your eyes,' says his mother, 'You're falling apart.'

And he hears her words, but can't keep his eyes closed.

'One light looks like all the others, and one shit also looks like all the others,' she says then, and even if it doesn't quite apply, something begins to shift because of it. Because of her remark, weeks later, instead of heading left to the train station Ruven goes right, to the estate, and there he rides a few times around the pond with the swans and the boat house in the shadows of a triple-trunked alder tree. He calls this thinking, and it could also be called a little bit of planning ahead, into the future.

On the estate is the house of Gosche Lunten, the steward, and his wife, Erika, who raises so many cattle and grows so many vegetables with her husband that the interior of the estate has become something like a farm again, and along with his steward's wages it makes possible a very good living and a large household. And every morning there emerges from this household a whole swarm of futures, that is, ten daughters with twenty pigtails.

'In heaven, I'll still be braiding the hair of all the angels,' says Erika Lunten at breakfast each morning. 'My hands are so accustomed to it. I'm useless without it!'

Ruven rides past the Luntens' house and Lene is standing in the garden, eyes glinting. She fingers her braids and says, 'Take me with you into the woods; the badger said that you play your violin out there.'

'If that's what you want,' says Ruven.

'If I'm not your second choice, then that's what I want.'

And then he's no longer alone and so his assumptions were correct. From now on, there is always something lying next to him in the leaves, a living bouquet of meadowsweet, and it looks up into the treetops and only occasionally says things like: 'No, not like that—it should be heavier and deeper here, then lighter there, and then it will be music. Do you see the beam of light there, how it falls through the foliage, everything there is always precisely attuned as if the sun were saying: It should be just so. Or the tree. The tree can't ever be too thick or too thin. It is always just right. But when you play that this way, it's not quite right. Oh, I don't know, I don't know anything about music. But I have ears.'

Yes, you have ears, thinks Ruven, you have beautiful and good ears. And he goes to the pond with the swans again and inwardly says goodbye to Rahel, or at least tries to: It will unfortunately come to nothing now, he thinks. Not this year and or next year or the year after next. One must know what one can want, and what one cannot.

The air is clear, the contours of the landscape are sharper again, as if the earth was remembering itself after a long summer. With a water lily in his buttonhole, Ruven stands in front of Gosche Lunten's house door and rings the bell.

'Go through the kitchen!' Calls Gosche from inside. 'The front door is jammed!'

'No,' says Ruven. 'Today I must go in through the front door.'

It goes on until Gosche gets the door open. He wonders at the fact that it's opened at all. No one has walked through it for the last 300 years.

'So,' he says finally, 'What is it, now, that can only come in through the front door?'

Ruven holds a deep breath. 'Your Lene . . .'

'Lene? You've had your eye on her too? You're not the only one.' Gosche laughs. 'I say you can have her, you sophisticated fellow! Take her with you, but make it fast. Mother! Lene! To the front door!'

They're here already. The coffee table is quickly set. But Gosche Lunten forgot to ask his wife. Erika Lunten, unsettled, pours the tea and cuts cake and helps them to the food and says, 'Yes, you can have her, but only when she's grown and you've become someone. Not until then. Until then, she stays where she is. Wherever money is, you'll find the devil. And where there's none, you'll find him twice. I've also said this to the young Peter Röver, who also came here fawning.' So she says. And that's that. Everyone falls into silence.

'Hmm,' says Gosche finally. Nothing more. And Ruven searches for the front door and wants to walk out backwards through it, as if that would undo what happened. Gosche simply shrugs his shoulders and says, 'We were much too rash. If she doesn't want it, she doesn't want it.' Then he shoves the heavy door shut and kicks it and Ruven hears the way he laboriously turns the key in the lock and curses at it.

'We won't get anywhere this way,' says Professor Bernhard. 'Self-abasement is nothing but another instinct. You must be more relaxed, cool yourself off. You are so entertained by your own inner drama. Anyone can see it! You're like a kind of changing Tristan chord.' He tells Ruven to fall back for once, to not show up for three weeks, give himself a rest; perhaps a bit of boredom will help.

Ruven falls back. He hardly speaks at all any more. He lies in bed, next to his violin, for hours. He fingers its lacquer, puts its back against his ear and listens to the wooden body inside. You are so light, he thinks, as he holds it up, so innocent. And yet you control me. You can kill me, you know it. But you have no heart. You take mine, my life, for yourself. The two of us will end up very much alone.

Ruven plays. Sometimes, throughout the night. He sits in the pitch black on a footstool and plays the violin. Outside, in its stable, the blind mare twitches its ears, and inside the house the violin sings, whines and prays under Ruven's fingers.

When the professor hears him twenty days later, he lifts himself from his armchair, stands and listens, and when it's finished, he claps, very slowly, three times. Then he simply stands there for a long time. Perhaps something has just passed before his inner eye, his own career: at fourteen he was already the first chair violinist in Frankfurt, after that he'd travelled widely around the empire and also crossed over its borders, he'd been to Berlin many times, especially Friedrichshagen, and everything had been fluctuating in the current of his music until he'd met that blow and found himself again in this city with its bricks drowning in oxblood, its draughty churches, draughty alleyways and bourgeois houses in which a spare, gestureless language was spoken, as if the citizens had to save their strength because of the weather. It's a language that exists in the far front of the mouth, without any music but with a kind of humour to replace it, which he unfortunately only first began to understand after many years here. Here, he'd established himself, pushed his Paganini students so far until he'd been in the position to further impart his violin pedagogy in one of the two rooms of his gloomy house. Here, he'd finally found a student, a highly gifted young man whose cranium refuses to absorb his theories but who possesses an ear and a sense of rhythm that makes the professor in his armchair go alternately hot and cold and finally feel something like envy arise in himself for all the pleasure he takes in this gift, because this young man stands there with a face with which a person can either fall in love or use every weapon of the heart and mind to keep away, so as not to lose oneself in it.

'You are ripe,' says the professor finally and wipes his eyes. 'For the moment. You're only missing the right instrument. A truly good instrument.'

Ruven scuffs the parquet floor and doesn't answer. He is gaunt. He is badly shaved. He has nearly exhausted his tears, and he knows he will not be able to raise any money for a violin that is truly good.

'I'll take care of it,' says the professor. 'I'll take care of it. My boy, you'll be huge!'

It storms on the way home. The wind changes direction and twists across the field. And the field, too, is black by nature or, at least, very dark, and Ruven doesn't have to search for long before it occurs to him why such colours can hurt so much. And for a while, he sees himself overcoming all obstacles and a door on Hamburg's Fontenay Street silently opens again.

Shortly before the estate he runs into Lene, and instead of saying anything, she just smiles and looks at the ground.

'Where were you?' He asks.

'I went by the nurse's for tea. I've told Emma about us. I'm supposed to tell you that you shouldn't be sad. A woman only grows better with age.' At that, she grins again and even laughs, loudly, into the air, spinning around with her arms splayed as if she wanted to display herself from all sides, and then she simply walks away, basket on her arm. She pulls her coat closed and doesn't look back again.

A black night follows the others. In the mornings, Ruven feels courageous, in the evenings, fear. Finally a Saturday arrives, and Ruven dresses up and travels to the city.

'You're playing with me on Saturday here, for a small circle of the right people.' The professor had made notes for it, a short list of names. Now those names are sitting there, drinking wine and smoking. Off to the right, on the sofa, there was even a journalist, who would later write: *The young artist commands an absolutely assured technique, and an incandescent, warm sound pervades his performance. His accomplished staccato is downright astonishing.*

The professor says a few words beforehand. He hasn't prepared a difficult program. 'Tchaikovsky comes later,' he'd decided, 'much later.' Instead there was Handel, Mozart and also something he'd written himself, a lullaby.

This prelude has something akin to a birth, particularly in the careful looks that measure up the young musician. They have heard him already, in the beautiful Jensen woman's house, but it's very different this time. He'd changed. It was as if he'd been sick. He looks so pale. And he plays as if he's alone, as if there were no audience in the room. And how he grips the violin, they can hardly trust themselves to watch, let alone clap. Afterwards, too, as they partake of the food on the table, they are almost slinking around, and it's only once they are in the corridor that they grow loud again, and confident, and judge the way that people are wont to judge.

Next to Ruven sits Marie Linde with her son, and this time she's also with her husband, the ophthalmologist.

'Do you remember me?' asks the doctor, and Ruven says no. He can remember neither faces nor names. 'I've heard you once before, in the winter, maybe two years ago. You played with a very old man in the Hotel Kaiserhof.'

Ruven remembers, vaguely. Old Goldbaum with the soup, the gentleman at the table in the back, the heavy fur coat extended to him as he left. The voice came into his head again. One must know what he can want, and what he cannot.

Dr Linde nods. 'It was one of my bad nights. I'd sold a painting from my collection that morning.' He looks past Ruven. 'It had once been a meaningful collection. But at some point, I became almost accustomed to selling. Circumstances change, and we must somehow go on living.'

From that point on the doctor speaks for two hours about art, asks whether anyone knows this or the other painter, discusses some Norwegian painter, until Ruven's face flushes red again since he can only ever answer: 'No, I don't know that one, no, not that one, either.' Then what does he know? He feels none of the pleasure that the doctor has for this or that painting. He knows how to make wheels, barrels, and little foals, he can listen and play music, but no one in the Preuk family has ever been interested in painting; and music, too, he doesn't play music just for pleasure. Work, it is work! And love, yes, perhaps also love. He would have liked to just say that to the doctor. Most of all, he would have liked to tell the man that he might prefer conversing with people who also understand him.

They change to a more comfortable seating arrangement out of woven basket. Ruven loses his balance, one leg falls over the other and he can't right himself. He is either too tall or too short for the creaky seats, and in the middle of a particularly arduous sentence, he glimpses black mud on the edge of a sole and shoves his right foot under a small coffee table. It wasn't designed for it and shakes perilously. Dr Linde nods amiably, nods indulgently and shakes his head: 'You know, these are hard times, even for me.'

I've lost the thread, thinks Ruven and nods anyway so as not to let anything show. And also so that he doesn't aggrieve the doctor's indulgence. It really takes all sorts of times, he thinks.

'Soon I'll just have the memories,' says the doctor, 'a good portion of the works themselves are already gone, to America, for all I know.'

Why America? Ruven's eyes search the room for the professor, and he only hears the doctor as if he's speaking from a distance: 'You should see what's still there! It is still a collection, yet!' Dr Linde stops himself for a moment. 'But what am I talking about! We should be discussing music, your music!'

A shiver up his back, Ruven suddenly sits very straight in front of his demitasse cup. My music? he thinks. Can I talk about the colours with him? Should I? Tell him that a tangle of colours always dances around me, when I play my music? He'd surely take me for a lunatic. He's an eye doctor.

'Tell me about the Norwegian,' says Ruven very quietly. His own voice sounds strange and fake. He'd never actually asked someone to tell him about something.

The doctor trims a cigar and as it smoulders, he leans back: 'The Norwegian, yes, we liked to call him that—I haven't seen him for a long time. Sometimes he writes to me, or to my wife.' The doctor glanced wistfully to the side. 'He's often not well,' he says. 'It's his nerves. He drinks a remarkable amount . . . well, it's also his disposition. He's a solitary man, tormented by pride and humility. And yet for a long time people would fall at his feet. Perhaps that only tore things further asunder for him.' The doctor remains silent for a few seconds, and smokes. 'It's quite precisely fifteen years ago that he was in our house for the last time. And he was often our guest, and stayed for a long time, too. He painted the most wonderful paintings!' His son laughs. A self-conscious laugh. He's barely older than Ruven, has delicate features, and laughs until a tuberculosis cough overwhelms him. 'Painted is not the term for it,' says the doctor, 'what he did was so new that a new word had to be invented for it. In the language of music, we would have perhaps said that it was the large, powerful transformation of the south into the north. He had killed the entire light of impressionism within himself and allowed it to be resurrected in a new form. But I'm talking too much again! What is more boring than discussing absent paintings.'

He looks down at the table in front of him and strokes his moustache. He likes talking, it sometimes feels like doing gymnastics, his blood gets pumping when he talks. There, his son, I have four, he says quietly, four sons. 'But you really have to see the paintings at some point. And the drawings! Treasures! We'll invite you, no question! Preferably soon!'

There's no rush, thinks Ruven, and feels embarrassed because he's ungrateful. But Helene Bernhard looks happily at him from a distance and comes over to him. She takes him by the arm and says quietly, 'That was good.'

As if marooned, he finds himself in his little room at the wainwright's again. He feels like a genie only recently freed from his lamp and already too big, inflated too much for his old vessel. He'd also smoked so much that he was staring dizzily at the ceiling beam.

He hears Gesche crying in the next room. She's always crying, these days. Ruven listens. He's alone too much. He's too agitated by all that was and by all that could still come to be. Norway, this earthy love by the sea, what was it that the doctor had said? The stones, bones, bodies, the wind and the splashing of the soul on the beach, one can almost hear it. The splashing of the soul—good heavens!' And Berlin and a black piglet? What sort of black piglet? A pub, with a name like that? And where had the professor been the whole time? And what had he himself been babbling about, for a trinket! Just remembering what he'd said made him turn red. It occurred to him he'd like to stand up now, to relieve himself outside somewhere in the lilac arbour, when the door opens and Gesche comes in. She slinks barefoot to his bed and at first, he thinks that she's sleepwalking but then she stops and stands still, her naked body in front of his face.

'Comfort me,' she says into the darkness.

Ruven doesn't think he's heard her right. 'But John?' he says, startled.

'Sleeping,' she says, 'Comfort me!'

'But . . .'

He knew about her. He'd almost always lived with her beautiful eyes. He'd known about her since his twelfth year, perhaps even longer. There had been a certain encounter before this one, too. One of the sort that a person never mentions, yet also never forgets.

It had been Gesche who had brought him the warm towel from the oven, on that Sunday when he was about eight years old and had fallen into the half-frozen reservoir and been hauled home, stiff and shivering, by John. Like the maniple of Jesus Christ, which the pastor had briefly mentioned, the white towel appeared in front of him and Gesche rubbed him back to life with it, so that his skin and her hands and eyes seemed to be burning.

And so he knows what's happening and looks now in the dark for cigarettes and smokes to gain time. He feels lightheaded. He is seized with rage, at the same time, because he is still living alone in this small room. What's the use of music if one would also like a proper life! If one would also like to feel that his whole body is alive! He grabs her naked stomach with his free hand and lies down on his back again.

'I'm not allowed to do that, Gesche,' he says finally and taps a few beats on her skin, until Gesche makes herself very small next to his bed and begins again to cry. In the dark, Ruven balls the fingers of his right hand into a fist. Then he kisses the part in her hair and says, 'Gesche, it is no solace that life is what it is. It hurts.'

In the morning, Gesche mops all of the rooms. At noon, she cleans the windows. She cooks onion soup and bakes onion quiche and peels and peels and as she works she weeps torrentially. She doesn't look at Ruven. She only cuddles more affectionately with John, but so much devotion is almost too much for him because it only puts him under pressure. To please a woman it's most effective to muster up a bit of manliness, John knows that. But what Gesche doesn't seem to realize is how in the middle of events a sudden, wholly unrelated thing can come to mind—he prefers to call it French foolishness—which happened to someone far away from the homeland when it was too cold, too hard there.

Who would blame a person for seeking his earned rest and warmth in the gender that had been responsible for it for centuries, after the taking of a homestead? But of course, after the taking of such a homestead, a taking that was necessarily violent, one couldn't quit this violence again so quickly. And it seemed that a person didn't have to speak for the French hussies to understand that, too, and that's why they didn't complain. Now, years later, when John lies beside Gesche and thinks back on it, it seems entirely different, especially when he pictures the French farmer, whom they shot dead like an afterthought. John imagines him resurrecting from the dead and paying a similar visit to Gesche.

Such thoughts always go through his mind at the crucial moments, leaving Gesche alone and only able to soothingly lisp: 'That doesn't matter. I love you, one way or the other.'

In December, Gesche puts a postcard next to Ruven's plate. On it is written:

Dear Herr Preuk!

We would like to put on a little evening concert here in our house on the 22nd of December, and as I will never forget your stunning performance at Prof. Bernhard's, I'd like to invite you to perform—with the request that you bring sheet music with you and provide your lovely violin playing for a small circle of listeners in our music hall, which is renowned for its acoustics. We'll provide a good pianist.

We ask that you take the 4.54 a.m. train and stay with us for dinner.

Please only inform us if you are unforeseeably pre-
vented from coming and in that case you may of course
do so by telephone at my expense (number on reverse).

It may interest you to know that we've had a violin
made for us that turned out wonderfully. Hopefully,
you'll be convinced of that yourself when you hold it in
your own hands!

With warmest regards!

I remain yours,

Dr Max Linde

'Go quickly,' Gesche says and laughs. She's brushed out the
suit and holds it out to Ruven. He rides the bike to the train
station. He just barely catches the train and after he arrives
in the city, he stands for a few minutes on the street until
Linde's son drives up in his father's car.

For the first time in his life, Ruven rides in an automo-
bile. Up until this point it had only been horse-drawn
hackney carriages or omnibuses, if it was anything at all.
But now the journey through the city is unusually comfortable and enviably direct. The young Linde bears right
on a curved driveway, at the end of which lies the villa. Just
as they arrive at the impressive house, the door opens and
the hostess appears, waving, or perhaps she's only lifting
her hand to her hairdo while she glances out at them. Her
gaze is distracted and full of emotion. Or perhaps she's
simply near-sighted.

She leads Ruven almost silently into the house. Inside, it's comfortably warm. There is something enchanting and sombre about the high-ceilinged rooms. A superfluity of mirrors multiply the palm trees and sculptures and brightly coloured empire-style furniture, and Ruven wanders as if through a fairy-tale castle; he can barely orient himself. This is really genteel, he thinks, and for a long moment, he keeps clearing his throat because something is sticking in it.

The doctor appears more stooped today, but perhaps that's only the effect of his youthful portrait behind him on the wall, in a blue and black sailing outfit. He's still at the best age there, with light-brown hair and sensitive, almost childlike eyes. His face, thinks Ruven, looks like a raw piece of meat. He must turn away, he's almost embarrassed that someone had allowed himself to be painted like that, and he looks around to see if Professor Bernhard is perhaps close by.

The doctor smiles. 'Yes, you see, these pictures hanging here are the ones I told you about. Come with me, I'll show you around.'

No, don't show me around, thinks Ruven, I'd rather puzzle through all of this by myself.

'You know,' says Linde, standing before a very small painting, 'it's not just that one wants to simply own these things. He's silent for a few seconds and looks down at the floor. 'Have you ever been in a large museum?'

Ruven shakes his head.

'Then you're not familiar with that moment in which you'd like to hold a painting and decide on a frame for it, to find a place for it, and want to touch it again and again.'

No, thinks Ruven, I'm not familiar. And he almost feels like laughing, to protect himself.

The doctor keeps gazing at the floor. 'It's not for nothing that possession is such a physical word. A large appetite, that's possession. To be allowed as close as possible without doing harm.' Here, Linde cautiously taps the frame of the painting. 'To breathe it in, provide for it, care for it. And to allow oneself to be cared for. One is really under the protection of the painting. A protection against disappearance.' He looks almost as though he has to tear himself away from the small painting.

He leads Ruven silently to the next room. They stand in front of a wide painting. It shows four boys in front of a white door. Hopefully they don't actually look like that, thinks Ruven. The doctor looks at the picture and clasps his hands behind his back: 'We will once have been.' He looks at Ruven, who is resolutely wishing that he were in the woods or in some village pub.

'A certainty that will allow us to survive after all,' the doctor continues. 'A certainty that justifies us, justifies what we are doing now. We will have been. Do you understand?'

Not a word, thinks Ruven, and he's discovered a noise coming from somewhere, perhaps just water gurgling in one of the modern radiators, but this noise is attracting his ear and he must pay attention so that he doesn't begin to hum along with it, *hm-hmm-hm, hm-hm-hmm*.

'Collecting art is purer appetite for life,' says the doctor. 'We nourish and are nourished. Only the bread that I offer is secular, it is only bread.'

The doctor goes to the next painting. A little cart with two goats in front of it, their short tails almost twitching. Everything is so scribbled and scrawled, as if the journey should be setting off soon.

Hm-hmm-hm, hm-hm-hmm, Ruven nods absently at the goats, moving his toes in his shoes to the beat, and searches for the melody.

'You know, sometimes I feel embarrassed . . . but come here, let's sit down.' The doctor points to a stool. On the table next to it there is a blue linen portfolio embossed with gold letters. Inside, there are etchings, stitches and drawings by the Norwegian: the Linde family. Ruven only sees the eyes, and he dares not look up again, as he fears the eyes in the doctor's face will appear less alive than those on the sheets of paper. What is drawn there, he wonders to himself. Purer eyes! Does the painter wish to demonstrate that we can see? Or that we will have seen? What does this Norwegian know about sight? 'Can he also hear?' He asks the last question in a low voice, and the doctor raises his eyebrows: 'Astonishing question! Yes, I think he can. You should meet him someday!'

But Ruven doesn't answer any more, so engrossed is he in the portfolio. And he is almost happy, when the somewhat impure C of the doorbell reminds him of the impending concert.

He hastily takes a glass of water from the tray held out to him in the music room and drinks a bit too fast, so that he must wipe his mouth. The music room appears huge in the mirror. The metal stand is ready on its three lean legs, a grand piano next to it, hardly opened as the room is not all that large—after the first notes, however, it's clear that it can handle music.

Ruven stands sideways to the audience, his eyes almost shut. He lifts the violin mechanically. He has a body, and it is suddenly in his way. He breathes in and out, but even as he takes in air he is thinking too many thoughts. He plays without glancing up. He doesn't see the lips of the apothecary twitching to the wrong beat; he knows nothing of the ill-wishes from the two music students in the last row; he doesn't see the hungry eyes of the older listeners, behind whose foreheads a word is perhaps forming that fills them with vague and unwarranted pride: Aryan! they think. He plays La Campanella, he plays because it's perhaps all that one can do when one is in the world, as the professor once said. For music isn't simply one thing among other things, but rather everything among everything else. There is a difference.

The pianist is very tall and accompanies Ruven somewhat phlegmatically. Her part is not particularly hard. Ruven plays blindly and simply, without breathing. He forgets to breathe, plays and plays and thinks: Tomorrow, I'll drive up the poplar road and visit Lene. And he plays on until he senses that someone is looking at his fingers. He senses the presence of someone who is both familiar and utterly foreign to him. Something horribly sincere that, like the violin, lacks a heart because it is only what it is. The gaze turns his fingers into lead and presses down on his entire hand until he opens his eyes.

The mirror fills half the wall in front of him. The mirror has a bright, staring gaze that he hadn't at all recognized at first. It feels to him as though these eyes had already gazed at him before and he has to pull himself together so that his knees don't buckle when it becomes clear to him that these eyes are his own. There he stands, doubled, and all at once his violin is only an object, his fingers reaching once around its throat. The pianist has so much momentum, she's been listening so little to Ruven that she plays a few measures further. And then it is silent.

A throat clears. Ruven doesn't know at what place he'd interrupted his piece. For several moments, he doesn't know at all what's happened. The pianist repeats the last measure again, as if to remind him. And so he sets off again and plays to the end but that doesn't enchant anyone any more.

The park is stiff and coated with frost. It glistens in the light that still descends from the tall windows. It's very cold, but Ruven walks on and on in the dark and listens with half an ear until he hears the footsteps of the pianist and just barely manages to step into the shadow of a yew before she overtakes him.

'Herr Preuk,' she says quietly, 'Ruven?'

He waits until she turns around and goes back. Then he walks further into the park. He has a horrible urge to gag. He considers simply staying outside. But the path inevitably leads him in a long arc back to the house.

Things must be finished, Ruven knows that. That he will be watched, he knows that too.

Inside, everything is civil and warm and atrocious. Sherry as aperitif, comforting looks, disappointed looks, no looks at all. Food is served, napkins spread over knees and glasses spun in conversation. Forks are stuck in meat and potatoes, sauces mopped up, wines emptied, and not a word is said of the incident. People merely smile more when they turn their attention to Ruven. They had already marvelled at those eyes. And they also try a little to conceal their disillusionment from themselves and from the others. For it would have been much too beautiful for such a picture of a man to also be a convincing musician.

The two students sit up as tall as their delicate spines allow, and speak loudly about this or that musical interpretation. They laugh fake laughs. One of the two even puffs his cheeks out and splutters, overexcited and half-drunk. Ruven sits mutely at the table. This humiliation. Better to rot alone than to burn so publicly.

'You're so serious, Preuk,' says the doctor, who doesn't see any further problems with the whole affair, even if he notices that the young man needs to be helped up again. 'Yes, take incidents seriously. Seriousness is the virtue that one loses first.' He looks at his hand. 'Do you see,' he says, 'how my hand shakes? And it is the most serious part of myself. I touch the world with this hand. But it shakes. Show me yours.'

Ruven lifts his hand slightly above his plate, the bow hand, absolutely still, it surprises even him.

'I knew it,' says Doctor Linde, 'Like the hand of the Norwegian. It was so still that this woman shot him right there, as if she had to keep the spot awake. As if she had to inflict pain on this body part in order to make it susceptible to that which wants out of there.' Sometimes, says the doctor, he thinks that people often don't have enough pain, not enough pain at all. He almost thinks that one must buy art solely because one doesn't have enough pain. 'Do you understand that?'

'No,' says Ruven very quietly.

'Perhaps this is also an unsound thought. Come with me,' says the doctor, 'I must show you something before the dessert.' He waves at Ruven to follow him into his study and closes the door. They sit down in two deep armchairs. Doctor Linde smokes silently, then points to a violin case lying atop his writing desk: 'Open it!'

Ruven stands up, seized by a feeling.

'I wrote to you about this.' Linde smiles: 'Play!' He nods at him.

Ruven tightens the bow. He brings the violin to his chin. It protrudes from his throat like a new organ. Still bowing, he stands in front of the doctor, then straightens himself, lifts the instrument and cautiously tunes it. Then he begins at the place where he'd frozen.

He sees the grand piano's accompaniment before him, as it had been. Someone quietly opens the door. In the next room, the apothecary swallows his last spoonful of raspberry parfait, and the racial wounds in his mind are healed in a flash. The senator's wife keeps her mouth shut and listens, so that her eyebrows finally descend again to their rightful place, just above her eyes, bestowing upon her face an ebbing tide that allows her husband's heart to beat more calmly, or in any case, the senator feels as though something dreadful has dropped away from him, and even the two students are sliding fitfully back and forth on their chairs as though they ought to escape, their long, thin-skinned fingers tapping nervously in time.

Everything spins on a bit further. The whole carousel of miracles and marvels. It even feels as though the temperature in the villa is climbing up by several degrees, and perhaps it is this new, proud, German heat that gives the guests such alarmingly red faces that contrast so inelegantly with their light-coloured hair.

'And?' Asks the doctor when the last note has faded away, smiling again, 'What do you think of the instrument?'

It lies on the table at the window. 'Take the violin with you to the country for a while,' the doctor had said, suddenly not able to look at him. Now, well, it lies there.

I should have left it somewhere else, thinks Ruven, it's draughty by the window. It is ice-cold in his room; the water in the washbasin is frozen through.

'Linde'sche, that's what I'll call you,' says Ruven, and he holds the violin close to him in bed, turns it this way and that, strokes it and cautiously scrapes and knocks. Linde'sche, he thinks again. What have we gotten ourselves involved with, there? Do you see this, Joseph, my second gift. At least for a while. I know you can hear me. Where you likely are, you can hear everything that's happening down here. And not a little is happening.

'Preuk is a complete and total loner,' says Peter Röver. 'As if we were no longer here. Preuk doesn't say hello to anyone any more.' He stands at the corner of the house with Fritz Dordel and Hinrich Werkzeugmacher's youngest and smokes.

'If he comes along down here, there'll be a conversation,' he says and holds the cigarette in a cupped hand. His ears are red from cold. He actually ought not to mind Ruven's solitude, but somehow he has a small suspicion that Ruven still has company in his solitude, and that company might be someone whom he does indeed mind.

'But we should be proud of him,' says Werkzeugmacher's youngest.

'What do you mean, proud?' Peter Röver stubs the cigarette in the snow. 'It's only because Preuk can't do anything else that he thinks he can do whatever he can. It's only because that dirty city swine loaned him such a violin, a violin that now no one here is allowed to touch, because it's supposedly so infinitely valuable!' Peter Röver spits and stands up straighter, and Fritz Dordel nods his head, and his otter-face is very pinched as he asks, 'Does Preuk have any responsibilities in the village? A bit of fiddling for the silent films should be good enough, eh? He's not to be trusted.' Fritz Dordel makes a hole in the snow with his shoe. 'Does he pay anything to the community? From what, then?' He raises his empty palms aloft and lifts his eyebrows high up to his hairline. 'From what then, from what?'

Ruven hears none of it. If anything, after the violin he only hears Gesche, who sings much too often in the neighbouring room. These sad, simple songs. Suddenly, he wishes that she would come to his bed in the night just one more time. And he cries, secretly, and can't look at others any more, least of all Gesche, since she'd said, 'Your eyes, Ruven . . . What's happened with your eyes? They look dead. As if it isn't you looking out from them.' She had said it very quietly while she washed the dishes.

'And what if it is me, and you just don't recognize me any more?' He'd asked. But she'd already left the kitchen. In that moment he'd decided to only keep on listening to music, for a long while. Pitch, strength, quality. What do his eyes matter! How to add a new note to the previous one without cracking the lustre, without doing a muffled stroke, that's what one must know! The rest is unimportant.

Now he can play masterfully without driving the notes forwards, now they are exactly as he wants to have them, as the professor had wished it. And after a successful lesson, Ruven one day says to himself, 'Sometimes I suddenly hear without my ears.' The professor is silent and pets the red cat to warm his hands. Then all he says is: 'Nonsense! Détaché and martelé are still too close. Separate and hammered are not the same thing! I don't hear a difference there. You must differentiate better between the two strokes, and let the bow fly! What are you pushing around there?'

At other times, the professor is very silent. For all of January and then February, too. Sometimes he is even reluctant. Should Ruven prove something to him, he asks him then. Should he should contribute something, show him that he plays this and that section in such and such a fashion? Ruven does not understand him.

In March, days come in which he takes the path through the fields, to the smooth ash. He doesn't climb up high any more, a man who wears a hat doesn't climb trees, but he leans on its trunk and listens to the *tee-ta* of the white wagtail. *Tee-ta* is all it sings, with no notion of how beautiful it sounds when everything is still brown and the wind is still. This happy, bright call. Ruven returns home with the *tee-ta* in his ear, and re-creates it. A short pause, and then again. But it won't come out right. It doesn't want to go, on the violin. It is like a 'No'. It won't come together yet. In the beech tree, it is a 'Yes'. Well, back to the professor and report it to him. However, the professor only laughs and says, as if to himself, but that doesn't sound strange, and sinks into his armchair and appears to fall asleep as if the thought had fatally exhausted him, because it simply had no end.

'I have,' says Ruven, 'The feeling that I'm more and more alone in my search. Outside, everything passes by, everything goes about its business, but the people look to me like corpses because they don't want be anything more than just not too bad. And inwardly, I'm standing still and failing to find the connection. I'm alone.'

He shouldn't, for God's sake, think about that, says the professor quietly. For God's sake, don't think too much! It seized him once, this *tee-ta*, this twittering resonance—at that he should leave it.

On his way home, Ruven runs into the nurse Emma Braren. It was as if she was waiting for him, and she insists that he come with her into her house.

'Coffee?' She sets a blue enamel kettle on the stove. He has never been inside her home. It is messy and warm and there are piles and piles of books. Ruven imagined this place completely differently, he'd pictured it tidy and somehow white.

'What do you want?' He asks, because she's not talking, just looking at him, although not like the Klunkenhöker woman used to. Without desire, rather mocking. She's perhaps thirty years old and her hair is chin-length. She fits in here even less than he does. Perhaps that's it. She smiles, she drinks coffee and smokes.

'Something about you is interesting,' she says.

'You hardly know me, miss.'

'The girls tell me enough.' She grins. 'My name is Emma, by the way.'

'And what do the girls say?'

'This and that.'

'And what's interesting about it?'

'Why don't you take some kind of wife? Everyone here takes a wife and then goes on and breaks her.'

She slings her arm over the back of her chair and crosses her legs.

Now listen here, thinks Ruven, as he considers the framed photographs on the wall. 'Do you have a husband, then?' He looks at her. She smiles. She is no less strong and alone than he.

She doesn't need one, she argues and smiles again and shrugs her shoulders up high.

'And why do you think I should take a wife, then?' Ruven isn't sure if the conversation is bothering him.

'This is about Gesche,' says Emma, and now she has an entirely different tone. 'If you raise her hopes any further, you'll soon be dragging her out of the reservoir.'

'I'm not raising my sister-in-law's hopes at all,' says Ruven.

'Be that as it may,' says Emma, and there is something contemptuous in her expression because she doesn't believe Ruven: 'There are also other women.' Emma looks as though she were trying to read his thoughts.

'Perhaps no one wants me? Perhaps I'm not good for them, and I'll destroy them?' And he looks at her eyes so that it comes out like a threat. And it is, perhaps. He himself believes more and more that something unhealthy is coming off him.

Emma looks at her watch. 'I must go, I'd still like to go to the district capitol today. If you'd like, you can be my chaperone.' She stands up and takes a hat from the stand. 'It's assembly again. The bus leaves at five,' she says.

These assemblies are actually supposed to be kept a secret out in the villages. There are barely any workers here, and the servants live too far away from one another to join forces. And besides that, while their lives do indeed seem boring to them, they have food to eat and will marry one of the maids one day, when they will move into the servants' and workers' houses where they can even plant a small garden, and life isn't bad. But it could be better. For that reason, a few from the villages find themselves going to the assemblies. Ruven hasn't concerned himself with any of this before. Politics. But something about the way that Emma's eyes are glinting now grips him.

First, however, he brings the violin home. These are two separate matters; he wants to keep them apart. Then he pushes the bike out of the lean-to while Emma waits in the road. She climbs on behind him, as if she belongs to him, and when that doesn't work because a few bolts are loose there, she climbs down again and he lifts her up in front of him, onto the handlebars.

They ride from the large village to the small village and to a small one again and then to a large one. They've been alternating like this for ever, the large German villages, the small Slavic villages. The large ones are constructed along the road and in such a way that the inhabitants have to see very little of one another; the small ones are arranged around a central square and in such a way that the inhabitants can see quite a lot of one another. It was designed this way, however, in olden times. Nothing here is Slavic any more, instead everything is very German and things only occasionally still end with an 'itzke' or 'ow', and the more the land bleeds and the more the Germans fear that someone wants to do away with them, the more German they become, as if someone there was distilling something from it, a drink for some kind of slaughter, and it's not safe to travel to the assemblies because no one here knows any more where the Reich or the Republic is heading and so, one invokes the smallest and commonest of common denominators, which is after all still German, and one quite simply has something against such Bolshevik assemblies because

one can do the math on one hand and see that if these
assemblies were implemented, one will most certainly have
less than before. And so Ruven and Emma can be glad that
where they are going isn't written on their foreheads, or
that Emma is at least wearing such a tight hat that it covers
her forehead.

Ruven hides the bicycle near the train station. Emma
is already sitting by the window in the bus and looks out
to where he's standing. In the district capital, they go to
Lindenmüller's. In front of the house, young people and
ducks pass by in a gloomy procession. The people's jackets
are black and blue, the animals' plumage is a dirty yellow
and while the animals complain in every pitch, the people
are silent and wear the expressions of those afflicted by a
dangerous new belief.

Emma opens the door energetically.

'Ah, Emma Braren, come in, come in! There's still
space over there.'

The innkeeper wipes his damp face. He knows exactly
what he's doing here and what can come of it, but he is a
man who had never wanted to be an innkeeper and who
had only inherited this inn. He'd actually wanted to study,
philosophy or theology, had even become a pastor to do so.
Now he pours out the wine in unholy amounts with his
wife as he ruminates on this and all at once, everything is
drunk, even the furnishings are unbalanced, hands leave

nothing on the trays, the Republic is jostling around and not united.

In the low taproom there are six tables and two windows looking out onto the street, their curtains are drawn today. The smoke-filled speech from the miller's boy, Heinz, is audible; visible is the bloodlust in the eyes of his friend, Willi. The innkeeper's wife turns the glasses onto the brushes and scrubs them lightning fast, up and down. Then she looks over at Heinz and shakes her head until his talk finally comes to an end and there is more light, and the whole room shouts for the main speaker, a shipbuilder from Hamburg, from KP Wasserkante, the Hamburg district communist party, who relays greetings from the leadership and reads something just one more time, as a reminder: 'By selling his labouring power, and he must do so under the present system, the working man gives over to the capitalist the consumption of that power . . . ' After every sentence, he looks at Emma, who nods or shakes her head in response. Someone calls out loudly: 'But today, the wind is blowing in a new direction, away from Marx! Today, there are fascists crawling all over the place!'

'Ah, well,' murmurs the innkeeper's wife and peeks at the door. She already has the liquor at the ready and turns the key to the cash register. She'd ruin it in the end, the one who has to restore order, the one who also serves something to the people outside so as to cloud the united will a little bit, and who will be washing up until daybreak what this young republic will have vomited up everywhere. She reflects on this and just when she allows the key to the register to disappear into her cleavage, a man with lots of paper walks in and delivers a report from Zetkin's speeches: These speeches espouse the view, and all communists are in agreement, that fascism, which imagines itself to be such a bully, emanates from disruption and decay of the capitalist economy and is a symptom of the dissolution of the bourgeois state.

The report declares that fascism is also unable to unify the various bourgeois forces with whose silent, benevolent patronage it came to power.

There are various conclusions to be made from this. The first is that one mustn't regard fascism as a coherent phenomenon, not as a 'block of granite' off which all efforts ricochet. Fascism is an ambivalent construct.

One must devote the most energy to taking on the struggle, not only for the souls of the proletariat that have lapsed into fascism, but also for the souls of the petit bourgeoisie and middle bourgeoisie, of the peasant farmers and the intellectuals, in short, all of the social strata that today, because of their economic and social conditions, are growing in their opposition to large-scale capitalism and beginning to engage in a keen struggle against it.

In response to the chaos of contemporary conditions, the enormous shape of the proletariat shall rise up with the cry: I am the will! I am the power! I am the struggle, the victory! The future belongs to me! Then there is singing. 'The Internationale'. And more liquor. And then a bit more singing.

Ruven is silent in response to it all. He'd given up a greeting to the badger, who had surfaced with his coat inside out and gasping for air from the mass of faces, like a sea lion in a flock of fishing seagulls, as he shouted: '*Cursed be their anger, for it was fierce; and their wrath, for it was cruel!*' Then, like a lame sheepdog, he'd walked around the assembly at a shuffling pace and had bellowed one more time: '*And I will give children to be their princes, and babes shall rule over them. And all the people shall be oppressed, every one by another, friend by friend; proudly shall the child rise up against the ancient, and the base against the honourable.*'

'Are you for or against us, eh?' Someone shouted out from the back, and Ruven waved the badger over to him and took him by the hand and then withstood the looks and all the rest, and tried to pinpoint the place at which he'd lost the feeling for the main speech. Perhaps it had just been too loud.

In the bus, Ruven and Emma are quiet. They've brought the badger along, he is sitting between them like their large made-up child. They walk from the train station on foot for a bit, until Emma sends the badger on by himself and turns into the path through the field that leads down to the river. Two rows of poplars here make rigid and stark lines, their branches scraping against each other in the wind.

'There were too many words for me,' says Ruven and scratches his neck sheepishly. 'I'd really just rather be playing music.'

'There were too many words for me, too,' says Emma, and then she laughs. 'A heart doesn't need so many words. All a heart needs is another heart. Without a heart, there are no brothers or comrades. I've been trying to inject some heart into them for months.' She looks up to the dark sky. 'A new world can't be created with just the mind. That's why they don't know yet if they like me or not.' She searches for something in her purse. 'But a heart also needs cigarettes, so that we don't end up with too much heart. At least that's how it is for me. Sometimes, I have to properly free myself from the heart, just like I have to also free myself from God.' She laughs again. A nearly silent, perhaps even sad laugh.

'I didn't know that you had anything to do with God, still.'

'It depends on your perspective. I don't go to church, of course.' Emma takes an energetic pull from the cigarette. 'You would be waiting a long time for that to happen! But despite that I feel that atheism is idiocy, a bad sickness.' She presses a smoky kiss to Ruven's cheek. 'A shame that nothing will happen between us. I like you. And Gesche's heart would be helped, too.'

The night has passed its low point and they are chilled through by the time they leave the river behind and fetch the bicycle from the train station. The ride home goes quickly in the dark, and they separate at the entrance to the village.

The lamp is burning at the wainwright's, and Mother Preuk is sitting in the kitchen in a circle of light and spinning. She always spins at night and speaks to herself as she does it, as if she were reading from the threads that grew from her hands.

'I don't need sleep any more,' she says when Ruven tries to send her to bed. It is beautifully warm in the kitchen. A cricket rubs its legs together behind the oven. It wakes up and chirps every time the oven is heated, and Mother Preuk takes it as a sign for winter when it chirps in the kitchen, and as a sign for summer when it comes from the fields.

'I hear what there is to hear,' she says. 'One sense is enough. A person must only understand how to use it. Everything belongs somewhere, all one needs to know is where.'

From now on Ruven spends his mornings in the nurse's kitchen, with her books. Emma chooses one without looking and reads loudly: 'O my soul, I took from you all obeying and knee-bending and sir-saying,' she grins and blows dust from the table. 'The man wrote a whole book only to be able to say at the end: sympathy for the superior people! Do you know what that means, Ruven, sympathy for the people? Did you know that I'm risking my life for it?' That's how she says it. A molar in her upper jaw has recently gone missing.

'Where's your tooth?' Asks Ruven.

'Gone,' she says, 'A treat for the young Röver boy and Fritz Dordel after the last assembly. We ran into each other afterwards. They just barely caught my scent, came out of the bushes like a couple of martens.'

'Caught your scent!' Ruven looks at her, disconcerted. 'But why the whole tooth?'

'Perhaps they wanted to proselytize to me. But I remain loyal to my ideas. That didn't suit them.'

'I can see that,' says Ruven, thinking that the two will be sorry for this yet. But Emma just grins and displays, not without pride, Röver's and Dordel's work.

'It's only such a shame that it's such a dead gap,' she says, 'and not like the ones that schoolchildren have. Those are the loveliest gaps I know, because something is certain to grow back!'

Then she goes out into the kitchen garden and digs something up and slaps the dirt off her knees and presses her hands in a cross. Sometimes the badger stands at the fence, wanting something from her. 'I see the hunger in your face,' he murmurs softly, and then Emma lifts her spade threateningly and says, 'Then you don't know me at all.'

Ruven is playing at the open window in Emma's front room, and behind him sits Lene Lunten, dreaming more of concert halls and evening soirees than Ruven himself. Peter Röver remains completely unaware of Lene's intentions and lulls himself into a sense of security with large-scale farming. She's made her decision, at long last. One must really just hear him play, she thinks. And watch him as he does, that costs absolutely nothing.

Emma leaves to do the shopping, closing the garden gate behind her, and leaving the two young people alone. The store is at the village's only intersection, it's visible from all directions. The shopkeeper, Schlappkohl, wears a grey smock, keeps his hair very short and combed to the left, and clears his throat constantly. The whole man is as clean as the polished counter in front of him. Outside of his shop hours, Schlappkohl raises rabbits, fat under black and white fur, and pheasants, which he delivers to the Heidkrug pub during the hunting season, before the hunting caravan with the local councillors turns up after it has failed to shoot anything again as a result of its raucous drunkenness. Schlappkohl also has a peacock that struts around as décor and cries out something like *meow* and spreads its tail feathers so that it can't fit through the gate. The village children collect what it sheds and hide the feathers in their treasure chambers in the attics, next to the mouse skulls and pieces of flint, and do a brisk trade with them in the winter.

Emma buys coffee from Schlappkohl as well as dry sausage and thread and receives a discount because she rubbed with a white towel all five of his futures, in the form of small daughters, and then laid them in his arms. This is not enough, however, for him to like Emma. Something about her is dangerously close to him, although it's also far from him. Perhaps they both love what they aren't supposed to love. Despite that, his wife is still fully in use—perhaps even with unusual frequency—as if this was a way to deflect a secret. And so one or the other little futures will be born in the Schlappkohl house, at least until the poor woman finally arrives at menopause, and each future must be properly separated from its mother.

Ruven is still standing by the window in Emma's front room, and he watches how the evening approaches: 'Four weeks to go and then it's to Hamburg for the contest. We'll see then if anything comes out of me. And if so, then I'll marry you. No matter how young you are.'

He turns around to face Lene and smiles, and they both sit down at the table, carefully entwining their fingers like a lattice fence, and Lene gazes at him and doesn't seem to have any fear at all of Ruven's eyes. She even surrenders to him something of her own vibrant blue, she has so much of it.

'I'm happy that you aren't going to Röver,' says Ruven.

'One never knows,' says Lene, grinning. 'My mother says you must first move out of the wainwright's house. It's too close quarters there, she says.'

'Yes,' says Ruven, 'it is close quarters.' And as he says it he thinks of Gesche's naked body, and he'd like nothing more than to undress Lene, too, and behold her. If it's only for a second, he thinks, and all in innocence. But then Emma is already back and standing at the garden gate, and she sends a loud warning with the lock, for she does not want to run into anything.

And then on the following Monday, Emma runs into something. A bundle of brushwood, incredibly long, that isn't hanging from the latch like the deliveries from the broom maker but is instead nailed to the lintel, displayed there disquietingly and full of spiteful intimations. At first, Emma didn't notice it at all when she went out to the chickens in the morning, but when she went back inside, something was in the way of the door closing.

'Someone wants to give me a good caning,' she says later to Ruven, who had snapped the twigs in half and tossed them in the stove.

'And who?'

'Perhaps a few fathers.' She locks the door. 'Or some brothers, too,' she says with a gloomy look and mentally goes through a few comrades.

It is a dark yellow day. The rainclouds hang down to the treetops. They must light the lamps in the kitchen, even though it is noon and even though this time of year the temperature at noon is 23 degrees.

'If you leave here, Ruven, I'll be alone,' Emma finally says, thoughtfully, and goes out to the garden only to return shortly, all pale, to the kitchen.

'Come outside with me,' she says. And then she leads Ruven to the willow next to the shed. She takes him by the arm and nearly pokes him as she points to a woodpecker hole in the trunk. It is an ancient woodpecker hole, the lower rim of it shines from the many comings and goings of small birds. Right now only a beak can be seen there, a beak that belongs to a fat bird, far too fat for the hole, and this bird cries and wrenches open its throat, which flashes yellow and competes with the twilight.

'Do you see that,' says Emma. 'The cuckoo was born there. The egg could fit, but now he can't get out again.' Ruven leaves to get a hammer and chisel. When he comes back, she's standing, still pale, in front of the willow and staring at the hole.

'What is so terrible here, Emma? Every cuckoo lays its egg for a foster mother, and this cuckoo's mother managed to lay her egg for a chickadee. She didn't give it any more thought. It's just a bird.' Ruven hits the trunk with the chisel.

'It's not that,' says Emma softly, as the cuckoo finally flutters out and disappears into the neighbouring elderberry tree. 'It's that something like that can be born in such a tight space that it kills him,' she says.

'But he's not dead.'

'Go practise, Ruven,' says Emma, 'See to it that at least you manage to get away from this place.'

'You're welcome,' says Schlappkohl in the shop, his posture very straight. The bell rings as the customers leave.

'He was staring at your fly,' says Peter Röver to Fritz Dordel, when they're standing on the street again.

'We'll have to break him of that habit.' The flask sloshes in Fritz's sleeve. The silence of the afternoon crackles. For the past three hours, the oak has been throwing its growing shadow towards the northeast. They sit in the shade until the dark reaches over to the entrance to Röver's yard.

Schlappkohl closes the shop for the day. He has other things to do after four o'clock on Saturdays. Schlappkohl has a small boy scout group. He teaches survival skills in the woods to boys between the ages of ten and fourteen. He also teaches resuscitation and general life skills. It's somewhat in service to the German people, but also for his own purposes. To Fritz Dordel and Peter Röver this is suspect, and so they keep an eye on it.

'What are you two doing here?' Schlappkohl asks Peter.

'We're waiting.'

'And? What are you waiting for?'

'For the harvest, you know that, Schlappkohl, for the harvest.' Peter Röver laughs, his Adam's apple bobbing. His laugh makes no sound.

'It's June,' says Schlappkohl, 'there's nothing to harvest,' and walks on. They watch him go. He is almost fifty and has a wife and five children, all of whom are girls. It is as if only girls were coming into the world here. For Schlappkohl and his alleged preferences, a tough lot.

Peter Röver walks home in the shade. Fritz stays in the village square. Others come; they stand in groups and don't speak loudly. Fritz has the floor, his droning bass the only thing anyone hears.

The candles on the windowsill slowly droop to the side. Outside, the sky shimmers above the fields. Ruven plays so quickly that his eyes can no longer follow the notes. Sweat runs down his temples. He stops and wipes down the violin. Gesche clatters around in the next room. She cleans the kitchen and the cellar as if a move were imminent. John reads aloud from the newspaper with his arms outstretched. 'The dollar now costs one hundred thousand marks,' he says and reads on, a bit arduously, Hamburger SV is the new German football champion with its 3–0 victory over Union Oberschöneweide, a barge broke apart on the canal, and then much more, Stresemann and reparations and and and.

'Politics is getting crazier and crazier!' mutters Gesche as she wrings water into a bucket, 'Make room!'

John lifts his feet, the scrubbing brush moves between the legs of the chair and back.

'Perhaps people are also getting crazier,' says Ruven and grins at her through the open door.

'The fact that it interests you at all,' calls Gesche to Ruven in his room, 'How is one to make sense of it. Or what are you up to with Emma? You're always going over there, and her attitude is very well known. But yours?' She wipes her forehead with her apron: 'Music should be enough.'

'One must be involved in things. Particularly when one makes music.'

'What's that supposed to mean?' Gesche leans in the doorway and smooths her apron until Ruven drops the violin from his neck and looks at her.

'Well, for a start, it doesn't mean anything yet,' he says, 'but what you're calling politics is actually horribly out of control, and perhaps one must do something that will push things back in the right direction. Emma says it's all so different from what people think. It's about something entirely different, she says. About love. A person is the fact of love, or something like that. I still have to think about that, but the way she looks as she says it—her expression and her face, I can almost hear it. That's why I go over there. Emma's sound is entirely her own.'

Gesche holds the damp rag at the end of her long arm, and the water drops beside her bare toes. 'Oh, Ruven,' she says softly and turns around. Her back has grown wide. Her whole body has curved forwards, like a withering leaf curling around an empty middle. There's nothing left of the tension between her shoulders that had once allowed her to proudly prop her beautiful breasts underneath blouses and aprons, so that the young men's neck vertebrae had nearly locked in place. From the next room she asks, 'When is your contest?'

'On the twelfth of July.' Ruven puts the violin aside and sits on the bed. Yes, everything is falling apart. You have to compose yourself, he thinks, stand up again and practise until it's dark, until you're playing badly and everything hurts. Why not just be normal, he thinks, calm and content with whatever you have or don't have. The two, three people, who really expect everything from you, they have to be put off, the appropriate excuses already come to mind, sickness, phrases, why you really don't have much more ability than anyone else. You could also put yourself off, persuade yourself that you are ruining music, that it's making you sick, he thinks. Playing this passage for the eighty-first time. And one more time, because you get nervous when you leave it alone. Because time is running away from you. Perhaps you just should stop sleeping, that's a way to gain time. And who should pay for all of this? Just one more year of this. And if it then comes to nothing, go to work. Only do what there is to do. And perhaps also finally grow humble.

Ruven plays. He stands and plays, he sits and plays, until the 12th of July. It doesn't feel at all like a summer day. And July is also the wrong time of year for such a performance. Who can accomplish anything great in July?

Three of the professor's other students are competing. One of them sits with Ruven on the train to Hamburg. His good suit and careful movements, as if a spotlight were already always trained on him. And how he smokes. He's long been accustomed to the imminent environs, has been surrounded by culture from the time he was born. When Ruven boarded, he'd just offered a sour smile.

A conversation never materializes, and when they arrive at the central station Ruven is already soaking with sweat, certain that every accolade was unearned and feeling a rising nausea in his stomach and a dull pain in his foot. The previous night had been nothing more than an arduous span of time spent in bed. He is tired and suddenly so confused, as if he had lost his way.

At the lyceum he lingers near the entrance. The nervous voices echoing through the lobby, the rush for the toilets, the greedy sinews on the backs of the mothers' hands. Ruven is alone. He is also the oldest one here. He makes futile attempts to make eye contact with people, the sounds of that morning still ringing in his ears, the clucking of the chickens and Gesche's clattering in the kitchen. How is one supposed to properly perform his role as a musician, in a place like that?

The small concert hall isn't full, and from his side room Ruven hears the teeming, coughing, clattering crowd. The Linde'sche lies in its punched-out bed made of velvet, its red wood gleaming like a well-groomed horse. Outside, a summer thunderstorm fades away. As if in a trance, the rain had spread across everything for several moments, the clemency of the clouds in the tired grass in the street. Ruven stands at the window. Professor Bernhard makes a noise, a cough, it is time.

Breathe into your belly, Ruven thinks while he wipes his fingers dry. He looks down at his clean shoes as he climbs the small steps onto the stage. Half of the audience is still awash in applause for the last musician, a favourite. The polished grand piano is wide open. Hard to believe the ceiling doesn't come crashing down, the Steinway has such volume, thinks Ruven. The notes dance briefly in front of his eyes.

The journey home happens in the dark. The spark was lost. First, second, and third prize were awarded, and it was only the already-printed documents that betrayed the jury.

Bernhard was no comfort.

'It is how it is, Preuk.' He looked bone-weary as he said these words, as if something grave had just become clear to him. 'Next year we'll try again. Until then, you quit it with the flirting.'

How disappointed that sounded, and how Ruven hated him in that moment. The professor should have kept talking, should have added some technical reasons, health ones, in any case, he shouldn't have left any holes into which this new failure could force itself. The acorn in granite, which needs just the smallest bit of water.

The bike is gone from the train station. It's two hours by foot. At least the summer night is mild. He fills it with thoughts of Lene. But she's far away now, too. The bad concert between them. But was it really bad?

The light is still on at Uwe Dordel's. Ruven knocks on the window. Inside, old Ils jumps up from her sewing kit as if she'd been caught at something.

'It's you! Come inside, before the gnats get in!'

The old man is lying on the sofa with holes in his socks. When he sees the violin, he laughs: 'Where is my little sapling coming from, in the middle of the dark like this? Mother, bring something to drink! Our violinist is paying a visit. I wanted to have a drink with somebody anyhow. I was at the horse market this morning and bought a colt. I'm starting to breed them now. The field up here is too sandy for crops, but it's just right for the legs of horses. And we don't want horses to just disappear completely from the world only because so many of them had to go to war.'

Everyone knows that the screaming horses had troubled Uwe Dordel the most. He'd had a harder time getting over that than he had the deaths of men. It was rumoured that he'd shot all of his ammunition into the heads of dying horses.

'And where are you coming from with your violin? May I?' Gingerly, Dordel opens the case and his eyebrows rise in astonishment. 'I've heard of this! Heavens! Such a parade animal!' Carefully, he takes Linde'sche and fingers the empty strings. 'And?'

'And nothing,' says Ruven. 'Fouled it up, as they say. Next year I can do it again, but until then—well, you know how close we live.'

Dordel puts the violin back down. Then he takes the chewing tobacco from the shelf on the wall and stuffs it in his cheek. He chews silently for a couple of minutes.

'You could move in here, you know,' he says. 'Perhaps muck out the stalls. Fritz, Düwel, I've given the boot. A son wants to be like that. A son is something different. Brings

me such shame with his rage, even scares the horses.'
Dordel grabs Ruven's biceps. 'And if I look at it this way.'
He smiles. 'Women also like to be carried. With your little
chicken wings, at the most you'll get a really skinny one up
there.'

Ils brings two small glasses and the bottle of schnapps.

'You'll move in August,' says Dordel and extends his
hand to Ruven. 'I still know my fiddling. At least you will
make something of it. I haven't gone far in my life. But I
can watch another go far. Watching, you know, is another
one of life's simple joys.' Dordel grins and drinks: 'Anyway,
besides, you can play something for us here, then I'll turn
Ilsche over here in a circle again and maybe she'll even get
a bit younger.'

'I can hear you!' Says Ils and sits up, half-offended. She
has turned a little red.

'Yes, yes,' Dordel nods in her direction, 'Just stay like
that. Or else you'll end up scuttling over to the neighbours.'
He looks out the window as he says this, and declares: 'It's
already getting light, Ruven. I have to go to sleep.' And with
that, he shows Ruven to the door, and Ruven goes out into
the night and thinks to himself that despite what he says,
Dordel is very much an old musician.

Four weeks later, very close to the day the new chan-
cellor Stresemann was appointed, a few pieces of furniture
totter through the village.

'That looks indecent, really,' says Mother Preuk quietly to her son, who stands behind her as she stares through the window. 'Furniture needs walls around it. Furniture under the empty sky, that's just not right. And bedclothes—never!'

There is much more, however, that won't be transported. A convoy is here for it. Snot-nosed village children on John and Ruven's carriage seat, and at the fence, behind a veil of salt water, Gesche. Inside, nothing has been overlooked. And everyone is relieved somehow that it's finally out—even John, who has known it for a long time anyhow. It doesn't shock him. He's collected enough shocks for this lifetime.

Dordel's little room has such a low ceiling that Ruven hits it with his bow arm as he plays. Gesche gave him gloves made of tough leather. 'So that your hands don't get sore,' she said. He kissed her on the mouth, and she let out a soft squeak.

Halfway there, Fritz Dordel is waiting in the road. 'Pff!' He goes, and pulls the corners of his mouth down south. He's living with Peter now, on the Röver farm, and doesn't show up at his father's house any more. He hasn't been by Emma's since he and Peter caught sight of Schlappkohl. But that doesn't mean much. No one can sit back and relax any more. Ruven had the general impression that one must slowly forbid oneself from sleeping, the way the whole country was hanging in the balance. That anyone still slept at all!

Often, he sits at the table late into the night with Uwe Dordel. Sometimes Emma joins them. When the two men resort too frequently to silence, she begins restlessly to smoke.

'Everyone here just waits around and gawks like idiots,' she says one day, 'like children standing at the shore and watching the waves coming in till suddenly they're tumbling over the children and ripping them away.' She shivers as she says it, this waiting terrifies her so much. 'But we can see the sea, how it climbs before the storm surge, before it goes over the dyke! And from land, we see its climb as a threat to money,' she says. 'Money is the blood of the country. The power of society dwells within it. Without money, power lies fallow. But it is also a question of measurement. Eleven million marks for a dollar! I call that letterpress printing! And someday there will come a haemorrhage!' She'd leant far over the table with these words, and as she finishes, she tosses herself indignantly back into her chair and looks at the men with defiance.

A few days and weeks close in but pass by, unused. Fall finally comes again, the flames on the edges of the maple leaves. There are some flames in other places, too. Emma brings a lot of paper with her from Hamburg.

'Read,' she says. 'It's still fresh! And that too!' She pushes something towards Ruven—*Equality: 'Towards the clarification and deepening of the socialist sensibility and thought of proletarian women,'* says Emma and grins. 'You can still read it—a man is a woman on the inside.'

Ruven stands at the table, the corners of his mouth turned down, and reads.

'And you want to hang this up here? Convert the town?'

'Relax.' She sits on his bed. 'There's a plan, Ruven. The movement must be spurred into action now.'

'Without me.' He turns slightly towards the light and reads the second article.

Emma smooths the blanket: 'I need your help, Ruven. Peter Röver and Fritz Dordel have respect for you, at least.'

'What am I supposed to do?' He asks, without looking up from the sheet of paper.

'Distract them. Give a concert! Here in the village, in the pub, wherever you want. Find whatever reason.'

'And you?'

'We!'

'Yes, all of you? What's your plan?'

'We're taking over!'

'What?'

'The tax. A republic, Ruven! We're founding a *new* republic! A Soviet republic!'

'Here?'

'Hamburg is leading the way!'

Ruven raised an eyebrow.

'You underestimate the revolutionary power of the present moment,' she says quietly, 'A new society will come out of it. Born and formed in the silence.'

'If you found a new republic here, then you'll also bury it here. And I'll be the one burying you, in the end' says Ruven.

'And when. It's about more than us!' Her cheeks redden. 'Play me a march! And then agree to help!'

'You'll get a bit of Ave Maria, and I'm not agreeing to anything. I'd rather be keeping an eye on things for you.'

And Ruven keeps an eye on things. He can hardly sleep any more, for all his keeping an eye on things. He quickly notices that Fritz and Peter seem unsettled, too, and he thinks that they'll find, at one or the other fixed point, an accusation or even just a suspicion in order to take Emma down. And so he also watches her.

But whom is he actually watching? Where had this woman got her fighting spirit from? Surely, not from Verdun and certainly not from her time with the doctor. This fighting spirit must come from an old life, and in this event it is, as it is so often, her childhood. For behind the name Emma there belongs a surname: Braren. Emma Braren, daughter of Sven Braren, whom she has never seen and yet whose inheritance she carries within herself.

During the night from 22 to 23 September 1916, Emma sat between her mother and her brother on the cold bench by the fireplace in the front room of a house with a low thatched roof and listened to a hurricane that was bearing down on their island. While her mother started to pray and attempted to soothe the wind with her quiet yowling sounds, Emma imagined herself, in that moment exactly as old as the century, as the thatch roof over their heads soaked with water and slowly sagged until those below it drowned or suffocated, just like some of the fishermen did under the sails of their capsized boats, and perhaps just like her father, Sven.

A deep-sea fisherman—that's what he'd been. As a boy he'd even been on one of the last whaling ships, before they'd ceased the hunt of those massive mammals because they'd been moving farther and farther into the north out of fear of the harpoons. Even the bravest men couldn't follow the animals there because the calculations for the journeys didn't make sense any more, and even the bravest began, at the time, to do the calculations.

But Sven Braren couldn't let the fishing and the high seas be, even after he was married. And so, the morning after the wedding he went out into the dark, even though the other fishermen were shaking their heads over the inkiness of the ocean and saying that this was no kind of weather. His body elated by the fulfilled night before, he crossed against the shoreward wind, straight away from his wife. She stood, still bed-warmed, on the beach and watched this back and forth, port and starboard, and something inside of her collided so that nine months later she brought twins into the world, a girl and a boy. Her husband never returned.

But the boy played with dolls, and the girl with a wooden sword. Even as a teenager, Emma was unmoved by feminine occupations such as spinning or embroidery. She'd have much rather gone out to the Kleiers' shacks, where the Kleiers, covered in slime, sat and rested from cleaning the drainage ditch. Emma would squat down low to talk to them, so that it would have been easy to look under her skirt if she ever wore a skirt, and she listened to their sorrows and hardships, and was even allowed a draw or two from their pipes. These errors didn't exactly bring her fame or glory on the island. Only never-ending strife with her mother and the deep disdain of the village girls.

During that night in September 1916, while the once-in-a-century hurricane flew around the house, Emma Braren resolved, before she be smothered under the mossy thatched-roof and the mossy relationships, to go onto the mainland and to Hamburg, where she began training to be a nurse when it was still winter. She was able to rent a room from Doctor Marks, then she quickly fell in love with his young wife. And so, she followed this man to the village and later to Verdun, never for his own sake but only to be close to his wife, and in Verdun, to escort her to the doctor at her request. After he bowed out of the war with an overdose of morphine, Emma had at first returned to his wife, until she remarried shortly thereafter and moved back to the city as soon as it was at all possible.

Emma remained in the village. She didn't know to what end. But she reflected. And she befriended the teacher, a thin man with books. And in one or the other of these books, she discovered an idea that she didn't let drop again. Perhaps it was closer to a question: What would it be like, if everything had gone a bit differently, a bit more justly? And how would life feel, if women had taken part in that justice from the beginning? This is more or less what she asked. And so she quarrelled with her comrades, 'You all have understood so much, you've understood more than others,' she said. 'But your eyes are still blind to the feminine!'

In October 1923, secret mail arrives. Emma stands in front of the window in her trousers. It is coincidentally another twenty-third, only seven years later, a Monday, a rainy day.

'Where should this go?' Ruven unhooks the window.

'Bargteheide,' she says excitedly, almost happily. 'You don't have to come with me, but you can!'

She takes the carriage and pair from John. Under the seat there's a flask with coffee and there's one with liquor. The whole landscape dreams a brown dream. The moss on the windward side of the oaks is saturated with water and glows dark green. Deeper in the woods it smells of mushrooms. Emma rubs her hands together.

'In the next life, we'll just gather chestnuts,' she says and knots her headscarf tighter underneath her chin. 'We'll just relax outside and gather chestnuts.'

On the eastern highway, there are two people travelling. Also with liquor under the seat, also with the brown dream, but an entirely different one; not at a working trot, but a gallop. They come to a stop at the crossing behind the woods, and take a swallow from the flask. The soaking-wet gelding crosses its right front hoof over the other and scrapes its shoe in the sand.

'Be still,' says Peter Röver. 'Bloody horse!' His feet stick out in large black boots. He hadn't inherited those. He'd bought them, simply because he'd liked them so much and because a German man doesn't walk around in clogs.

It grows light up ahead. Emma and Ruven reach the edge of the woods; they still can't hear the stomping gelding.

'Stop,' whispers Emma, and Ruven obeys. They suddenly notice the horse with the steaming mouth at the crossroads. Emma immediately makes a perfect right angle with Peter Röver's horse and cart.

'Eh?' is all Peter says. And then, after a gulp: 'Where to?'

'How is that any of your concern? Are you lying in wait for people here?'

'What people?' Peter laughs silently and glances at Fritz questioningly. And then, without laughing, he says to Emma, 'I'd call it something more like a wild boar hunt. It's October, you know. Shall we do it together? Sound the call?'

'Leave us alone,' says Ruven, and he wants to get going again.

'No, no, no!' Peter gently moves the long whip between them, 'You both aren't understanding me.'

'What is there to understand?' Emma's face smoulders.

'Oh, you know,' Fritz interjects, 'for example, that your beautiful, expensive violin is sitting in my father's house, and it's so cold there . . . '

Peter nods, leans back and sticks his left thumb behind his belt: 'Someone should heat it, isn't that what you mean? Otherwise, the walls will get damp.'

'You won't get it, Fritz, you know that,' says Ruven.

'What are you talking about?' The otter puts on an innocent face, but it began to twitch anxiously. 'Have I said something . . . ?' He turns to Peter, who pulls the gelding sharply to the right and strokes Emma's face with the whip as he rides past.

'You need a shave!' At that, he cracks the whip once between his horse's ears, so that it jerks and strains its long legs towards home.

Emma breathes in sharply. Ruven pushes his horse into a trot.

'He won't do it,' he says.

'And if he does?'

'Then I won't be a violinist. Then it'll finally be decided. And by Fritz, of all people.'

They travel on.

'I can't bear this, you must turn around,' says Emma. 'I'll continue on foot.'

'It's not up for discussion.' Ruven adjusts the carriage awning. He is completely damp under his jacket, even though it's autumn, and not at all warm. Perhaps he should have given a concert in the pub instead of storming the barricades with Emma while in every bush an otter or a Röver son is cocking a rifle.

'Then go back and catch up with me tonight. Take a horse from old Dordel, he'll give you one.'

They travel further. Then Ruven stops the horses.

'Promise me you'll take care of yourself.' He presses the reigns into her hand.

She nods. 'I've already endured all kinds of things.' And then she kisses him farewell. 'If we don't do it, somebody else will,' she says. 'And if that happens, it will be an entirely different kettle of fish.'

Ruven raises his hand in farewell and then heads back in the direction of the woods. He walks for a good hour and stares furiously ahead, not down at the path, but instead as if he might see the tracks from the one-horse carriage suddenly swerve.

They travelled in a beautiful curve, again in a gallop, until they finally caught up with Emma again, so that a little behind him there would be a kind of right angle made out of two horse-drawn carriages, while Ruven walks to his violin. But behind the sharp bend in the path, a bit further to the south, there stand two new shapes. Fritz and Peter weren't expecting them. They don't know these shapes at all. But they are armed with rifles, and one of them cracks in the air so that Peter can hardly restrain his horse, and then everything descends into chaos.

The violin gleams in its case. Ruven picks it up just once and plucks the strings and thinks that he'd like to return to Emma, if the saddle and tack wasn't all gone.

'Düwel,' grumbles old Dordel, 'I always hang it up there!' And points to the wooden handle on the wall. 'Someone has cleared it all away.' They don't need to speak aloud what they are both thinking.

Ruven sticks the violin case under his arm. He's already walked far today, and it's dark when he arrives at the wainwright's. He explains everything very fast while Mother Preuk shakes her head, stands up and tries to grab her cane, but Ruven waves her off: 'Leave it, Mother. This isn't a time for looking, it's a time for doing. What shall I do?'

'What is there for you to do in the dark? Walk on foot to Bargteheide? You shall stay here.'

They sit in the kitchen, glancing up sometimes at the cane leaning in the corner, and keep on turning up the wick in the lamp.

'The way she looked at me, Mother. A person rarely looks at you like that.'

'Then go,' says Greta Preuk finally, and her lip quivers a little as she says it. 'But take care of yourself, my boy.'

Ruven walks through the damp woods. The mist moves over his face. The owls shift noiselessly in the trees. Halfway there, it is day again, and three-quarters of the way, he encounters a constable.

'Turn back! You can't go here! Turn back!' He'd shouted in his uniform, as Ruven would later tell his mother and John. He was out of his mind with excitement. So much revolution, so far out in the country! He had mud stains all over his uniform. Still he kept walking, and Ruven glanced back at him and was of course moving forwards, unfortunately much too slow. There was the lame foot, but also some kind of resistance that stirred inside him. And then, he heard a shout or a call coming from somewhere behind the yellow linden trees. They shot, he would say, and ran off. He imagined Emma, how she laughed so suddenly loud. Again she was the first in line, this marvellous woman. She would give away all her teeth for the good things. Then he'd started running faster; fear had gripped his throat. Up ahead, the road was blocked by fallen trees and everything was scattered and howling through the morning and trying to saw through the barricades. A cold rain fell and softened everything. The few women in skirts, brown up to the tops of their knees—how they tore out their hair—and men, whose hats were ripped off their heads. He leapt to the side, into the field, and ran around the barricades until someone yelled: 'Stop! Hey, you! Halt!' And then he was suddenly conscious of how few Emmas there were in the world, that there was only the one. There he was, and as Ruven would tell it, he was running through the churning place when a cry came from the middle of it, where they were wrenching an elderly man around—he was apparently the town's head clerk—and yelling, 'Soviet Republic Stormarn!' They stuck their arms up high and clearly looked frightened. They had apparently seen the city police force arriving and so had disappeared into brick buildings, those red boxes that someone lacking all taste had put up in the middle of the place. When Ruven turned around, an entire armed troop was closing in on him. He asked after Emma once more but no one knew anything. Then finally, near the front wall of the house, he saw a coat waving with its opening at the back. He grabbed the badger by the shoulder and the badger immediately began to whimper, 'She hasn't come! She never showed up! *Simeon and Levi are brethren; instruments of cruelty are in their habitations. O my soul, come not thou into their secret; unto their assembly, mine honour, be not thou united: for in their anger they slew a man, and in their selfwill they digged down a wall!'*

And then there appeared in Ruven's mind a horrible image of a gelding and two Adam's apples which leapt through the night wind and drank liquor. What was it that those two had wanted, he asked himself, and it was with this question in his head that he finally ran back home.

He'd tell the whole story when he was sitting with John and Mother Preuk at the table in the dark with his mother smoking her pipe in silence.

But he's not quite back yet. It's not yet night, and definitely not midday either. Eleven o'clock chimes from the church tower when he finally walks across the bald field of lilies-of-the-valley. From a distance, he sees John's carriage in front of the house. He exhales in relief.

When he opens the door, however, everyone from the village is standing in the front room and craning their necks, mute and abashed. The door to the other room is ajar. Several murmur something when they see Ruven, they press their hats into their hands. Finally, John emerges from the room. Behind him, Ruven can see several women and two naked feet on the table.

John takes him by the shoulder. 'Come,' he says and pushes him past the room and into the workshop. He goes over to the workbench and toys with it unnecessarily. He's searching for words. 'The horses and the carriage went through the fence,' he says finally and pushes some wood-chips into a small pile. 'She was hanging with her foot in the reigns,' he says and lifts his dusty hands in front of his face. 'I didn't recognize her.'

Ruven stares helplessly at his brother. The many boots from the village scrape in the front room. The men go to the pub. The women stand around in the garden and inside the house. Today, they don't touch anyone else. They stand there, proud and withdrawn, as if they were the last women in the world.

Ruven goes into the room. Mother Preuk has laid a cloth over Emma. On the floor, there's a bowl filled with reddish water.

'Emma didn't lose her mind. Not she.'

Mother Preuk takes Ruven by the arm. 'My boy,' she says softly, 'oh, my boy.'

On this night, there are only potatoes with salt. They all sit together in the kitchen at the wainwright's. The police haven't come. They had first to put an end to the

Soviet Republic. And they did it, too, and it wasn't difficult—the local revolutionary force was much too weak. Those who took part will be in the Gollnow fortress in Pommern for a good one year. The fallen barricade trees yielded thirty metres of firewood for the head clerk, Trede.

'That is all that those people from Stormarn, those courageous strikers, accomplished,' says Ruven and stares down at the tabletop.

Gesche pushes the plate away. 'You don't say,' she whispers and looks at Mother Preuk, who glances first at the clock and then at Ruven.

'Do you think that she could have gotten up to something with a man, yesterday?'

'Emma?' Ruven closes his eyes and sees Emma vividly before him. Her mouth, the knowing smile, the powerful chin. 'Of course not.'

'Of course not. But the men got up to something with Emma.' Greta Preuk rubs one hand with the other.

'Give me the pipe,' she says. Then she stuffs it and smokes. 'That, my boy, is what's known as politics.'

He'd like nothing more than to turn back time, to begin once more there, where he could still have decided differently, perhaps even against the violin. Instead, he stands in the ophthalmologist's mansion again and stares through the tall windows at the rainy park. He's cold, even though it's June. He stares at the dripping beeches, the black yews and a white statue in semi-profile. He turns and glances over at the mahogany table. In the middle of this circular table lies a sheet of paper on which a woman can be seen. Her naked skin, from her groin upwards, is white, as is her delicate throat, and she looks as though she is sleeping. The doctor's guests gather around. They examine her closely, especially her throat, so that they don't stare at her breasts. The face of the sleeping woman is framed by dissolving hair. Next to her, a sad embryo with small shrunken arms is crouching, as if he were also too cold.

Doctor Linde stands close to the front, bending over, and seems to have almost forgotten his guests. 'Virginity, desire, birth and death,' he whispers excitedly, 'everything is here to see! What a gem!' And then, despite his words, he shakes his head sadly.

A nervous art dealer in a fashionable Stresemann suit nods with simultaneous pride and disappointment, and presses himself between the guests and the paper. He fumbles awkwardly with a transportation map so that the print on the table is disappeared from view, and speaks loudly about virginity. He'd hoped to sell something to the doctor again, on this special day.

Ruven remains apart; he must collect himself. He's supposed to play for them afterwards. His hands cling to the lining of the pockets in his light summer trousers. You participate in everything, he thinks. Perhaps you'll learn it someday. But maybe you should leave, too. Only, where to? Ruven thinks back on his past year, especially on the winter. Really, he thinks, the whole year was a winter.

It was weeks after Emma's death before Ruven was able to play again. He had stood in the damp interior of the church and kept playing the same note. The familiar light struck dark and loud in the evening, when he finally walked out of the building and stood still on the top step and looked down at the ice in the river. All he remembered was that down there between the bald trees was where he had once stood with Emma.

Now everything there was frozen. It was only deep in the ground that the river was slowly pushing itself towards the sea. Ruven stood in the cold for far too long. Finally, he left the courtyard and walked across the heath, between and through the juniper trees and onward. He carved a crooked path. A stiff February wind was hard on his tail and it drove him forwards.

The light was still on at old Dordel's. In the stable, the stallion scraped at the wall of his stall and gnawed on the wood of his hay feeder. Ruven stood in the walkway between the stalls, took off his hat and wept. Not once at Emma's funeral—which would have made anyone cry, only five people had walked along behind the coffin, everyone else had stayed home because of fear or politics—had he shed a tear. He'd only counted how many curtains were surreptitiously pushed aside by a hand when they walked by. And they walked everywhere. They were going to be seen, fully seen. They made a diagonal path from the wainwright's to the churchyard. They went especially slowly across Röver's freshly raked yard, so that the dog barked and barked until he finally stood mute and shaking at the end of his hanging leash and watched the funeral procession.

'She'd be dead now anyhow,' the shopkeeper Schlappkohl had said later in the pub, 'she shouldn't have mixed herself up in politics, it's not a woman's concern. And hopping off to these assemblies isn't one either.'

'Isn't it?!,' Ruven hissed in his face.

'Nah,' another man offered his two cents, 'he's right.'

'He's right?!' Ruven asked.

'It was obvious something would happen to her. In the circus, something always happens at some point. And this was a circus. *Soviet Republic Stormarn*! She could have also accomplished that more easily! With simpler tickets for admission. Or had she only . . . ' At that, he got one. And then another, from the right. By the time his nose had begun to bleed, Ruven was already at the door.

Now for the first time, in the narrow path between the stalls, he shed tears for a while. Then he wiped his face with his sleeve and headed inside the house.

At the table sat Uwe Dordel, mending his riding boots. He guided the half-round leather needle like a cobbler, with hands like that of a bear.

'There you are.' He didn't look up. Dordel never looked up any more. Since it had been rumoured that Fritz was involved in the matter with the nurse, he'd been silent. And his Ils, even more. Although nothing could be proved regarding Fritz. He had, admittedly, been sitting and boasting in the pub all day, but one gave no credence to his words, particularly since the young Peter Röver claimed that the whole affair with the nurse wasn't them, it had all happened differently, but how exactly, that he didn't know, just that it was someone else. And so they called it an accident. An accident is an accident, they'd answered when someone asked about it. The absence of Fritz Dordel that immediately followed was suspicious all by itself. He was simply no longer there. It was rumoured that he'd gone to Hamburg to join a contingent of the German National People's Party, but that wasn't certain either.

Old Ils helped Ruven out of his coat. Then she looked at him unhappily: 'Where can I show my face, now? Everyone will stick out their tongues when they see me coming! I've never had anything against Emma, but I do have something against them.'

'So it is.' Uwe Dordel cut the thread with his incisors. 'And it will keep on getting worse. ' He nodded in Ruven's direction. 'And you? It's incredible that you can bear it here at our house. You're the one person with good reason to shun us.'

Ruven sat down at the table.

'You had nothing to do with the matter, I'm sure of it. But I'm going to leave anyway—I'm going to the city. It's too closed-in, too cramped here.'

'I thought you would,' said Dordel, finished with the boots. 'But let me at least help you move a few of your things, so that people see that you're leaving in peace.'

The next morning, they loaded up. It wasn't much. For his mother, or because he was going to the city this time,

Ruven threw a couple of blankets over his belongings and tucked them in tight.

As they rode down the mountain and through the village and up another mountain, they were almost giddy. The February sun helped a little, but the flask of herbal liquor helped even more. It ran down the oesophagus and made sunlight down in the belly. Uwe Dordel even sang quietly to himself.

They took a small detour across the estate and to the steward's house. Ruven still wanted to say something to Lene.

As they clattered through the gate and onto the estate, all at once two hundred pigeons scattered into the sky and turned in their whistling circles. At the last moment, Ruven glimpsed the hawk. It had disguised itself and fluttered like the pigeons before it seized one. So it goes, he thought. One can only hope to recognize the hawk in time.

They stopped in front of Gosche Lunten's house and waited there until Lene arrived at the fence. And then they both stood there without any idea of what to say to one another, Lene turning a crimson red and Ruven a bright white.

'When I become someone, I'll come and get you,' he said finally. 'Wherever money is, you'll find the devil, and where there's none, you'll find him twice, your mother says. Good. We couldn't manage two devils, but one—we'll be able to handle that.' Then he went back to the wagon. As he climbed on, he glanced back at her again. Lene was standing still, her quaking back turned towards him; she didn't turn around again.

'Should we be embarrassed too?' Dordel asked and cracked the whip loudly, and they arrived at the outskirts of the city sooner than Lene was able to stop crying.

The canal bridge was covered in ice. Business reigned on the street—carts with wood and turnips and coal, cars and single riders, their horses sent into a terrible panic by the engines. Sacks and jackets were tossed overhead from one person to the other, and somehow it became a fuller and more interesting morning—Ruven and Dordel saw a great deal to their right and to their left, until they came to a stop in one of the ditches in front of a door.

The house was ancient and lopsided and its weather-beaten facade leant over the street. The stairs behind the house were so narrow and the roof so low that only the mattresses could fit through. They had to pull up the bed frame with a rope and then they only just managed to fit it through the window. But the window, too, was ancient and small, and the table had to wait until someone had an idea. The chest full of sheet music and clothing went up the stairs. Yes, that was it—the room remained without a table.

Uwe Dordel looked around: 'Not even a stove here.' He wrapped his arms around himself.

Ruven shrugged. 'I can sit downstairs in the kitchen. Otherwise, I'll play myself warm.' He looked at old Dordel a bit helplessly: 'Well, then.'

'Yes, OK.'

Ruven listened to the wagon, how it clattered emptily over the potholes, before it turned at the water's edge and couldn't be heard any more.

'Come here,' called the landlady, in a dress the colour of pumpernickel, and pointed to the meagrely set table in the kitchen. Her flyaway hair was tied in a bun atop her head and she held herself stiffly, her arms pressed tightly to her sides. She reminded Ruven of the wooden knitting spool that Gesche used to tie shoelaces back home.

The landlady was a frugal widow. She cooked in portions that were more like the leftovers of something decent and moved busily back and forth in the icy flat, a disquieting, seemingly endlessly thirsty creature of perhaps fifty-five years. At one point, she stood with her arms crossed at the window and said, 'You'll only be served today, you know.' Then she suddenly turned and looked at Ruven for a moment too long, just like the Klünkenhoker woman once had, from top to bottom. Then she glanced at the wedding photo on the wall behind the table. There was a black band tied diagonally over a corner. She looked at Ruven again, and he hurried with his baked potato, thanked her and stood up, stooping under the roof.

The widow left the kitchen door open from then on, so that he heard her, and she, him. Then one day she began to sing, with an alarmingly dramatic soprano: '*Do, re, mi, fa!*' Ruven took the violin in his hand, as if he had to protect it and its sound. He forbade himself from listening to the landlady's screeching. He breathed loudly when he played. He played until his throat bled, a weeklong, sustained inflammation. He played the violin with the pain and against the pain. He played the violin so fast and so well that the people below in the snowy alleyway stopped and listened.

The professor was less impressed. He had his concerns, a second stroke, and this time it had almost robbed him of speech. His sentences wouldn't come in time: 'I'd like . . . to wash your fingers . . . you play . . . that . . . so messily,' he said one day in March. 'Do you want . . . to have a conversation with people, or do you want to be . . . a musician? With your tempo . . . you're not showing me anything.' The professor stroked his collar of cat fur and struggled to stand up, grabbed the Linde'sche and rested it at his chin. Then silence. A pause of perhaps seven beats in which he suppressed all of his fragility in order to muster up enough power for the first note.

'Not . . . power,' he said then, slowly, and put down the violin again, 'It's courage that's needed . . . to really . . . begin. In the moment you begin, the note . . . approaches you . . . and you hear your own . . . music. You hear what music is . . . to you. It can . . . drive you over the edge . . . because you suddenly . . . have an idea of what we are, yes, I believe . . . indeed we are . . . mostly . . . music! Every . . . part of our body should . . . play along. The whole . . . person plays the violin! His . . . feet, his shoulders, his bowels!'

The professor looked at Ruven with his one eye, wide awake, almost happy, while the other seemed to sleep underneath its powerless lid. 'The minstrel contest . . . at Wartburg castle, Ruven, is not . . . yet decided. You must choose whether you're a jack of . . . hearts . . . or of . . . clubs.'

'I don't understand.' Ruven stood without his violin as if he was naked. His arms hung down weakly: 'I really don't understand.' And he looked into the fireplace, where the beechwood glowed and a willow branch popped and burst.

The professor shrugged his still-mobile shoulder: 'I myself . . . encouraged you. I wanted . . . to drive you out of something. I thought you would drown . . . in delusion. One can drown . . . in delusion. One can even . . .' But not a word followed, and the professor looked in front of him into the empty room, until he finally spoke again: 'Don't play music . . . slower than it is . . . on purpose, just because you . . . are afraid to go too fast.' Then he locked eyes with Ruven. 'But now . . . you really are too fast! The piece is . . . not *so* . . . fast, you know.' He let his head sink. 'I think . . . the tempo goes something different,' he nearly whispers. 'I have to put . . . the stroke . . . somewhere . . . do you see?

A point of honour, that the hand . . . is faster than the . . . mouth. But you—you'd better take your . . . silence. I know, you sometimes suffer under it, but . . . it is now closer, perhaps . . . it is even your . . . form.'

Ruven doesn't answer. What does he mean by my silence, he thinks. When nothing comes into my mind, that's not any kind of form.

'Now . . . ' The professor, looking almost embarrassed, lifted the violin and played the piece at an astonishing tempo. When he finished, they stood opposite each other. For several moments, they held each other's gaze.

'What do you . . . think?' The professor asked quietly.

'Nothing,' said Ruven.

'That's good.' Bernhard nodded. 'Music . . . is no accompaniment. It's enough, when . . . the ear thinks the sounds.'

Helene Bernhard set up the tea in the study. The little dessert forks, the expensive cups from Copenhagen, as if it were a special day. They sat across from each other, and Helene stood off to the side yet again, looking at her husband, who slowly and laboriously blew smoke into the air from a cigar in the corner of his mouth.

'Everything . . . goes. Our . . . time is up,' he said. 'We'll pack . . . the luggage. I'll pack . . . sheet music, a cat . . . and a wife . . . in my suitcase.' He laughed quietly. 'The old ones are moving on. Even the . . . eye doctor's walls are . . . almost empty. He's wrapped up a Rodin, a Manet . . . and a Munch. Such paintings won't . . . ever exist again.'

Ruven looked at him, not understanding.

'You didn't know . . . that? He's . . . selling the collection. All of it.' Exhausted, the professor leant back and wiped his mouth with a handkerchief. 'The museum director . . . is trying to save some of it . . . for the city, but they don't have much money, and the doctor . . . needs a lot.' He glanced at his wife, who was leaning her head to the side in the armchair and quietly watching him.

'Money . . . ' He let his eyes slowly close and almost seemed to fall asleep. 'When you hear money . . . you think of the future,' he said quietly. 'We always think . . . we must buy into the future. But let me . . . tell you, the future, we'll get it . . . for free. It will come on long legs. And . . . your violin, the doctor won't . . . sell it. He won't want to be the one . . . to have taken away . . . a young musician's . . . instrument.'

Ruven felt the chair in his back. For a moment, he'd had the impression that it was gone and he was about to tip down to the floor, or even deeper. Oh, well, he thought, then the doctor's sense of honour was about to save the young Preuk's ass once again. For a while he looked out into the courtyard: 'What do you mean by the minstrel contest?'

'I'm glad that you . . . ask.' The professor was surprisingly awake again, his hands mobile. 'I mean that Heinrich

. . . von Ofterdingen worked with a power . . . that we call . . . Klingsor. With it . . . he almost won . . . the minstrel contest . . . , the war of . . . art . . . the poker game . . . of spirits, with the power of . . . intelligence. An interesting and . . . splendid . . . power. Its background . . . however, is inescapably . . . black. All splendour has a . . . dark background, that is its . . . nature.' Here, he professor raised his index finger. 'The black jack of clubs . . . wins everything. Against it, Wolfram . . . puts up his . . . little idiot from the woods, one of those from . . . the kingdom of children . . . and lunatics, from the . . . school of hearts. From the perspective . . . of intelligence . . . there . . . is no . . . way that this naive and . . . capricious heart . . . can win. It will, however . . . at some point . . . win. That's what I . . . meant,' said the professor.

I see, thought Ruven, so I'm supposed to be this idiot from the village? The jack of hearts, who isn't worth much in the big game?

'Music can do . . . everything—it can heal or . . . destroy, like us,' said the professor keenly. 'I . . . even say that it's like a person, and . . . you can compel people with it. But if . . . you want to be a real musician . . . then you must . . . not go to the . . . school of . . . magic . . . or of . . . intelligence, but . . . the school of hearts . . . and in certain respects . . . become stupid. That's where you'll . . . find . . . artistic power.'

He took a sip from the tea, which had long grown cold.

'Don't misunderstand . . . me. I'm not talking . . . about the violinist . . . playing at the mountain spa! Or . . . about the blubbering of the violinist . . . when the stupid soul, the German soul . . . bleeds to death in the orchestra pit! I'm talking about . . . the purity . . . of sentiment.' He gently hit the back of the armchair with a flat hand, pushed himself up slowly and added, as if to himself: 'They're . . . far too often . . . confused.'

Months and months of practice went by without the professor going on again about the purity of sentiment. Two years weren't much for this, he repeated every afternoon. Two years were nothing.

Summers in the attic room were hot, winters cold. Ruven moved through dance halls and pubs and played for a hot meal. On Christmas, he even played for one in a brothel. The women were waiting for customers. They were standing and sitting around, bored and slouching.

'Amen,' said one of the women when Ruven finished his piece. Her face was tired of men. Her black hair, the feathers, the glinting earrings made of brass, the smell of powder and soured wine. Others were reading, one slept on the green upholstered bench. They even had a tree, with glass spheres and a bit of gold. It smelt of fir sap. Ruven stayed overnight and drank with the women who smoked him with half a look. You'll have to get used to this, he thought. Today, this is what you're a part of. This is the way the world is now.

'What about us interests you?' asked the women. He'd said, 'Nothing,' and had gone home in the morning.

He had to give music lessons again in order to make his rent. He bent and bowed the thin little arms of wealthy Hanseatic daughters under the throat of the violin. The spoilt and pallid children's faces stared dully at the sheet music.

He recalled all of this now at the window in Doctor Linde's villa. One grows accustomed to serving, he thinks. And to solitude and pain, somehow. Growing accustomed to things suits some people, it ruins others, but no one can escape it. This is how far I've come.

It is the 23rd of June 1926. A rainy day. The table and chairs that had been set out in the garden are brought back inside. Ruven hasn't eaten anything all day. He had, before he arrived, walked around the city twice, he'd even run on the city walls. Then he'd picked the professor up and driven with him to the villa. On the way, they'd both been silent, until the professor, smiling, had said, 'Yes, playing something on the violin . . . for a world-famous . . . painter isn't easy.'

How right he is, Ruven thinks now, and, you're standing here now, you should give it your best. He remains apart from the group, which, led by the ever-hopeful art dealer, has been discussing the print for the past half an hour. Ruven tries to concentrate.

There are, besides the professor and a few museum people, other guests. The young, famished women are half-hidden under their cloches, which lends them a sulky aspect. With the transportation map under his arm, the art dealer moves towards two businessmen standing between feathered palms by the door to the terrace. He speaks in a loud, conversional tone about the death of Paul Cassirer and Chaplin's *Gold Rush*.

To hear him talk, thinks Ruven. One can only hope all of this talk of gold rushes and overseas doesn't end with him dancing in a little banana skirt.

'He's from the capitol,' whispers Linde's son, who had quietly positioned himself beside Ruven, 'A very ambitious man, that one.' He looks at the clock.

'When should I play?' Asks Ruven, a bit too coldly. Why does he feel that every other person's emphasis is a criticism of him?

'Now, actually,' says Linde's son, smiling, 'But the main guest hasn't arrived yet, he's still at his hotel. We don't do him any favours with these sorts of receptions. He hasn't been a guest here for years.' He looks at Ruven thoughtfully. The painter had been rejected here, too, he told Ruven, or at least he'd felt that way back then. And perhaps he was hurt even more deeply than he was elsewhere, because here—and now the young Linde speaks very quietly—he was received at first with such warmth.

In Berlin, they had at least laughed him out, so he'd known immediately where he stood.

Linde's son turns to the guests and asks for their patience. It could be a little while longer. Surely the artist must be resting from his visit to the museum this morning, he says and nods to Ruven. 'Are you familiar with the Norwegian room?'

'A magnificent assemblage!' The art dealer intrudes before Ruven can answer.

'I say, the province has really saved something there of international . . . ' He cleared his throat, 'import!' When nobody responds, he adds: 'Sometimes one has a better perspective out here, where so little is happening, than when one is in the middle of things.' And the painter himself used to like it here, too, he says. The tension of the capitol had just downright shattered him. For the capitol, though, one must also be extraordinarily resilient. Resilient around temptations, too, and that's the heart of the matter. The young art dealer only says, Red wine! in order to resist. He strokes the breast of his Stresemann suit. The painter has always indulged his darker sides a bit too much, he says. He begins to stutter. Perhaps o-opium also played a role. Or too many Romance or Russian influences. The capitol is simply overflowing with far too many foreigners. The only thing missing is the arrival of Mussulmen in Berlin! The man laughs shrilly, realizing he's got carried away. But he can't stem the flow of his own words. He says that the painter was apparently also quite taken in by his own so-called visions, visions that in such a city lead quickly, of course, to hallucinations, because of the crystalline underground, everything built on top of sand! And so the painter gives more credence to his own double exposures, in a way, than he does to reality.

'You think so?' The young Linde turns to Ruven: 'How do you see it?—you're an artist yourself—do you believe in the existence of multiple realities?'

Good Lord! What does the man want? Ruven looks past him, frightened, at the large wall mirror, in which he can see the group from behind.

'There are moments,' he says quietly, 'When I'm walking down the street and I suddenly hear an entire movement, with all the instruments. It started happening when I was just a child. When it happens, nothing on the outside changes. It's just that an orchestra appears.' Ruven turns to the art dealer: 'If that's what you mean by double exposure. Understand, the street is there, perhaps someone is driving his cow to be milked, or someone's getting a coal delivery, someone stumbles or turns around to look at a woman— and suddenly there's an orchestra playing to it all.'

The young art dealer looks at him disdainfully, but he also seems a bit puzzled. At the same time, the white door opens in the mirror behind Ruven, and a tall, grey-haired man of about sixty enters the room: the painter. At least it could be the painter. The sudden silence of the guests speaks to it. Not a comfortable moment, not least for the one walking in. His proud face has a shrunken effect. His lips look like they never open to speak, so distinct and beautiful are they when they're closed.

The doctor gives a short welcome speech. The encouraging art dealer claps the longest and pushes himself closer to the guest of honour. He must, however, quickly distance himself again, because he's suddenly seized by a bout of sneezing. 'A bad allergy,' he says much too loudly. 'Some kind of flower or grass. The park is really just full of it.'

Ruven tries to make out the Norwegian's voice from where he is. Then he goes to tune the Linde'sche. Helene Bernhard accompanies him again. She plays Bach, Sonata in C minor. They'd managed to bring a harpsichord into the villa for the special occasion. During the siciliano, Ruven looks at the painter again. He's sitting by the window in a small armchair and keeping his eyes closed. He doesn't emerge from his absorption, even after the allegro. He also doesn't clap, as if he'd forgotten that he's the guest of honour, that everyone is observing him and the only reason they're here at all is, in fact, because of him.

The doctor nods to Ruven. The second piece: Mozart, something light and June-like. When it's all over, the painter raises his head. He smiles so infinitesimally that it might not be a smile at all.

Ruven goes into the neighbouring room and is fitting the Linde'sche smoothly back in its case when the doctor enters the room: 'Please stay for dinner. Then I can introduce you, and you can have a conversation!'

A conversation! Ruven thinks as he accepts the invitation. What else. He sits on the small sofa by the card table. The twilight feels pleasant. He closes his eyes for a moment. This crowd never ceases to exhaust him endlessly.

The remaining guests have left the villa. Even the art dealer had to go, although he'd tried to make himself interesting by talking loudly. Only the professor and Helene, the painter and Ruven are remaining, and they sit with the doctor and his wife at the table.

The meal is worthy of an impoverished multimillionaire. Even if it is the blanched and carved outcome of six poorly paid hours in the life of a solitary cook who not once in her entire existence has walked through the front door of the villa. She's given her best. It smells rich and good. And there is the silverware, starched napkins, damascene roses and four open bottles of wine.

Ruven has trouble following the conversation. There's an attempt to find a connection between Marx and Buber; there is disagreement about whether hysteria is really an illness—the doctor has decided against it—there is talk about the stock exchange and Zionism, it goes on for hours and the wine is good. Ruven picks up countless names: Hamsun, Przybyszewski, somewhat mumbled, Blavatsky, Bruckner, and here the gazes wander over to Ruven, Wallace, Gershwin, they're looking at him invitingly, the violinist who has trouble guessing at the correct sequence of cutlery and smiles politely into empty space. Finally, the painter tells the table very quietly about his estate in Norway, about the dogs, about painting outdoors. He almost only paints outdoors.

Ruven thinks, when he hears this, about playing violin in the forest, about Lene and Rahel, about fresh foliage and colourful skirts, and tries in vain to break the shell of his crab. Rahel was aristocratic without having to say or know very much, he thinks, and doesn't notice that the doctor is going on at length about how Ruven once asked him about hearing and whether the painter can hear.

The Norwegian glances at Ruven. His look is severe. He nods. But then he turns to the doctor, as if what is to follow is not directed at Ruven at all but instead tailored entirely for his host. He had been dependent on patrons for so long that he had become accustomed to letting them feel their own importance, despite his own pride. Yes, he says, that is a large question and yet it hardly seems answerable. If he answers the way he'd like to answer, one will quickly take him for a lunatic or, worse, a visionary.

'What is hearing? I don't know.' The painter smiles. 'Or perhaps we could phrase it: what is the relationship between colours and what a person hears?'

Ruven pushes his crab to the side. Its deep red embarrasses him.

No, the painter continues, one must start over and ask why sounds and colours alike are able to touch the soul at all, when one considers them as simply waves and vibrations. 'What is, then, the soul? And where is the little bridge between the one and the other? That's what we're asking. What kind of bridge is this?' He smiles. 'And does it have a railing, hmm? We must ask everything before we can talk about hearing an image, because it is then that we can also talk about the fact that hearing is a binding material, an in-between. And I paint colours in this sense. Indeed, they don't depict things but instead connect the one to the other. The relationship between figures in a painting shows itself in the colours. A girl and a woman grow together in the black of their dresses. It makes a daughter and a mother out of them. Perhaps . . . ' and he turns towards Ruven again, 'music is such a contract between us and the other. The dark dress that turns us into children of another mother.'

A dark dress, thinks Ruven and glances sidelong at the painter's proud profile. And suddenly, the thought strikes him that the people gathered here will all die before him.

He closes his eyes for a second. They are already at the finale, he thinks, presto; and I, perhaps the second movement? Andante. A bit sluggish somehow, and there is still so much to come. Then the serving girl takes his plate away, although he isn't even close to full yet, and Professor Bernhard whispers faintly, '*Ach, this . . . black lake . . . underneath me . . . have you . . . ever read . . . Nietzsche?*'

'No, but the black lake speaks to me,' answers Ruven quietly and takes an indifferent sip from the Château Margaux.

'You're a musician,' says Doctor Linde, anxious not to take note of the listless sipping of this wine from 1900 and to pull Ruven into the conversation. 'Musicians always seem to me the most genial. Sometimes, though, I wonder what's the point of playing the violin if people are too afraid to sing any more?'

'Why . . . do you think that people . . . are afraid?' asks the professor, who hasn't noticed the doctor's attempt to bring Ruven into the conversation.

'Because everyone who wishes to avert death *can* only be afraid,' says the doctor vigorously. His face is all red, like the others'. The chemistry of their organs is finally beginning to respond to the wine. The substances coalesce hazily. And in the midst of the striking of the clock on the mantle, the doctor says, 'What's noteworthy is only that the more people fear death, the more they love it—they have deteriorated to such an extent that they deem the face of death to be alive. They should see and hate the ugliness of death. The ugliness and finiteness of naturalism. But still, they love it! That is the idiocy of these new times. And that is also why they feel that our guest's paintings, with their swimming surfaces and rough contours, are altogether unattractive—the art is forced by the will to be fashionable, that's how they put it. In secret, they even say: The painter paints people's faces so messily! That's no kind of painting! He's just trying to scare up all the ugliness in the world! They say: The artist is seeing double! I say: Whoever believes in the truth of simple sight is in the wrong. The eyes consider themselves the most intelligent sense and are too easily content with the outer nature.

This is how they talk, while in distant India, they're still battling the consequences of the March plague; in Paris, they're constructing a new cabinet; and at the wainwright's, a chick grows a feather dress. And so the world goes on, the poker game of ghosts. With and without ugliness, with and without fear. Things surface and disappear.

Ruven stifles a yawn. He drinks another glass of wine. Helene Bernhard bends over him, much too close.

'And what does . . . death . . . mean to you,' asks the professor, turning towards the Norwegian.

'Death? Death is the eye of the needle, through which a person must travel to arrive at the sun,' he responded softly. 'Death is the truth of the earth. It is, in a way, objective. One must not assign a value to it. It only becomes bad if one doesn't want to regard it as a necessary passage. When one wishes to remain, to remain on the earth, or, we shall say, with the earth, when one wishes to rid himself of death, then one has reason to fear.'

'Quite possibly,' Doctor Linde gestures for more wine, 'and the worst is,' he also opines a bit more softly, slurring his words a bit, 'Hardly anything that humanity accomplishes *doesn't* come from this fear of dying. Everything, architecture, politics, education, religion, is ultimately nothing more than the visible physiology of fear! People clutch at what already exists, what's obviously concrete, because they are *afraid* of change! Of development and surprise, of the open form! They believe more in the end of form than in what's forming!' Doctor Linde lifts his glass. The Norwegian lifts his glass, too, but in Ruven's direction, and asks with a hazy sheen in his eyes, 'And what are you afraid of, my young friend?'

Ruven can't sustain the eye contact and looks down for a moment when he hears the question. He was hoping for a very different encounter.

'You're asking the musician?'

'Who else?'

Ruven searches for a sentence, a single intelligent sentence. They've gone a bit too far into unknown territory for his taste.

'I'm sometimes afraid of just . . . music itself,' he says finally, looking directly into the others' faces with his transparent eyes.

The painter raises his eyebrows. For a moment, the two consider each other. It grows so still at the table that they can all hear the ticking of the clock on the mantle. For a hopeful second, it feels to Ruven as if they both know what secret they share. If the doctor were to ask him, in this moment, whether art was serious for him, he would surely hit him in the face. He would lunge at him, at him and his good fortune and his undimmed notion about helping artists. He would put even more of a shine on his well-shaved face and bluntly explain: 'We are not meant to be helped! *That* is our secret! We aren't meant to be rescued—it's not about *our* rescue!'

But there's no spark in the painter's eyes. He's alone here. Here, they don't want to know what is acting in him, in Ruven Preuk. He really is taken for unsophisticated. And for the first time in his life, he's irrevocably aware of it.

The well-sprung gong in the clock on the mantle strikes the expired hour.

'Here, I must . . . confess,' says the professor, who can't bear such moments, 'I also . . . fear . . . that music will grow ugly. It dies away in . . . perfection. Why should it . . . be played faster and faster . . . and more and more perfectly?'

'Perhaps because we'd grow bored otherwise. We don't feel anything any more. Everything must grow stronger, more intense, saltier,' says the doctor. 'The eyes, too, need more and more light. Otherwise they can't see anything. Only boredom.' He stands up and picks up a cigar box from a side table. He sniffs at a rather large and fat cigar, tenderly trims the end, holds it over his gas fireplace, turns, lights it and disappears, puffing away in a cloud. 'A Maduro,' he says, 'a true cigar. So much power, so exotic! Where were we? Oh, yes, at boredom. Boredom is the real revolution, I think. Call it quiet leisure. Leisure is a revolution. But most people are afraid of revolutions.'

The painter smiles at all of them. Then he lifts his glass in the professor's direction.

'What's crucial, however . . . is,' the professor says, 'that one doesn't find boredom itself difficult to tolerate. That's when one finds it preferable . . . to start a war, in a pinch . . . against oneself. One attacks . . . in order to avoid being attacked . . . by something unprecedented.'

'The unprecedented never attacks,' says the Norwegian quietly, now very serious. 'It only overcomes its own shyness now and then.'

He looks out the window at the garden. It will soon be light again. He glances at the empty bottles on the table, takes out his pocket watch and smiles almost sardonically: 'Too late and too early. With these kinds of conversations, they merge into one.' Then he turns to face the others again: 'Sleep is the second condition for all that exists. Gentlemen, good night!'

Ruven sits silently at the table for a while. The professor hardly looks at him. It attracts none of the others' attention, but Ruven feels the solitude expanding around him.

'You can do . . . a lot, a whole . . . lot,' the professor had quietly told him, 'But . . . you've got lost. Music is nothing you . . . need to fear. With this . . . attitude, you won't draw any . . . following. You are never to chip . . . away . . . at your aura . . . in public! Never!'

'But you yourself talked about courage . . . '

But the professor had already turned away.

It is September. The year needs its exhalation. Outside, the damp garden, the asters and heavy crowns of the apple trees; underneath them the fat, fully stuffed hedgehog. A Sunday at the long table in the Lunten kitchen. Eight daughters are still there. The parsley that Mother Lunten chopped with the mezzaluna lies atop the jacket potato, the carving fork sinks into the pork rind as Gosche slices the loin. The summer savoury wilts delicately and overcooks between the string beans, Gosche distributes the food, and then: 'Come, Lord Jesus, and bless this food.'

Lene eats in tiny bites.

'What's wrong?' Asks Mother Lunten, taking her daughter by the chin.

'Nothing's wrong. I've only just read the newspaper.'

'And that's ruined your appetite?'

'No. It's just . . . Ruven's professor died.'

'And?' Gosche looks down at his plate.

'And nothing. Only now Ruven will travel far away, perhaps, since he doesn't have a teacher in the city any more.' Lene's head sinks low and she says very quietly, 'I only thought, perhaps I should . . . '

'You should nothing,' says Gosche loudly. 'He should! He should come back here and say whether he wants you or not. And what he's earning by now!'

'You know, though, that he hasn't got too far yet.' Lene stares at her beans.

'What's on your beans there?' Her mother asks, and clears the table.

In the hallway, Lene takes a coat from the hook and tosses a quick glance at the mirror. She's grown more beautiful. Her cheekbones and dark eyes show more character. Outside, she goes to the pond. The last leaves of the alder trees are floating on the smooth surface. Then she takes the path across the fields to the wainwright's.

Mother Preuk picks dried mint off the stems and piles them in a large tin. The fresh scent of the leaves fills the whole room. 'Sit down, Lene.' She gestures to a chair and whispers a few other words under her breath. Little stories. She talks with Nils. She does a lot now.

'Old wheels are prone to crack,' she says to Lene. 'That's why Nils and I must become friends again, else we'll feel like strangers later on, at heaven's gate.'

Lene takes a seat at the table and looks at the old woman for a long time. Mother Preuk is wearing three aprons on top of one another. Lene waits until she's finished talking, then she says, 'I need advice.'

'Are you in the marrying mood?' Mother Preuk laughs. A quiet, friendly laugh.

'Don't know,' says Lene.

'Invite him to Christmas. He should play something for Gosche and Erika. They won't want to keep you as an old maid! They're no fools. And the boy, he'll go his own way. Not to say he'll be rich, not with his fiddling, but the two of you will live. He's done the numbers for me, they show that one really can get somewhat far if one can be frugal.'

'I can,' says Lene. 'And I will.'

And so a violinist from the city is invited for Christmas. It is done the way it is done. Always a bit of a production. Everything must be set up just right for Christmas, anyhow. The windows will be washed, the stove wiped down, floorboards polished, and then comes the cooking and baking, so much cooking and baking that the stove never cools any more. The curtains are starched and the silver polished so that it glistens preciously from every corner. Even the stables are whitewashed, the walkways swept and the hens' nests filled with fresh straw.

'As if our guest will be sleeping with the hens,' says Gosche and grooms the cows so that their hides gleam. And then the Luntens walk all around and take it all in, and for once they are very happy with what they have.

On the morning of the 24th, Gosche carries armfuls of firewood into each room and piles it up against the stove. To finish, he heats the water boiler. For the last time this year, he trims his fingernails and cuts his hair short, and for the latter, Gosche makes an extra trip to the barber in the neighbouring village, so that the evil beast doesn't get his hands on a little piece of human during these holy nights in order to prepare his keratinous body for dooms-day—an image that the pastor, a bit Jesuit-like and with a damp annunciation, had so often helped his parish to envision. And so, protected and secured both within and without, they welcome the young Preuk that evening.

He arrives in a suit with the violin case under one arm, and trudges through the snow in a heavy coat and fur cap. First he shakes Mother Lunten's hand, then Lene's father's, even tapping his heels together as he does so, and then finally each of the daughter's. Lene has positioned herself at the end of the row, and as he takes her hand, she can't bring herself to look up and so doesn't notice right away how much he's changed since Bernhard's death.

There's a gift for everyone. For Ruven, a briefcase for his sheet music, and for Lene, a purse.

'What am I meant to do with this?' Lene asks, and Gosche grins and says, 'For a thing like that, one really must travel a bit farther.'

Then they sit, freshly groomed and hungry and each one with something new in their lap, even the lead farmhand and the milkmaid, who sit at the table today. Ruven tunes the violin, lowers it and waits until the room grows silent. Then he clears his throat and looks at Gosche and his wife, lifts the violin to his chin and plays. Brahms. The Linde'sche sounds today as if it knew what was at stake. But so as not to make everyone too comfortable, Ruven links the sonata to a Hungarian dance, and throughout the room the hanging corners of the winter-damp wallpaper shake.

Ruven had thought it over well. It must hit the mark the first time; there wouldn't be another chance. He looks around at the many eyebrows, meandering up and down, they don't often hear music here, and when he's finished it is silent again for the first time, just like before, until the milkmaid isn't able to swallow a sob and Gosche Lunten begins to clap. And then the lead farmhand also claps his paws, twice, and Lene drops her gaze and brings herself back to the present.

They are all tremendously hungry after the concert. Their faces grow red in the half-darkness. There's hardly any air, already, from the many candles. Gosche sits with his polished Christmas goblet at the end of the table and quickly wipes under his chin with a handkerchief. 'What a thing,' he says. 'Where did a sound like that come from?'

Mother Lunten serves the food, first soup with fried pearls of dough, then the goose, enormous, stuffed with apples and onions and dripping with fat, along with dumplings and red cabbage. It all sits heavy in their stomachs, well, then a little glass of quince liquor, just before dessert, and then berry compote with cream. And no word of marriage the whole time, and also no word between Lene and Ruven. There are only glances, and also a little bit of something with their feet under the table. How they press against each other, how they confirm the other's presence through the cowhide of their shoes and then up above nearly choke, happily, on their potatoes. And then the snickering of the sisters, all of them with those light eyebrows and their hair blond as tinsel. Anyone could grow light-headed from so many girls' eyes that are scouring everything, inspecting everything, overseeing everything as it suits their mood until their father finally lifts his glass, allows a brief pause, and then says, 'If I am not mistaken, it seems we have two lovers with us at the table. Let us drink to their love and to Christmas! Yes, don't look at me that way, Preuk, you can have her! What's she supposed to do with a handkerchief here in the village? Bring her to the city. But be sure to look after her well.'

The glasses are brimming with elderberry wine that sloshes onto the cuffs of shirts and blouses, and Lene drinks her glassful in a single swig. Then she runs out into the night, and her white brows twitch above her dark eyes as Ruven stands quietly beside her and cautiously and uncertainly puts his arm around her.

'If you go into the stable now, perhaps we'll hear the livestock speak,' says Lene.

'And what will they say?'

'That Lene's leaving.'

The wedding is in May. All the stable doors hang open, bedecked with white cloth. In the yard, a large square is set up and everyone is invited, except for the Rövers, none of them are wanted here. They are all aggrieved today, sitting with their son and the rest of the brood at home, and letting the pigs cry out for their feed for a long time. Old man Röver is the most hurt. He balls his six fingers in his pockets; Lene's choice seems to him a funeral song for the Rövers' masculinity in general, and that does not make old Röver very happy.

'They should stay away,' Gosche had said. 'My daughter will marry whoever she wants. And whoever sows a storm reaps no sun. They'll see.'

Already that morning someone had arranged it all on a table to the side: a roast, jellied ham hock, brawn, liver-wurst, sweet and sour herrings, smoked eel, potatoes, baked, salted, mashed, compote, pudding and quark, coffee in pitchers, wheat beer by the barrel and whatever else fits.

'The purest ceremony,' says old Ils Dordel and keeps herself close to Mother Preuk, who will surely strengthen her spine against malicious gossip. But people have long since stopped talking about her Fritz. Truthfully, they were all glad when Emma was gone. They don't have anything against newcomers and to each his own and all that, but not here. This is what they think, and they don't suspect that that was only the prelude, the rest of the song is still to come, with the refrain only somewhat delayed but already in their blood, everything beautifully in time. *Put work and salt into the butter in May, and it will be fine and healthy each day.* Thus work the spirits of the time, the good like the bad. They've long since known where it's all headed. In this moment and on the ground, however, they just go to the church, in a cloud of perfume, with shiny shoes and dabbed cuts on chin and cheek from shaving. Ruven plays the violin until everyone, old and young, is sitting in the right place. The juddering of the pews, and among them the pastor, hurrying as always, waving to the west door and to Gosche Lunten for him to come out with his daughter and bring her in already, so that everything here can move forwards.

Ruven puts the Linde'sche down next to him and steals a final glance at her beautiful lacquer. And then he stands before the pastor, extremely nervous because the whole village is watching and because he's just as uncomfortable here as there in his city clothes and all the high German, to which he's grown accustomed. And also because he has just the slightest guilty conscience as he stands opposite Lene, now giving herself to him so completely, because all of his thoughts are going to a distant Rahel, and also to a week ago, when Ruven loaded his meagre belongings onto old Dordel's wagon again, and this time it wasn't Gesche's but the landlady's pale face that watched him leave.

The landlady, the knitting spool, whose shriek of *do-re-mi* from the hallway was of course anything but the fulfilment of a dream—but she was tenacious, and eventually almost in heat like a cat. Once she hung her pants on the drying floor in front of Ruven's room; once she just left the door to her bathroom ajar; she began to cook more and more often, even abundantly, for him. And so it came to be that one evening, after three glasses of wine, Ruven didn't pull back the hand that his landlady, with a brittle laugh, had pulled onto her left breast. For the briefest moment to Ruven, it didn't matter to whom the body under this pumpernickel fabric actually belonged. And so he unbuttoned all around the widow, clung tightly to the woman as his dizziness increased, and so she clung to him, too, and he disappeared from view in her embrace. A bit later, when the landlady began to cheer underneath him on the kitchen floor and slapped his naked backside, he awoke from this elevated blood circulation and abruptly became aware of the situation. Frightened, Ruven pulled back, but none of it could be undone.

'A bit farther over here,' hisses the Pastor, gesturing with his yellowed tobacco hand. Lene is already walking inside in the organ's breeze, with a veil and all the trappings; her natural beauty is hardly visible underneath the clamorous needlework. But Ruven doesn't need to see anything. *He who courts the girl next door is well aware of what's in store*, indeed. Now there's just each of their loud I dos and loud sobbing in the background, Mother Preuk making another goodbye, she'll never be used to it.

'Well, then, where two . . .' says the pastor and for a moment has a bit of déjà vu, or perhaps he simply hasn't prepared his text. 'Well, then . . .' he makes a movement with his head in the direction of the exit. And everyone is outside and stepping hungrily down the steps, the band in front with all of its brass, the couple followed by the little bridesmaids, chaste oak leaves on their heads, the parents behind them, the head of the village council, even the baron and his wife, the miller and all the rest, going down the road on foot all the way to the estate, and then a little farther still. Lene has her veil open so that she doesn't stumble, and behind her walks Gesche, pale, next to John, the stiff stems of her bouquet of lilies-of-the-valley wrapped tightly in her hands. Afterwards, she boldly sits beside Mother Preuk at the table, only two places down from Ruven, so that she hears his voice all day long.

The long prongs of the silver forks, the heavy handles of the knives, the requests for more sauce or a bit more wine. The unbuttoning of jackets and waistbands, the intermittent sips of liquor and speeches and poems.

'Them and their Goethe pasties,' whispers Gosche Lunten, when old Jacobs with his shaky voice recites a piece of *Hermann and Dorothea*, and Gosche loudly interrupts: 'Music!'

Hinrich Werkzeugmacher plays with what strength remains, and Dordel, too, starts fiddling again and even his wife joins in with a cello, her legs placed carefully on its left, Ils is nearly sitting sideways, good God, this is not a cabaret! Her knees are decorously closed, and she plays not a bit worse than the others.

They've taken the dance floor from the village pub. It had required an entire day with a bubble level and little blocks of wood to make it level. 'Instead of a bubble level now, we could just have some liquor later,' Gosche had said. 'It'll come to the same thing.'

But for his wife, it was not the same thing. 'We will not start this,' she'd answered him, and returned again and again to check on things, walking beautifully and slowly back and forth across the dance floor.

In the afternoon, they hear the car horn in front of the farm gate. Doctor Linde has made an extra trip out of the city. He takes a seat next to the bride, and she shyly observes his table manners and barely trusts herself to open her mouth.

Who is this posh gentleman, asks Frau Jacobs, and as she serves the cake she suddenly curtsies at everyone like she has a corn on each foot. He's a multimillionaire, says Ils, all agog, and she spills her coffee into her saucer. 'He's Ruven's patron,' she whispers, while she secretly pours the coffee out of her saucer under the table.

At that moment, the doctor stands up and taps his glass and folds his hands behind his back. He looks at Ruven and begins to nod lightly in front of him, as if something is becoming clear to him for the first time: 'Dear friend, I know that you've stopped believing in yourself.' Then he doesn't say anything for a long moment. 'I still believe in you. But I know that that won't help. Perhaps what will help is the violin that you've been playing for so long. It's not quite a Stradivari, but it is still a very good instrument. It should also be entirely yours.' The doctor pauses again, and then: 'I've always cared solely about my collection and about beautiful thoughts. I've missed public events because of it. Now others care about them, and I'm too old to change anything in politics. Change something. Try to play music that will ring on after the coming catastrophe. It is the only thing that remains for us; such is the direction the world is going towards. Our culture has long since abandoned its peak and is hanging by a rope from those gloomy German eagles, hanging in limbo above the abyss. You must preserve it until the next peak, or at least until the next hill. Then we will, you'll recall, at least have *been*.'

At that, the doctor sits down and bows his head. The guests, baffled but also somehow moved, stare at the cake platter.

'What kind of catastrophe?' whispers Gesche.

'What kind of hill?' asks Lene.

And thank God, Gosche begins to clap and waves Frau Jacobs over with the liquor and looks questioningly at Ruven. He only gives a quick nod. Then he smiles, a bit sad perhaps, stands up and goes into the house and comes back with the Linde'sche. He shows it around and then plays. It's a piece music written not quite by an eagle, but by the golden cock, Rimsky-Korsakov. Singing, howling, whistling, wailing, crowing. The eyes of the guests zigzag from the doctor to Ruven to Lene to Gosche, and their faces all alternate between red and white. And finally they clap as though they have been tasked with hunting a whole flock of cocks from the farm; they're all jittery and a bit relieved that it's over. It's unbelievable, this Preuk can impress, thinks old Frau Jacobs as she serves herself more of the heavy poppy-seed cake, even though she's already quite full.

Later, Ruven brings the doctor to his car, and when they arrive, there he shakes the doctor's hand for a long time. They both know that a double bar line will follow. This melody is ending. That's that. What's to follow will play somewhere else.

Around midnight, there are pies and marzipan again, liquor and coffee. Gosche puts out the candles and screws down the wick in the lamp. For the wedding night, they must have the room farthest back, of course. Mother Lunten has arranged everything. She's burnt cherry-wood in the stove, so that it smells good and simple. Perhaps this is the last wedding night of its kind. On a little table, far from the stove, sits the violin case. The eagle is in its night flight, with no sense of where it's headed.

'Don't look back!' Gosche says in the new morning, pushing Lene out the front door, 'You'll like it in Hamburg, my child.' He hands her a purse full of money and says, 'One must give when he still has warm hands and then he'll have his own happiness, too! This whole business of bequeathing when one isn't around any more, it's nonsense.'

Ruven and Lene only take with them what's necessary, which is their tired and shaky bodies under fresh summer clothes. In a few days, John will drive the rest in the big carriage to the train station, and surrender it there.

Now they climb, their pockets full of wrapped pieces of roast, onto John's single-axle trailer, and he brings them to the train. In front of the white train station he pulls on the reigns and looks straight ahead. 'I'll be standing here again at Christmas,' he says. They shake hands and Ruven and Lene go to the platform.

They're alone in their compartment and soon eat the cold roast and don't have much to say to each other because their faces are still hurting from the endless smiles the day before. They doze for close to an hour. The night hadn't been for sleeping but instead for something more like an incredulous fumbling and sudden permission, with strange hair in a face and a heavy arm or leg atop a stomach, they'll have to get used to it.

They step off the train into the main train station. It's nearly impossible to understand the loud announcements. Where are all the people going. And how they all look! With a single glance Lene takes in the Hamburg women and their elegance, the fashions that are here already, and, blushing, grasps her own new purse tightly.

They travel to Blankenese. From there they go on foot until they reach the water. Pear trees blossom on the hillside, and the tall beeches bloom chartreuse. They see a confusing image of stairs, small fences and low-lying houses, behind whose panes fine china and ships in bottles gather dust. The tall flagstaffs are like lances in the tiny gardens. Everyone lives together there, captains and beach aristocracy, and their children grow up together beside the greasy water.

Ruven and Lene walk a bit farther along the waterfront until they arrive at a white gate. A beautiful juniper tree is growing in front of the house, and there are two narrow rooms on the uppermost floor, one that slopes backwards and the other forwards, with a view of the water. Just as Lene looks up, a steamer pushes itself downstream, very close to the houses, and sounds its sad goodbye. People stand in the sand on the shore and wave with hats and scarves, and Lene suddenly has a lump in her throat.

'Where is it going,' she says.

'South America,' says the landlady, Inge Voss, from behind her. 'The whole world travels through here.'

'Do you like it?' Ruven had already politely sent the landlady away and turned the key.

'Like it!' Lene throws herself on top of him: 'Now let's have a child!'

In the village, John and Gesche sit in the kitchen. Gesche has already wrapped twenty-seven lily-of-the-valley bouquets with bands. They stick up stiffly from the bucket, to be sold. Twenty-seven hands full of poison. Under the stove the chicks peep in the warmth.

'So it is, and so it now remains,' says Gesche. 'For some people, there isn't much at all. Some are just simply there.'

John doesn't say anything to that. What should he say, anyway. He just strokes his chin.

'There are some regions,' Gesche says, 'where a person might ask, what was first, humans or boredom?'

John looks Gesche mutely in the eyes and then says something about how one could also ask whether the boredom isn't always in the same place where humans are to be found. And then he holds eye contact for so long that she almost begins to feel ashamed.

'Perhaps,' she says quietly. 'And perhaps something else will come along and one will be useful for something.'

At the same moment they hear a noise from the next room, and when they open the door and look to the right, Mother Preuk is sitting there in the armchair and staring straight ahead in a wholly unnaturally way. Very slowly and equally as unnaturally, she lifts her hand and points to her cane, which is leaning on the wardrobe.

'Take it, Gesche,' she says weakly. 'That is your inheritance.' Then Greta Preuk closes her eyes and is no longer useful for anything, ever again.

Well, the doors are bedecked again, this time the workshop doors of the wainwright's, the good white linens hang on them again, but first three days are waited through and twenty-seven tautly wrapped lily-of-the-valley bouquets are placed on the corpse. The neighbours are hardly able to summon their sympathy, the scent is so dizzying—it's a warmer day, and the corners of Greta's mouth are beginning to leak, so the scent of the flowers blends with that of decay until the parish clerk screws in the coffin lid and Greta Preuk is carried slowly and with dignity out of the wainwright's.

It's a long funeral procession, this time. Everyone joins in, the whole village and the neighbouring village, too. For Greta Preuk knew well what people wanted and what they must do, and she said what there was to say. She was the only one of her kind, and her kind was truly rare. A bedrock, Greta Preuk, albeit not in years—she was sixty at the most, although weathered like a fencepost from her long wait for death. And again, they regaled and feasted and celebrated loudly against this death. What a fat spring this was!

'Into the world and out of the world—both cost money,' says Gesche and spares nothing. And so after five days, Lene and Ruven are already back again.

'Not a good sign at all,' murmurs old Ils. 'If that won't be an ill marriage. If it doesn't . . .' and she doesn't finish.

Well, to the railway once again, with cold roast in their luggage. So it is: fate asks nothing. It travels its own path. And that is why there is also, soon, no child for Lene.

A music teacher and leader of a quartet, Ruven is always out and about. The summerhouses with turrets and green-tinged copper roofs are hidden between beech trees and rhododendrons. Ruven stands at the heavy park gates and takes a pull from his cigarette before he starts to play. Most of the time he plays the second part and the ship owners' wives take the first, and then a glass of wine. They play Vieuxtemps and Mozart and whatever else goes with beautiful clothes, while outside, in the shrubbery and on the water, the Hitler Youth become hard and fast.

Meanwhile Lene sits at home by the juniper tree and peels potatoes and quinces. Or she sits at the window upstairs with needlework and watches the ships. The virgin voyage of the *Monte Cervantes*, which is close to a hundred and sixty metres long. Almost not a ship any more, thinks Lene. And all the other luxury liners with their restaurants, their smoking lounges, libraries, everything's been thought of. The ships move up and down with every ebb and flow. The river has a heavy, old breath and a dress made of oil. And then there are the foghorns in November, which cause everyone to walk around with a shudder all month and put up their collars.

Lene shops for groceries frugally, she cooks and sets the table for two. Sometimes she's sad, sometimes happy, sometimes it storms outside and sometimes inside the house. A young marriage. There are nights, however, when the wind is still and when Ruven lies atop her and sometimes sings, too. Or he wakes her with his hands, when he comes home late, and pushes himself underneath her, until she's entirely awake and it becomes clear how well she understands some things about herself and how fond she is of Ruven.

However, one evening Ruven says quietly: 'I never thought that nothing might happen here in Hamburg. So much is always happening here. Why not in my life, too?'

'Be happy,' says Lene. 'Start small, end big.'

Ruven stands at the window and smokes. 'I can't do it any more, be happy,' he says. 'Perhaps I never could.' He throws the cigarette out the window, turns around and pulls her towards him by her skirt. He presses her against the wall, and she almost suspects that he's crying. He doesn't seem at all capable of finding joy, any more.

Ruven begins to really seek out joy, burnt and fermented joy. Joy is joy, and he has a lot of company on this point. Heinz Egon and Lilian Harvey sing from the radio at the Alte Seile. The barmaid has swollen hands; she breaks glasses and curses. In the black-tarred courtyard, she smokes eels and blubbers, '*Somewhere in the world there's a little bit of luck . . .* '

Many months pass this way. But a lonely child of the gods doesn't fall because he's looking upwards but rather as soon as he averts his gaze from heaven, well, Ruven has begun slipping downward. And as if he wanted to help move things along, a person suddenly arrives at the white house on the water, ten o'clock in the morning, June 1931, a pale gentleman in a trench coat, who knocks with a bit too much confidence.

'What do you want, sir?' asks Lene in astonishment. Almost no one ever visits.

'Is Ruven Preuk present?'

'Present, present!' grumbles Ruven from the front room and positions himself in front of the man, a little hungover and one-and-a-half heads taller than him.

'May I come in, perhaps?' The man takes off his hat and ushers himself into the room.

'Please. Coffee?' Lene feels proud. A daughter of the estate steward, she is. She straightens up her beautiful head and everything turns blue-blooded around her. Then, in the next room, the coffee grinder between her knees, two cups, a bit of milk and sugar.

'And?' Ruven sits facing the man, the window at his back, the other sees him only in silhouette and is slightly blinded, which briefly rattles him, but then his confidence returns, a confidence preserved through business dealings, and he finally begins to speak: 'I've been informed that a valuable instrument worth approximately five thousand dollars, from the estate of Doctor Linde, is to be found in your custody. The violin is listed in his insurance, and must now, due to enormous debts, be ceded to one of his creditors—in this case, me.'

The man moves as if he already intends to stand up and seize the violin.

Ruven doesn't stir.

'I've come to ask politely, sir, for you to surrender the instrument to me, or, if you'd like, to buy it off me, which in your case would probably be sensible . . . ' he looks round the room and also glances at Lene, 'As it doesn't quite look like five thousand dollars in here, if I may say that.'

'You may,' says Ruven. 'But you may not take the violin with you. It is not available for purchase. Just like my wife. A wedding present, I'm sorry.'

But the man will not be deterred. He fingers the shiny cheeks just above the edge of his beard, bends himself far forwards, and says with sour breath: 'In that case there must have been documentation of the gift, or a contract. If the piece wasn't struck from the doctor's property list. Do you have anything like that?'

Ruven looks to Lene, who is standing behind the man in the doorway.

'Do we?'

She shakes her head.

'Then unfortunately you must, sir . . . '

'Unfortunately you must your ass, sir, and leave! Or I'll call the police! Unfortunately!' Ruven stands up, and all that roast that Mother Preuk administered to him when he was a child is asserted. It's probably also the mucking out the stalls, and years, now, of climbing the stairs on the hillside. Everything together adds up to a certain physique, and then any 'sirs' don't go on for much longer. One more movement with an outstretched arm in the direction of the door and the man slips off, a trench coat with a bit of gentlemanly residue inside, and says something about the district court and the police.

'Yeah, yeah.' Door closed. Ruven takes Lene in his arms, she is white as milk yet also finally, after four years of marriage, hopeful. But it is still very fresh. He might become a Wasserman, if everything goes well. And such stories, now.

'He won't come again,' says Ruven.

And he doesn't come again. But a few days later a letter from the unknown gentleman's solicitor comes, nothing in it but an appointment, although it could well be enough for a miscarriage.

They stop at Gesche's and John's. They don't want to visit Mother Lunten until everything is finished. 'So that a shock doesn't send her off before it's time for her to plait the angels' braids,' says Ruven.

That evening, they sit mutely at the table. Ruven glances at Lene over and over again. She had insisted on coming with him.

'One really feels very criminal,' she says.

'Criminal means something different here!' Gesche cuts the sausage into thick slices. 'You two should really see how everyone has changed here. Always marching, Peter Röver importantly at the front, up and down the main road. And then in the evening, around the oak tree, standing at attention, and then the torches are lit. Today Peter came up to our fence afterwards. He kept spitting and clearing his throat until there was nothing I could do but notice him. All he says is that he thinks things really haven't been hap-pening for you, Ruven. And it's probably because it was a worthless Jew who taught you the violin, says Peter, and, well, nothing at all could come from that.

I don't understand a word you're saying, I told him. What do you mean, worthless? I asked, but he only laughed and said, We'll just have to wait and see who will soon be deciding on values here. And with that, he turned around once, saying, 'Now it's us Germans' turn,' and left.

'To say that it's someone's turn—that can be taken in different ways,' John responds. 'Not necessarily that it's going to end in catastrophe again.'

'This is just a beginning, though,' says Gesche, 'some kind of beginning. No one has noticed it. But it's where the gardener sleeps that the devil sows his weeds.' She stands up quietly and raises the weights in the wall clock. 'And what do you have planned in the city tomorrow?'

The golden crank purrs in a circle. Ruven shrugs helplessly. And then they go to bed, or at least they try to. Ruven tosses and turns for hours.

'Are you not sleeping at all?' Lene finally asks.

'How am I supposed to sleep? When the child comes, everything is going to be even harder. I'm also wondering about how the badger is doing. If Röver is talking like this . . . and I haven't seen him for so long.'

'You don't live here any more, you know,' whispers Lene. 'And a child, first of all, doesn't cost anything. Not everyone has to be as expensive as you.'

The next day they travel, shattered with exhaustion, to the city and the law office. The place is dominated by frantic activity, doors open and doors close—why is so much happening there? Is everything here switching owners? All around, people wear expressions like they're at a horse market. Ruven and Lene struggle to orient themselves. He who plays music can't do anything else, even the simplest things. They are stalled until the afternoon.

'But the appointment was for eleven o'clock,' Lene tells the clerk, close to tears.

The creditor in the trench coat doesn't arrive until three, as if the thing had been deliberately delayed, and he's now puffed up with arrogance; his eyes soon linger on the violin case that Ruven has laid on a side table in the entrance hall. Then he's even taking the Linde'sche out of its case and handling it so roughly that it is obvious he cares not one whit about the violin. And as if he'd touched something forbidden and triggered some kind of secret mechanism, there is a rattling coming from down below, at the front of the building, and soon it's coming from the stairs and then it resounds, loud and feminine: 'You let me in now, sir, and quickly!'

Erika Lunten doesn't hold back her rage. She raises her hands to the side, her hands that so love to plait braids, and with a torrent of Low German she plaits the trench coat together so that he nearly drops the violin out of fright. But Erika Lunten refuses to wait so long, and instead she's soon occupying the solicitor's office and snapping her handkerchief at the table so that the papers flutter all around.

'It's hot in here! You must let the fresh air in!' Then she pants and says, 'So, so, so' and, 'No, no, no. You've already settled accounts here! What do you want then, paper or violin? Paper, you say?' And then she slaps an envelope towards the solicitor. 'There's your paper! Just ask! Everything here is by your arrangement! You could have had that arrangement much sooner. But who knew that in the city such a wretched piece of paper was worth so much.'

'Wait a moment.' The solicitor hadn't been able to get a word in edgewise the entire time. His thin hair was still billowing from so much rage-filled panting opposite him.

'Please!' She says, quietly sucking in air through her nose so that a bit of oxygen comes back into her brain.

The solicitor takes his letter opener made of brass and tries to make it glint somewhat threateningly. He opens the letter much too slowly and reads. Then a deep breath in and quickly out again.

'It is, in fact, a documentation of the gift, truth be told. In light of this, and to and for it, and the way I see it . . . ' he murmurs, 'Well, then the matter has already been settled.'

'That's what I've been saying!' Erika Lunten rises once again to say something else, but then manages to swallow it down, because of her good manners, of which she clearly has more than the pale gentleman standing outside in the entrance hall. She grips the violin proudly, gestures at Ruven and Lene to follow her, and swans off, down the stairs and up the street, and even outside, she doesn't say another word, instead she steers them over to the pastry shop and orders something with a lot of sugar and even more cream. Then she forks it in as if she had a day of battle behind her, and finally looks at Ruven and Lene, pleased.

'And?' she says then, almost embarrassed. 'Can I venture a guess then, that the letter that you two left behind after all the wedding celebrations, left behind for years, is important? This whole mess over a slip of paper!'

'Well, we had no idea,' says Ruven, avoiding her gaze.

'Don't sit there now like you're flying a flag at half-mast. I didn't throw it away, at least! Everything is all set now, anyway. You mustn't let yourself be pulled all around on a leash like a doted-on dachshund. Or like the badger . . . ' she says. But she doesn't say more.

'What's happening with him?' Now Ruven looks at her sharply.

'Nothing is happening with him.'

Now Ruven grows almost harsh: 'Tell us, Mother, what is happening with the badger!'

'They pulled him all over the place. This is a few weeks ago already, now. With a leash around his neck, the Röver boy and the others, until old man Röver came with his whip and drove all the little buggers off. And then the badger started up again with prayers and thanks. Then Röver whipped the badger, too, one time, and said something like: Shut your trap. Since then, the badger's disappeared.'

'We must go looking for him soon, Mother,' says Ruven quietly. 'So that they don't find him before you do.'

But there's no badger to be found, for now.

'No need to hurry,' Röver chimes in August in the village pub, 'As soon as the autumn leaves begin to fall in the forest, then we'll nab our prophet.'

Autumn comes and the cold does, too, and the leaves go, and the prophet stands stripped of his leaves, so to speak, in the bald woods, and can't move out of fear, and he stares at the slobbering dogs straining in front of him on their leashes.

In the new year, on the 6th of February 1932, Lene goes to the hospital in the morning and thinks that the child is on its way. But it doesn't happen. It doesn't happen at noon, either. The midwife, Küstermann, looks up the tides in the newspaper. 'The tide is coming in at three,' she says. 'Women who live so close to the water take care to hold themselves to it.'

At four o'clock the daughter is there. In one arm, Ruven cradles the little girl with the fiery red flame atop her head. How tiny you are, he thinks, how complete!

They name her just like the wife of Doctor Linde: Marie.

Mother Lunten hauls all of her silverware to the Elbe. She needs three days to arrange the baptism celebrations. The water in the river is very high and very deep. The seagulls perch on the poles, their beaks to the wind. The ice floes crunch and slide onto the sandy banks.

Finally, they celebrate the baptism: Marie Elisabeth Preuk. Her christening gown droops down deeply on the fourth generation and soon afterwards will be meticulously wrapped again in paper. They can't all sit for the meal, the young people stand. They talk soft and loud.

'Six million!' says Gosche and then something about the homeland. The conversation is a bit Germanic, or at least anti-Romantic. Because there exists some kind of connection between the six million and the French, the way

Gosche sees it. But it's also, somehow, anti-Polish and anti-Russian. The white sun wanders downstream, and at around four it's already sinking into the pink. The group goes back to the village. The house on the water grows still. The panes in the window glow in the evening light, and the juniper tree keeps its scent concealed until spring.

Beautiful years come for the young family, but a second child doesn't come. Every day has its own shape. Marie shapes the days of her parents, shapes her own palate, shapes castles in the sand. Ruven doesn't take his money to the Alte Seile but instead to Lene and Marie, and buys his wife dresses made of good material. 'We are too poor to shop cheaply,' he says then, and smokes by the window. At the table he now wears a napkin in his shirt collar.

Slim and put-together, Lene walks along the bank of the river after each meal. She pushes the white wicker pram on its little wheels. She likes to speak to the people who work by the railing. The people sing the old folksong: *'There are bandits in the for-est, hee holla ho. There are bandits in the forest . . . '* And when she can walk, Marie hops to the song, little right leg, little left leg, atop the sewer lid's iron castle: *'One, two, three, four, five, six, seven, all the Frenchmen went looking for heaven, but now they're in Moscow in the deep, deep snow, crying out oh no, oh no!'* And other old German rhymes. And the river flows, the wide world always in the picture with her. One of the first photos of Marie alone:

rolled stockings, ramrod-straight legs, short skirt, blouse, shoulder-length hair, with a bow tied high across her forehead. It is 1937, Marie is five years old. She smiles.

She also smiles when she cooks something with Lene for Ruven, or when she sings something with Ruven for Lene. She is fuelled by the love between the grown-ups and loves along with them and above and beyond them, when the years and the work have worn down the adults and they hardly engage with one another any more. Lene has a camera, she takes pictures. Only of Marie at first, later of Inge Voss, the landlady, too, she has an interesting and intelligent face; then of the captains' widows, pilots or the other neighbours. She works her way farther and farther into the harbour, up to the shipyard gates. Shift change in winter, shift change in summer, she photographs everything and hangs the prints on the wall in long rows.

'You're gifted, you know,' says Ruven one morning as he contemplates the pictures. 'I had no idea.' Then he looks at Lene, who is standing before him in her green dressing gown. She has her hands in her pockets as if she doesn't know where to put them. The room behind her looks so cramped that Ruven feels afraid. He frantically opens a window.

'No, I knew it,' he says softly.

Lene's cheeks break out in red blotches, and they are both shocked at how long they've lived together here without seeing one another.

'And you?' she asks. 'What will become of you? How long will we live here in Hamburg? Shouldn't we borrow money, finally, and rent a hall? Or do you want to go on like this for ever?'

'No.'

'Well.'

The next day, Lene writes to her father. Gosche Lunten arrives in person with the money.

'As I always say, give with warm hands,' he says. There is still time for it. One doesn't die so quickly. Nothing is freed so quickly either, and Ruven also needs run-throughs and practice time. He sits by the water a lot. One time, he sits there into the night. When he walks into the house and encounters Lene, she asks, frightened, 'What's wrong?'

'Nothing's wrong,' he says. 'Or, no. Earlier today they kicked a man in the face, up at the train station. A woman threw herself on top of him and tried to protect his head. Then they also kicked the woman in the face, and shouted, and soon she didn't need her face any more anyhow.'

Lene stares at him, appalled. 'And what did you do?'

Ruven avoids her. He has to laugh. He laughs, disbelieving, a good long while and finally says, 'I did nothing, besides think about my fingers. I . . . thought about my fingers!' And about Rahel. But he doesn't say that aloud.

August of 1939 has already counted twenty-five days. Ruven pulls the dusted-down suit towards him and stands for a long time in front of the mirror, considering his face in the glass.

'You have to leave,' says Lene, standing very close behind him. 'It's late, Ruven, you should be on your way already.' They make eye contact in the mirror.

'A good horse jumps at the last moment,' says Ruven. Then he turns around and faces her, kisses her forehead and sets off.

She sees him off until they're downstairs in front of the house. Then he walks with the violin case along the bank of the river and looks around one last time. Lene stands in a white dress in front of the house, with Marie holding her hand. A gust pushes through her hair and through the juniper tree. The house's windows are as white as the eyes of the blind.

The hall is nearly full. It's an oppressive evening. The wind isn't strong enough to blow into the rooms. People stand with sweat on their faces and the women look pale, even though it's the end of August, and everyone talks nervously and quietly, looking around at each other constantly.

They look as though they're afraid, thinks Ruven, and discovers his own shadow on the wall. This fear, he thinks, is rising up from the evening like a mist.

At just this moment, Lene is sitting on the steps in front of the door at home, and her gaze follows a ship upstream. Without looking, she knits a coat for Marie. Marie is digging a deep trench in the sand on the bank. Lene knows that it's a moat for a castle.

A couple of men in black uniforms come walking along the water and stop beside Marie and speak to her, and one of them laughs loudly into the twilight. Lene eavesdrops, then she's on the garden path, that is a mistake. She runs across the soft sand to Marie, so slowly it's as if she were fleeing in a dream, and grasps the child's hand: 'We don't speak to strangers.'

The leader hesitates but then quickly recovers.

'But I do know you.' He pauses. They look at each other.

'Yes, Fritz Dordel,' Lene says slowly, 'but I didn't know that we were using the informal 'you' with each other.'

Dordel shrugs and turns to his comrade: 'Take note of the house!' he says, then looks at Lene in a particular way again and adds: 'Beautiful face.' And then they turn around to go and Lene is left looking at black backs. The men have pulled their belts so tight and their trousers so high, it looks as though they had needed to hold something together.

Ruven's concert is a great success. It's even mentioned in the newspaper. For a whole week it lies open atop the bureau. Then Ruven cuts out the article. 'All the things one wants to have, just because one has briefly caught scent of the wider world,' he says.

The week ends with a daybreak at four forty-five in the morning, when the Polish farmers are just setting out to milk the cows or sharpening the blades of their scythes and walking to the meadows to cut the feed. The camomile is still curled from the dew, the women walk together in long skirts and aprons, their white headscarves tied tightly at the back of their necks, and everyone is still protected by just a barrier gate, but what is a barrier gate anyway? A sign, but a sign alone protects very little, and to what avail when the old signs are new and contorted and, well. When the old sun ruptures.

Six years of torching.

All of the old wooden time is incinerated. And so what happens, then, to a violinist and his ears and to everything else, too. How many violinists are being wiped from the picture, how many musicians, how many varieties of music, millions of varieties of music that were everywhere before, in the rooms, on the paths, and in the rows of beans. No deed without a song, no sawing wood, no igniting wood without a voice. A whole way of life. Not only in the shtetl, but everywhere. And then suddenly nothing more. Suddenly everything is as if it's been torn away. Suddenly the memory is simply burnt. As if a demon had severed the connection, but in truth it is oneself. In truth, one carries out the undertaking oneself, the whispering and murmuring of the times, the extinguishing of the whole testament of the ancients, in which one ignites them, the children of Abraham, the children in general, the singing ones. And then: nothing more. Only silence.

'War is a story that cannot be told,' Inge Voss says to Lene one evening. By the sixth month of war, she's already holding the death certificate for her husband, Otto, in her hand. Pale and composed, she sits with Lene in her living room and offers her quince bread.

'Or should one really tell the story of what happens when a body that has been grown and loved over many years, a beautiful and living body, is hit by a grenade, its organs simply ripped into shreds?' She looks intently at Lene. 'I don't know where Otto died. But did he kill, too? Did he kill children? You know that we always wanted children. And should one tell the story of how an innocent face that has barely seen anything of this beautiful world is forced to watch its mother be smothered by a shot to the lung, until that innocent face loses consciousness itself under unimaginable straits? Do you believe that war can happen without that? And should one tell that story?' She slowly shakes her head. 'War deserves no language, no stories. It is no material. It is the end of all material, I think. A person only goes into it. And no one really comes out again.' She closes her eyes because Lene is crying.

Ruven is in the war, too, he'd gone into this war with a rucksack made of pelt. He hadn't said, 'Until next time', only 'Farewell'.

And Lene must, well, live, and she raises Marie and waits for letters from Ruven, but there is nothing in the letters. The whole city is flying flags, always flying flags, on houses, factories and ships, *Victory, victory,* they say, *Greater Germany*! But there is nothing of that in Ruven's letters.

In the winter of 1941, in the middle of the night, someone knocks on the door. It is a frightened knock. There's no time for Lene to fetch her dressing gown, she must go to the door in her sheer chemise. She opens it carefully and draws back. Behind Inge Voss in the stairwell stand two other people, an old man and a young, very beautiful woman, Lene is able to make out as much in the light that falls from the apartment onto the three faces.

Inge Voss is so out of breath that she cannot speak. She only looks at Lene in such a way that Lene moves quickly to the side and leaves the entryway free. Frau Voss is already opening the attic hatch from the floor with a hooked cane, and the ladder falls, then the two people climb hastily up inside. None of them utter a word. They also don't say their names. Only their breath is audible, heavy as if from taxing work.

That's not a safe place to hide, Lene thinks, forcing herself to supress a sob. She's afraid, an attic is no place to hide! And in her house, too, which clings so closely to the hillside that the next house begins directly above the roof. And how is one supposed to hide a person, anyway? A person is perhaps only in the world at all so that he or she can be seen, thinks Lene. Such thoughts whirr through her mind as she opens the door one more time and listens carefully to the stairwell.

Inge Voss stands on the cold floor. She glances at the ceiling and then at Lene, who is pale and leaning against the doorway, waiting. She holds Lene's gaze until her breath is finally even again. They still don't know each other very intimately, although they've known each other for a very long time. They drink tea and listen to the radio together, too.

'Thank you,' says Inge Voss then, quietly, and closes her eyes for a moment. 'Thank you, Frau Preuk. You are a good soul.'

'Why are you doing this?' Lene asks the next evening after she's switched off the radio and the screeching of the Führer is still in their bones. 'And why do you trust me, Frau Voss?'

She stands up, then pulls the curtain a bit to the side, and looks out the window to the river. It flows and flows, black and heavy, as if it knew where it was going.

'I've known the two of them for a long time. My niece used to be their maid. They helped her quite a lot, back then—today she's a schoolteacher. And you know, Lene, we can leave things be,' she turns around, 'but we can also do them. When we leave them be, then we aren't proper humans. And proper humans are what we want to be, you know. You and I.'

Lene nods. From then on she brings food and candles up to the attic, and sometimes an attempted smile. They barely speak.

The nights above the rooftop are clear and cold. The frost magnifies all sound. The frost gives itself over to the river, so that the river solidifies. Then the old man begins to cough, at first only occasionally and then over long stretches of time. Lene lies in her room below and eavesdrops. What if the neighbours hear this. She thinks about Ruven. She cries out of fear for Marie. Then she stands up and pulls the attic ladder down.

'Come into the apartment,' she says softly.

That's too risky, whispers the woman.

'At least for a few hours, please, come in, I've covered all the windows. And it will be harder to hear you down here.'

Lene makes tea. The man and the woman sit at the table with grey faces. The woman is beautiful nonetheless. The symmetry and colouring of her features don't recall life at all, though. She tries to smile. Her lips are cracked. They still don't say any names. The woman asks about Marie and even smiles a real smile, for once. Then she gazes for a long time at the photographs of Lene and Ruven on the wall. Bewilderment paints itself across her face. Then she looks towards the music stand in the corner.

'Your husband is a musician?'

Lene nods. The woman begins to cry.

'Come now, why are you crying?' Lene carefully replenishes her tea.

'I miss music,' says the woman softly. 'And for a moment I thought I recognized your husband from before. But that must be a mistake.' She draws a breath as if she wanted to say something else, but then she seems to immediately use all her strength to supress it. She grasps the wrinkled hand of the old man. And he looks over at the photographs, too. His eyes widen slightly, he starts to cough again. It seems unlikely that he will make it through the winter.

Then the two climb back into the attic and speak excitedly with each other up above for a long time. The coughing can be heard all night long. For days and nights on end, the coughing is heard on the hillside. A bit of gossip with the milkman, a bit of gossip at the baker's, no one wants to be a traitor but there are things that must be reported, and reporting isn't betrayal, they say to themselves. Reporting isn't betrayal. A certain arrangement, an order, has also been established.

And there stands Fritz Dordel at the door, he snaps his arm out in salute, nearly hitting the doorjamb as he does it because there's no room for such gestures in here.

'Why aren't you in the fields?' Lene asks, sending Marie over to Frau Voss with one look.

Fritz Dordel turns red for a brief moment, and then: 'Have enough to do here. Important things.' Then he grins: 'And so we are using the informal 'you'!'

And then he's back to being very businesslike: 'And how is everything with all of you here? Everything clean?'

Lene shrugs and acts impassive: 'You can look around, if you want.'

And that he does, even looking under the bed right away; he doesn't notice the hatch to the attic. But isn't that a cough? Dordel kneels in front of the bed and listens. Lene pulls herself together and moves in a way she's never moved before. It's not a beautiful movement, but it's inviting. She wears a blue skirt and long stockings, and her legs are taut. Dordel keeps kneeling on the floor and raises his gaze to her in astonishment. His Adam's apple bobs up and down. 'Well, so you're one of those. That's what you're worth?'

This is what Marie is worth. Lene looks directly in his face, she suppresses a chill. She thinks of Marie's small hands and the down on the back of her neck. The Adam's apple bobs up and down again and then the light goes out as if by itself. Lene turns the key in the lock. And what follows pleases Fritz so much that for more of it he's plainly prepared to let one two three Jewish sows run for now. This Lene has always driven him wild. But he'd never thought her capable of such business acumen!

'What have you done with that man from the Gestapo?' Inge Voss is mopping the stairwell energetically and barely makes room to let Lene through. Lene just stands still and waits.

'The old man coughed so loudly, what should I have done?' She sits down tiredly at the top of the stairs. 'I know that man, and he is ruthless—but if a child comes from this, then you must help me,' she says.

Inge Voss straightens. 'Forgive yourself, Lene.'

'There is nothing to forgive.'

And a child does come from it, a Dordel. It shall be helped with soapy water and a knitting needle. They send Marie to the baker. 'Run!' Lene holds her in a tighter hug than usual as she sends her off, nearly frantic, only able to keep breathing in, a dry weeping. And then, again: 'Run!' And with the last of her strength and one of her rare gazes directly into the child's eyes, she says, 'Don't be afraid. Everything will be fine.'

Then Lene lies down on the kitchen floor. Inge Voss has brought a woman with her who knows how to do this. The icy tiles underneath her, the assistant's poking. But It is ensconced in tissue and has its own rhythm and with every second grows against each and every external will, as if it knew of its rights and its innocence; it will not allow itself to be pierced.

Lene, in contrast, disappears. She makes room for the Dordel.

'How am I supposed to raise it, when I can't love it?' She asks Inge Voss.

'You'll simply do it.'

Later, Lene is standing by the juniper tree and thinks back on those words and walks with one foot after the other and looks to the river. She can no longer touch her own belly. Her hands shake when she feels the child moving inside of her.

Dordel pulls on his boots upstairs. He's coming almost every day, now. He is very friendly to Lene and even looking forward to the child, although it's more and more in the way during his special visits. He acts as if everything is going perfectly. He describes the dangers of the war and the front while glancing at the photographs of Ruven out of the corner of his eye as if Ruven had already been killed in action. Meanwhile, Ruven is writing to Lene more and more often from the loneliness of the war, but Lene can hardly open the letters, she is so ashamed of herself, for she has almost grown accustomed to Dordel, she is lonely, too. She even disgusts herself less. She catches herself primping, combing, listlessly, but she does comb. Because now it is two bodies.

But the juniper evaporates in the April sun. Its berries are in their second year and Lene walks past them daily, white from their poison. She plucks a handful and then another and stores the berries in a glass. And Fritz comes and goes, he brings sweets for Marie, he strokes Lene's hair and takes a long time for himself. To Marie, he says that he's reading something to Mama, German poets, and they need quiet for it. Here, he's an entirely different person. On his way up the stairs on the banks of the Elbe, he sheds his skin, in a way. He also has a new haircut. It conceals his otter forehead a bit. And so he likes the way he looks much more. But again and again, almost compulsively, he glances secretly at the photographs of Ruven. In seconds, a sneer and then something like affection alternates in his expression, sometimes deference, too, but then there's only hardness and stupidity again. He never asks once about the attic. Sometimes he even thinks he'd let it go entirely, if only Lene wouldn't turn away from him.

But in September, when the time arrives, Lene speaks with the pale woman under the roof: 'Inge Voss will care for you.' And then she travels with Marie to the country, to the estate, and knocks on the steward's front door. She has been feeling the contractions for days. She hadn't told Fritz that she was leaving. He knocked on her door for a half an hour, and then understood, and slowly and meaningfully thought to himself, 'All right, then.'

It is silent around the steward's house. The dahlias stand regally at the fence, as if they knew that they would be allowed to spend the cold winter on a straw bed in the cellar. Lene knocks a second time.

'What do you want in here?' Erika Lunten calls from inside.

'I must come in there,' says Lene, 'Open up, Mother.' The door opens tiredly, and Mother Lunten freezes when she lays eyes on Lene.

'Are you dead or alive?' She says and takes her daughter by the shoulders. 'What is happening to you?'

'I'm not well.' Lene sits down. She says nothing about the juniper berries. She knows that it's too late to change anything. Lene's mother shoos Marie into the next room with Gosche. Lene sits on the chair as if she hoped to remain there. Her mother rubs her shoulders, pulls both combs from her own long braid and resolves everything, and Lene leans her head into her mother's soft belly until it is dark.

'Should I sing you something, child, like before, when I undid your braids at night?'

'Yes, sing me something,' says Lene. And then she listens with closed eyes.

'Like a silent room,' her mother sings the old lullaby about moonrise: 'That's just how some things are—' and she stops, because Lene has started to scream.

At five o'clock a boy is born in the back room, they name him Friedjof, as if he were a comfort; but Lene—she's eaten so many juniper berries over the past several weeks. She takes the little one in her arms one more time and thinks, I was wrong, I could have loved you. But then she grows weaker and weaker. She asks for Marie again. She strokes Marie's red hair one more time. Then she asks for Ruven, but she can't wait for him any longer.

It smells like blood in the death chamber. Gosche and Erika, the sisters and Aunt Gesche and John stand in the weak light and don't say a word. Their eyes are sunken, they hold one another's hands or shoulders. Marie is alone. She doesn't look at the adults. She emerges alone from the night and alone she goes back into it. Suddenly they are all without any notion of heaven, even Aunt Gesche, who has always known something comforting to say. Now, she just says, it takes quite a lot of deaths to ever grow accustomed to them.

Marie stands with her back to the bed and to her mother. She forces her eyes open, and outside is the autumn and it dabs its blood.

'Where am I to go, now?' asks Marie. She sits on Gosche's old chair at the window. She rocks slowly back and forth. Aunt Gesche is standing in the room with Friedjof in her arm. The baby is tightly bound in a swaddling blanket, as if Aunt Gesche were carrying a large grub.

'You'll come and stay with me, the two of you,' Gesche smiles faintly. 'You can come and stay with all the other chicks under the warm stove. And the Linde'sche and Joseph's violin, we'll also pick those up soon.'

'Who is Joseph?' Marie wants to know, and Gesche tells her the story at the window, and in Marie's imagination, Joseph takes on the shape of the landscape—he's a stake, a tree, a mill.

'I'm imagining how Joseph spins when he fiddles,' she says.

'Yes,' Gesche answers softly, 'he always turned in circles when he played.'

The fields outside are harvested. The rooks and seagulls swing through the air. Again and again, Marie goes into the good room and observes Lene's pallid face. Her chin wrinkles but she gathers herself together so that she doesn't cry.

'She's not sleeping,' she says.

'No,' says Gesche from the next room, 'she's not sleeping.'

They carry the corpse out through the front, as if through little gates of paradise. But then Gosche Lunten takes a few long timber nails and hammers them slantwise through the door and into the old frame, groaning in despair: 'Now it stays closed for ever! Never again will anyone ever walk through it! Not in, and not out!'

The funeral feast sticks in all of their throats. With the elderly, this means something different. But when someone dies young, and Lene at that, and moreover because she perhaps wanted this—no cake will ever be able to sweeten that.

'If only one could properly cry,' old Hinrich Werkzeugmacher says and rubs his balled hands in his eye sockets. And then they pat Gosche's upper arm, pursing their thin lips together, and then they nod once, and go.

Nothing about Lene's death is reported to Ruven. Only what one can report to the front, that he also has a son, they write, and that he is a joy. When he's allowed to return home from the war for a short time weeks later, John meets him at the train station in Hamburg.

'Where is Lene, why isn't she here?' asks Ruven.

John isn't able to meet his gaze. 'You must come with me to the village,' he says.

For a long moment, Ruven looks as though he wants to turn around and board the train again, which is beginning to move, hissing and packed full with young life.

'I've felt it,' he says. 'I'm alive. And she isn't.'

Later, with Marie, when he places something on the grave, up on the church hill between the poisonous yews, it surprises him how much life suspends itself when someone arrives and when someone leaves.

'This is so clear in the world,' he says, 'one can break it into pieces like bread.' And Marie nods to that, but only because her father is nodding.

All the things we missed, thinks Ruven, all the things we overlooked and didn't say. And what we shouldn't have said. And he sees Lene before him, in the tapered space, and he counts backwards and counts himself into the trap where he can't cry for Lene, because the birth of this boy argues against her and against the boy, for the son cannot be his.

'Do you remember that time that you defended me from father, and played at the slaughtering party?' John says in the evening after dinner, as they both sit by the oven and smoke. 'Since then, I've always felt that I owed you something. I always knew that the day would come.' He takes three drags. 'We will care for your children. They'll have a family here. And your violins, you'll get those back, too, and then perhaps you'll still come to something with all that. We were too late there, unfortunately. They'd cleaned out the whole apartment and taken everything. Apparently, Lene had hidden a man and a woman in her attic. I didn't believe it, but Marie had such an expression on her face when I asked her about it. She knows something, but perhaps she doesn't know herself exactly what. She talked about a man in uniform, though, who came to visit and spoke Low German with her mother. Lene once secretly called him the otter. You know who the child was talking about.'

I have you there, Fritz, thinks Ruven, and he's suddenly so hot that he has to move away from the fire. Yes, she would have spoken Low German with you, Fritz, with who else? And he remembers the night that John had mentioned, the night in front of the big house, under the wide sky, when Lene stood next to him for the first time and the clouds of their breath mixed together as they spoke in the frost-cold. She only spoke Low German with old acquaintances, never with strangers. And it was even a slaughtering party back then when we met each other, he thinks, and you are dead, Lene, because between then and now the slaughtering party spread across everything. An international butchering. Pigs and non-pigs, my little Lene. But how does Fritz figure in? And who else did you have in the house?

'Do you still believe that we'll win?' he asks suddenly.

'Win!' says John. 'We're next, I've said that already. It's only going to keep on going ass-backwards, now.'

'And what they're doing now to the Polacks,' Gesche says, inserting herself into the conversation, 'that's going to destroy us, you better believe it.'

The three of them stare into the embers as if there were something there and one could read it. They say nothing for a half an hour. And then, as if they'd finished reading, Gesche says, 'The baron is picking up women in the neighbourhood, they say, and ordering them to his hunting lodge. The young and the old. Once, I hear, he had them dance. A hoppledy-hop around the table and on top of the table, between the plates. The baron supposedly directing them with a pistol. And then they had to pick up bottles. But not with their hands. And the baron laughed, supposedly. Worn-out Polack hags, he laughed, supposedly, until he had tears in his eyes. The farmhand saw everything, all of it, and went on and on about it, as if he just wanted to name-drop.' She stares into the fire again. The clock makes a quarter circle.

Gesche then leaves the brothers alone at the oven. She goes and pushes the bolt closed and turns the key twice. A bit undecided for a moment, until she finally turns and says quietly as she walks out, 'The boy can do nothing about any of this. Try to love him, Ruven, whoever his father is; otherwise he'll grow up to be wicked.'

Ruven travels back to Hamburg. He'd inquired with acquaintances beforehand and learnt a few things. That Fritz is in the Gestapo, for example, and takes care of enemies of the state and Jews.

Those filthy people kicked the bucket, along with Frau Voss, the woman next door tells Ruven when he enquires. But whether the head of the police was named Dordel, that she doesn't know, in fact she doesn't know much at all, she says, as she thinks back on it.

Who were the two? With whom had his wife been living, Ruven asks again and pushes a bank note into her hand, which she immediately sticks in her apron pocket.

She doesn't know anything, the neighbour says again. People change places so often. Perhaps it had been communists, although they had had those Jewish profiles. And his wife? She'd heard that she had gotten sick.

'Yes.' He doesn't say any more. Ruven turns away stiffly and walks up to the city. His limping has grown worse again. Ruven takes the train for a stretch, then walks again on foot until he's at the bank of the Alster River, long, short, long, short, and aimlessly past the houses, long, short, his Morse steps saying only: Save us, save us—in English, well, two syllables; no one can expect rescue from the German.

As if by accident, Ruven lands on Fontenay Street in front of Jakub Golbaum's villa. He struggles to compose his expression. The villa is unlocked. Inside, all the rooms were all emptied, the dining room, the blue parlour, years ago. But somehow he can hear it, as if it were hanging in the walls: Grieg, G major, second movement, Rahel at the piano, the quiet way she proceeds, and then the violin: *Taa-da-daa-dee da-dee-da-da* . . .

Ruven stands there for far too long and hesitates, because something is holding him back, because his eyes can't turn away from what's lying there in the corner, between the torn-down curtains and tattered books. But he's too tired to take the few steps and look to see what it is. He's too tired for everything. There is nothing more here. The house doesn't smell of people, any more. They've been gone for far too long.

The women were sent to the prison in Fuhlsbüttel, the neighbour had said. The man, they'd—and then she'd just pointed to her temple.

It is not very difficult to find Fritz Dordel's office. When Ruven walks in, Fritz is cleaning his nails with the tip of a letter opener. A fire burns in the fireplace. It's the old world that he's burning in there, and he'd done it calmly, too, revelling in strangers' things. He'd gotten the desk from a solicitor, desk lamp from a doctor, chair from a pianist, Chesterfield armchair from an industrialist family, the gramophone had belonged to a university professor, and he fingers all of it with the self-satisfaction of a conqueror, and all he'd needed to do for all of it was pick up the telephone.

'Ruven Preuk! Look at you. The prodigal son.' It doesn't occur to Fritz that he might get up. Or perhaps he forces himself to remain seated. They're almost related now, after all, even if they weren't exactly announcing it in the town square, and Fritz also doesn't believe that Ruven knows anything.

'What brings the successful musician here, to my wretched house?' He laughs a fake laugh. Ruven feels the sweat under his arms. He doesn't know what he wants here, yet. For a few seconds, he simply stands there and listens to Fritz's voice. It's turned oddly clear and cheerful. As if he weren't Fritz any more. The buzzing overtones are as good as gone, he's even almost elegant. This is not quite pleasant. Also not quite pleasant is his new ability to sustain eye contact without blinking.

'And?' Fritz pushes the letter opener slowly into a red leather case. 'Have you lost your ability to speak? Well, I suppose you were never very chatty.'

'No,' says Ruven, and takes a deep breath: 'I'm looking for a . . .'

'Woman?' Fritz interrupts him. 'Already? I heard what happened to Lene, what a tragic thing. But the child survived? A son?' Fritz lifts his eyebrows questioningly. It's impossible to tell what he's feeling.

'Yes, if only all of us now took a year to mourn,' he says almost shrilly, 'Right? We would hardly get ahead, then. Let's mourn while we can, don't you think? After all, we're in a war.' And this last word comes out like a screech; it almost sounds like there's a note of fear, or despair.

But of what is he supposed to be despairing? A yearning for Lene? Or because Ruven's wife preferred poisoning herself—that much, at least, has finally filtered down to him—to being connected to him, to Fritz Dordel?

Perhaps it's also just now occurring to Ruven that it must leave a strange impression, when a man goes searching for something else so soon after the death of his wife. Perhaps he also thinks for the briefest moment about how Lene wasn't only his wife but also a shelter, perhaps this marriage was a shelter, too, marriage in general could constitute a shelter, a shelter from the great and terrible encounters that so few people can bear, and those who make use of this shelter should account for why they are actually doing it. And with a strained voice, he says, 'I wasn't talking about a wife. But is my wife a victim of the war, then?'

For a moment, Fritz can't find the thread of the conversation again. He bows his head and gives Ruven a predatory look. And then he laughs anew.

'What do I know? I'd also hoped for a different fate for her. Such a superb German. Ask the pastor, though, he'd have said something.'

'I don't know what the pastor said. I didn't bury my wife, I was at the front.'

'Yes, now, we all have our obligations. My condolences, in any case.' Fritz looks suddenly bored. 'Well? What are you looking for?'

'My apartment has been stripped because people were apparently being hidden there. And my instruments have disappeared. A valuable violin, among other things.' Ruven stands up straighter. 'I demand that my violin be returned!'

'Just a moment.' Fritz lights a cigarette. 'Demands won't be discussed here. Yes, we've confiscated your belongings; I heard something about the matter. Your wife wasn't hiding people, however, she was hiding Jews. And which ones might interest you. There was a very interesting similarity of names between the two flea-bitten half-cadavers in your attic and your old violin teacher, the one who could supposedly play the violin so much better than my father.' Fritz looks at Ruven expectantly.

Ruven grasps at the chair next to him, but doesn't sit down, instead he supports himself on the back of it. What do you know about me, he thinks, how much? And quietly, he asks, 'Goldbaum?'

'Goldbaum!'

'You found the Goldbaums in *my* house?'

'I thought the same thing!' Fritz flashes awake and leans over the desk towards Ruven: 'It's like that old proverb, whoever finds the old keys, eh—' it slips out of him, and he's clearly annoyed by it, 'doesn't need the new ones any more, or something like that. Although, both keys are gone now. They aren't to be found again, Preuk. You should know that.'

Against his will, Ruven sits on the chair. His mind floods with thoughts, looking for connections between two life stories. Had he had something to do with this, somehow? Did Lene and Rahel meet in his house? His Lene and his Rahel? And then as if they were suddenly standing before him and affirming their answer to this question, very briefly and perhaps for the first time Ruven genuinely feels an unnameable feeling for Lene.

'You found Rahel Goldbaum in my attic,' he says more to himself than to Fritz.

'Me? No.' Fritz is already lighting another cigarette, he's so excited now. 'I wasn't there. I'm not here to clean your house. I organize.' But the name is enough for him. These names could, after all, be struck from books, from hearts, or wherever else. They would be done away with, repotted, all those gold trees—*Goldbaum*—and silver apples—*Silberapfel*—and rosebushes—*Rosenstock*. No more handouts for them. You earn what you earn! For a moment Fritz falters, then he's in control of himself again and looks at Ruven with frozen pupils. A smile, as if his face were made of poison. Fritz will ask after where they were taken. Ruven shouldn't think he can bring them back, but if Ruven is asking him, then he'll look into it. Ruven has stood up again, he has trouble staying upright.

'Yes, Fritz, please look into it.'

'What was the name again, exactly?'

'Goldbaum, Rahel.'

Fritz disappears into the next room. The matter is even more interesting than was to be expected. How pale Ruven had looked, and how he had so quickly forgotten his violin!

A young man goes through the list. Fritz stands closely behind him and looks over his shoulder. Yes, Goldbaum, Rahel, is still there, but could that be the right one? Fritz goes back to his desk.

'Come again tomorrow,' he says, 'bye, bye . . . ' and he stares into space. 'Yes, like old Joseph used to say. Bye, bye. And his daughter, Sofie. They tolerated you well. Many people tolerated you well. Those were the days, eh? But you've changed, Preuk. Bye, bye, I must look into this further, eh.' Yet again this ugly interjection slips from his lips, but now his elation drowns out all shame.

Ruven leaves the building as if he has blood poisoning. He barely manages to find a small hotel near the train station, and sleeps in his clothes.

The next morning, he wipes his forehead and neck with a damp cloth and smokes a cigarette as he walks down the street. He only has two thoughts: Your heart, Rahel, beats twice as fast as the hearts of others, and your heart, Lene, doesn't beat any more at all.

Fritz instructs his secretary to pretend that he is out of the office for two hours. And then, in a pressed shirt, he sits at his desk. He's in a good mood, he's been in a good mood all night long, he doesn't know what's gotten into him. An idea had come to him, one after the other, just short of brilliant. He's not at all accustomed to it. He'd pulled the address of this Goldbaum, it wasn't hard at all to find, and headed there in the evening, as if he was on the scent of something. Goal, scored: Ruven Preuk. Bye, bye! Times have changed. To wit: in the clutter and under a pile of curtains Fritz finds a violin case, and very carefully he puts everything together. Around midnight the thrilling idea occurs to him and he creates a bit of light in the backyard in an old brass drum, which he had erected there for the destruction of disagreeable things.

Now the violin cases sit on the desk from the solicitor, the short, grey-haired man who had stood there so still, no, he'd stood there like an idiot and refused to understand that he was a zero, already erased. Next to the first violin case are two others. He had pushed them aside when the men showed up in the warehouse with the furniture. He had remembered that much—that at least one of Preuk's violins must have been very valuable.

Fritz pulls out the desk's middle drawer and pushes it shut again when Ruven walks in. His mouth pinches shut and he shakes his head, signalling hopelessness.

'Nothing to be done for it, Preuk.' He lifts his eyebrows high and lets them fall again. 'You can't have her so easily. But we aren't brutes, you know, you can send her greetings.

And here,' he points to the cases, 'you can also send her something, as a keepsake. And let's put it this way—we're going to play a little game, just like Joseph used to do, a kind of shell game.' He's grinning. 'I've switched around the violins a bit. One of the three is Goldbaum's violin. You can guess which case it's hiding in, and if it's the right violin in the case, then perhaps we'll turn a blind eye. The other cases you can have, of course. They belong to you, after all.' Fritz shrugs. 'Write something nice to her. Write, for example, that you forgive her for being Jewish.'

Ruven cannot answer. His lips are so dry that they feel as though the skin has grown together.

'Can you not forgive that? Then just write nothing, I don't care,' says Fritz and glances at the cases, suddenly looking as though he'd like to leave.

'Let me write something, Fritz, and I'll also take a guess.' Ruven feels the way his lips rip apart.

'Good! There's paper and pen right there, but quickly!'

Ruven looks at the violin cases, then writes *Rahel* on a piece of paper and folds it together and gives it to Fritz. He slowly fingers the cases. In one of them there's the Linde'sche, in one the violin from Joseph and in the third the one from Goldbaum. He tries to divine Fritz's thoughts. In which case did he put Goldbaum's violin?

Ruven's hand stays on Goldbaum's violin case. He feels nothing, as though the case was empty. Well, only Joseph's violin could be in there, he thinks, it is so small it's almost not a violin at all. The Linde'sche case is the same as always. Then Ruven grips Joseph's heavy case, it almost feels heavier than the violin from Goldbaum, and Fritz reaches for it. He is struggling to suppress a grin.

Ruven lowers his gaze. 'Then I'll be going, now.'

'Yes. And you can take the two other cases with you, we'll let you know if the woman recognizes the violin.' Fritz points, smiling, to the door. At the last moment he shouts: 'Haven't we forgotten something?!' And snaps his arm up.

Ruven takes the violin cases, glances once more at the third, closes the door behind him and goes downstairs and onto the street without a salute.

A window is open up above. Ruven can hear Fritz laughing. He takes the bus directly to the train station and then takes a train north. He then travels on foot to the wainwright's. He arrives in the evening.

They've cleared out a room for him, he goes into it now and puts the two cases on the table. He stands there for a while in the dark and wants to pray. Then he lights a candle and unclasps them.

There is only a violin in one of the cases. In the other, there's a laugh, a jeer, as if it were coming from deep below. Shocked, Ruven shuts the case. Then he opens it again, and again a laugh comes out. Ruven tumbles out of the room and outside into the winter. There's a sharp pain in his back. He runs from the pain in his back. He grasps at the place where it hurts. The sky is alight with stars. The houses lie still, large and humpbacked in the darkness, and in the houses these people who no longer recognize each other.

Ruven runs across the fields towards the forest. Between the trees, he stands still, and props himself up on the closest one. Then he slams his head against the trunk until a noise emerges from his throat, as if he were hollow inside. Then he returns to the house, sheds his clothes in his room and goes to sleep like an ancient man.

'Ruven is unwell,' says Gesche in the morning. A howling can be heard coming from his room, and then a desperate moaning. John drinks his coffee. With his left hand he rocks Friedjof's cradle. He doesn't answer. *Tip-tap* goes the rocker on the floorboards.

'Do you know what he brought with him from Hamburg?' Gesche shakes something in the pan. 'He brought violin cases. But one is missing a violin,' she says. 'It only has wood ashes and a couple of wires inside. But he won't say a word about where he got the cases. He won't say a word about anything at all, he just makes noise.'

In this way, three days pass. Then a whole strip of skin on Ruven's back bursts open.

Gesche boils lemon balm, rips up an old bed sheet and dips the pieces in the brew. She takes the last of the honey, too, from the earthenware jug. Then she turns Ruven's shivering body onto its stomach and spreads the honey over the burst blisters. On top, she lays the cloths. Wherever danger is, or wherever afflictions are, Gesche is always calm and attentive.

She also discusses warts and wounds. Mother Preuk taught that to her. You can't pass this on to everyone, she had said back then. One doesn't pour milk into a barrel of sauerkraut. Mother Preuk was well versed in it, and one afternoon she had taken Gesche aside and only said, 'Let's go a ways into the woods, I have something to give to you.' And then, in the woods, Gesche was supposed to step on the little toe of Mother Preuk's left foot, grip her around the throat and look over her right shoulder and never forget again what she saw there. And so Gesche did it. But whether it was just the forest that she saw there or very possibly something different, whatever it was, or nothing at all, she had never disclosed to anyone.

'He has shingles,' says Gesche in the kitchen, 'And what a case of it. People have hanged themselves over less.' She washes her hands for a long time. 'Don't let the children in his room, and take those violin cases away!'

John goes into the room. He's back soon after.

'He doesn't want me to take the cases. I'm to leave the cases next to each other, like a married couple in their tomb. He thinks they should stay together for ever, now.'

'That's bad, then,' says Gesche. 'He shouldn't hear anything about the other one.' And John nods to that, his lips pressed tight against each other, for he himself would also rather have not heard anything about the other one. Why had it been him, of all people, who went into the forest hunting for pigs that day?

He had crept all around for four hours without a single trace of game. But then he'd found something else, head over heels, hung by his feet, already fallen halfway down, the clean white bones falling apart, most of everything already plunged into the anthill that was situated directly under the branch.

John didn't need much time to recognize the coat, and to conjecture everything else as the remains of the poor badger. And he only needed a little more time to run back to the house and disappear for the rest of the day in the workshop, out of which Gesche could hear his hammering and beating until late into the night. And when she checked the next day to be sure everything was in order, she found he had built nothing, but instead clobbered everything to pieces.

So it was. But they won't tell Ruven about this. It already takes Ruven enough time to get up again. Then for weeks he walks mutely around the garden, until a large package arrives. It's the old black violin case, the one that Nils constructed long ago, and inside it is Joseph's violin, as it had always been inside it. A note from Fritz came with it: *Frau Goldbaum unfortunately doesn't recognize this instrument.*

Ruven looks at the three cases for a long time. Goldbaum's, with the wood ash, comes in the middle. 'Who knows why we fall in love,' he finally says. Then he begins again to play.

'All three of them must be played,' he says quietly, putting a hand on the empty case, and sings Schubert and Mozart. Then he cries for half an hour, then he sings again. The tears coat his face, which also makes Gesche cry. Afterwards, they listen to the radio. The icicles grow like long spears along the roof and down in front of the windows.

'Everything is destroying us, now,' says Gesche at some point, 'so hold yourselves together.'

Fritz's office is, as always, well heated. He is alone; he's sent the young man away. On his desk there are papers, more requests from Ruven that he rips up. He also rips up a photo of Lene and lights the remains in an ashtray. A suitcase is beside him.

Fritz picks up the telephone and gives instructions. An hour or so later—he spent the entire time looking out the window—the door opens and a slender figure enters the room and stands in front of the desk. Fritz turns around and scrutinizes Rahel Goldbaum, who, despite the weeks in detention, sports a tidy haircut and looks clean. She hasn't let herself go yet, thinks Fritz, perhaps a little disappointed.

'Sit down, please.' He points to the empty chair. He bounces his left leg nervously. So much has just occurred to him again that he hardly knows where to begin. The matter with Ruven Preuk seems to awaken a talent within him. The violin guessing game was an excellent one. Much more interesting, however, would be if Ruven wasn't only living with an empty violin case but also with an empty faith. Faith is empty anyhow, thinks Fritz, pure self-delusion; there, as Obersturmbannführer Heinze once noted, the communist pigs were correct for a change. And here he, Fritz Dordel, has the opportunity to prove it. Ruven Preuk would go on living believing in something dead, in a dead Rahel! And he, Fritz Dordel, would be the only one who could destroy this belief or preserve it. A kind of god for Ruven. Lord of the truth and lord of Ruven's love, or something like that. His thoughts on this are making his heart race, so that he has to take a deep breath before he addresses the figure on the chair again.

'What are you thinking, why are you sitting here?'

'I don't know.' Rahel's eyes search the desk. There's no red transport ticket. Instead, papers and passports.

'I'm making you an offer.' Fritz leans back and lights a cigarette. He blows the smoke across the desk. He could die laughing. How red she suddenly turns! She blinks as if she doesn't know whether it's day or night. What kinds of thoughts are women always thinking. As if there were no other possibility in their minds but to think of fornication at the first glance from a man. Hilarious, how her gaze lowers and her face trembles. What does she think she's sitting across from? A whoremonger? A Frenchman, or what? Fritz takes another deep breath, then says quietly, 'I can provide you a new life, but only under three conditions, please listen closely: You never disclose your old name. You never contact old acquaintances or relatives. You never come back to the north. If you do any of these, you'll be dead.'

Rahel looks at Fritz silently. She doesn't seem to have understood.

'You are free, gold tree, go! Here, a new name, papers, something to wear. You'll take the next train to Frankfurt, then travel on to Munich—you won't be so out of place there, with your particular features.'

Rahel still doesn't move. But then, with a sudden movement, she stands up, grabs the papers, leans over the desk, taps Fritz on the forehead and whispers: 'God bless you.' Then she takes the suitcase and, without another word, she's gone.

Fritz stares out the window for another half an hour. God bless you! He tries to think of something funny. Bye,

bye, he thinks. But there is a spot on his face, precisely on his forehead, like the muzzle of a revolver. Fritz goes to the washbasin and dips his face into his water-filled hands. When he looks in the mirror above the basin, he only sees two small eyes.

Many streets away, Rahel Goldbaum takes brisk steps down the pavement. No one takes any notice of her, although she feels as though her head is burning. 'Gertrud Meidner,' she says under her breath. 'My name is Gertrud Meidner, I live at Schmiedegasse number three.'

She reaches the train station just in time. The platforms are full of hats and helmets. She remains still in the middle of the crowd and slowly stands up taller. She lifts her chin and straightens her own small hat. Gertrud Meidner. Then she moves through the smell of sweat and clouds of tobacco and disappears in the vapour.

Ruven, too, falls from view for a while. He has to return to the front, and the war knows no evening on which one could or would speak of it, and also no night. In this war, the nights lose their twilight shroud for all time, they become forever suspicious and lose their last possibilities.

And Ruven also loses; the war is the end of all talent. And the end of so many stories. And perhaps it would also be the end of his own, if it weren't the case that something grew back again, the reverse of art, in a way.

Marie is eleven, almost eleven and a half. It is the year 1943 and July. The English are planning *Gomorrah*. Marie is far away when the aeroplanes delimit the zone above Hamburg with flares and then drop phosphorous. Far away, when forty thousand workers and their wives and children shrink in the firestorm to the size of dolls, because revenge is always revenge. Far away, when the western quarter of the city is spared because the connections of the upper class are always the connections of the upper class.

Marie guilelessly climbs trees, jumps over ditches and mows through tall grass with a flat hand.

The child flies around all day, thinks Gesche, without sense or reason, like the butterflies, the large whites that alight all around the pond, looking like a trim made of foam. The child understands so little.

Gesche puts the newspaper away, rubs her eyes and then points, smiling, at Marie and says to John, 'That is what health would look like, if it had two legs.'

Outside, the cows bellow. They send their long tongues up their noses. The peaceful clouds stand still above them. The summer is hot and dries out the marshes and ditches. The warblers rub their wings together night after night, and the people in the houses lie awake.

On one of these overly hot summer nights, Ruven is to be seen again, because he unknowingly ties himself to Marie's fate. He lies with a shot leg in a sickbay in Southern

Russia. He had only been in the region for a month, an almost suspiciously short time.

'A few weeks, perhaps five, then you'll be fit for service,' says the doctor. Next to him, stands a pale nurse. She's tied her hair back in a severe bun. In her service to the German soldiers, she turns the snow-white blanket over for Ruven and supports him as he stands up. It's quite dark there in the sickbay. There's not enough power for lamps and other such things. But the woman seems almost to glow. Hilde Klemm is her name. Daughter of a conductor from Kiel, well, a good contact then, too. A bonnet-wearing hope that he might pick up his music career again somewhere. Ruven sees the way she tugs her apron into place when she enters the overfilled tent. The tugging of her apron has such a soothing effect on him it is as if the woman were tugging the images of the dead, piece by piece, from his thoughts. That anyone in these times could still be at all anxious about something like a smooth apron. He'd like to remain close to this white, clean fabric, to go home with it somehow, whatever and wherever that home might be. Well, he puts himself in Hilde's hands. And she takes him in. And? Will life get any better?

Hilde has an invincible will, a will like the blows of a hammer. And so, an arrangement between her and Ruven is quickly established. It concerns the employment of a housekeeper—Hilde Klemm will do it. It will mutually satisfy certain basic needs, for it's also with the hope for a cultivated life in a musician's family, the one that she knew in her own childhood, that Hilde requests a transfer to the homeland and then travels northward and knocks one day on the door of the wainwright's. And because the hammer blows of her will catch everyone's congeniality off-guard, Hilde is able to soon make clear to the entire world: It is not acceptable for the children of a musician to live with a wainwright, and the way that Aunt Gesche still takes Marie onto her lap is not at all good, in fact, it's almost unsavoury. She has her principles, after all, and so she takes the children with her to Kiel. She's been assigned a small apartment there; the coats of her predecessors are still hanging in the closet.

There's only a single room for Friedjof, for Marie there's just a cot on the floor. They'll find a proper house for us eventually, says Hilde, staring at Marie's red hair as if its colour were a contradiction against the decent house.

It feels too cramped to Marie at Hilde's, and too cold. And then comes what always comes. Shall one call it hate? How Frau Klemm shoves Marie. The girl is always in her way. Night after night, she can't sleep, perhaps bad memories or because Marie and Friedjof are lying on their pillows like young apples and with their innocent sleep are generating a rage-filled wakefulness in Frau Klemm, as if there were secret scales that were never to drop on the side of innocence.

In the mornings, there's more and more shoving. Sometimes Frau Klemm believes Friedjof is watching her as she does it and thinking certain thoughts. So she barricades the children apart from each other. And somehow it always happens that one receives an apple and the other does not, first the one, then the other. Friedjof chews around his and Marie comes in, Hilde hides what's left so that it always looks as though the one grants the other nothing, until the children don't know at all any more who is on what side.

Ruven hears nothing of all this. Hilde only writes what she wants to write and soon she's ending her letters with an intimate *Your Hilde*. Then she licks the envelope and seals it shut with a snap of her thumbs. Sometimes she stays seated for a few extra moments at the secretary desk and grips her stomach.

Later, she makes a round of visits with the children. Hilde goes on many visits. Marie and Friedjof are always with her so that everyone sees that the German people are steadily increasing. She also looks all around her and asks about flags and about the attitude towards victory. These harmless activities provide her with an extra income as well as satisfaction.

'Wouldn't you like cake, child?' ask the women as they raise both the cake platter and their eyebrows. They don't allow themselves to comment on anything. What they're thinking is never clear. They have something to complain about, but they act unruffled. They've sent their sons to the front. That's far too much for a conversation over coffee. 'Marie?' And before Marie can answer, Hilde's voice cuts through the afternoon: 'She doesn't need anything. We are at war. Your last ration of flour shouldn't be thrown away so frivolously.' She pinches the girl's leg under the table as she says this. She wants the children to grow accustomed to measure and discipline early, she says. One can't emphasize often enough how becoming these virtues are in the German people, and so on—naturally—and the others don't want their watery cake any more either, and they purse their lips tightly and make faces as if they were absorbed in thoughts of the nation. And in the very back of their minds perhaps they really are thinking of it, or perhaps they're thinking of nothing at all. Outside, the sparrows sit in the trees and freeze. They don't see the difference between a peaceful and a non-peaceful time. They anticipate the winter. They ruffle their feathers and see, far below them, a woman in a grey coat finally emerging from a door, departing with a small child in one arm and a girl holding her hand.

At home, Hilde takes two cords and ties Marie's legs to the chair. She is nervous. The latest news, the weakening army. She pulls the cords tight: 'A woman must be able to hold still.' Then she stands at the window and looks outside at the snow and the sparrows.

'Your aunt can't stay still, either,' she says. 'If we didn't have people like your aunt, then we would have had more force for the war.'

'Do you like the war, then?' asks Marie.

Hilde strokes the girl's cheeks and smiles a beautiful smile. Then she says very steadily, 'The war is a duty.'

Marie nods. She remains on the chair until evening. She also has to knit, right and left, while Hilde stands behind her and watches the child's fingers so closely that the left stitches fall from the needle as if by themselves. The whole piece must be undone, and Marie begins all over again. She keeps on knitting every night in her dreams, right, left.

On a Sunday, Marie draws with chalk on the floor, hops from square to square and sings: *'There are bandits in the fo-or-est, hee-holla-ho!'* It's a friendly Sunday, and still very early and very quiet. Marie hops forwards and backwards, forwards and backwards, one, two, up, down, *hee-holla-ho*, with her arms, too. If anyone could see it, how well she moves and beautifully her skirt bobs up and down as she does. It would make anyone happy. The world knows nothing more lovely. The glass jar is happy, too, and shatters for joy. The shards glint and fly as far as underneath the cot.

Hilde pushes the broom under the bed and pulls it and the shards back out again. Her face clouds with anger. Her eyes are very blue. Marie moves to the balcony door and tries to reach the brass handle once Hilde is finally standing in front of the mirror in the next room. She tightly pulls her hair back again and rubs her wrist. Then she takes little Friedjof's hand and exits the house with him, simply leaving Marie to lie in her room. A friendly Sunday, early and quiet.

Hilde just barely arrives at the church on time, she walks in the door as the organ's prelude fades away: *God showeth His good will to men, and peace shall reign on earth again, O thank Him for His goodness!* And a few days later, with a bitter voice, at the baker's: 'We have no idea how it could have happened.' The handkerchief moves over Hilde's face. 'You know, I've been thinking, the girl should really be sent away for an education, she is so wild and defiant!'

The baker looks over at Marie, who is barely able to stand on her legs. 'Why so wild?'

Marie is silent.

Little Friedjof says quietly, 'Hit Aunt Hilde!' Hilde pinches his arm and the baker knits her brows together. 'You hit your aunt? What were you thinking? Do you want your father to be ashamed of you? When he's doing so much for us, as a soldier?'

Marie is silent. At home, she writes a letter to Gesche without Hilde noticing:

Kiel, 20th of January 1944

Dear Aunt!

I want to die.

Your Marie.

Days later, Gesche is standing at the door, her mouth a narrow strip, another vertical line between her eyes: 'What's going on here?'

Hilde Klemm smiles. 'What's supposed to be going on?'

'Why would Marie write something like this?'

'What did she write, then?' Hilde waves Marie over, her eyes dark and dangerous: 'Do you have something to say to me?'

Marie bows her head. Gesche tries to read the child's expression, but it's all a mess. A child is not so stable in the world. Sometimes the child goes to take a step and doesn't get up again. Some even talk of children who, after they were slapped by someone whom they held in high esteem, simply up and died, from illness, from overwhelming disappointment. And so a child is, for the shortest while, an undisappointed person. Well, a child's rate of growing up can also be seen in their rate of disappointment. But in this mess there's nothing to be seen, and Gesche turns helplessly to Hilde: 'Won't you offer me something?'

'Of course.' The whites of Hilde's eyes. She turns her gaze to Marie and takes her by the arm and pulls the child with her and is always by her side and doesn't leave her alone with Gesche for even a moment. The tea remains without milk and sugar, the bad times, careful instead of caring. Gesche takes sip after sip until she finally puts the cup down.

'Give me the child to take back to the country,' she says firmly. 'Marie just makes more work for you, and you can keep Friedjof.'

'I'll tend to things myself!' Hilde's eyes are wholly disquieting. 'And I will not discuss it with you either, Gesche Preuk. See to it that you become a woman of the times. We are destined to be a great people!' At that, she stands up and straightens her dress and points in the direction of the door. 'I'm sorry, I have other matters to attend to. Next time I'll have more time for you.'

'And I'm sorry that you must postpone your duties today,' Gesche replies, and then she also stands and makes herself tall and wide and has haunches like a logging horse and she achieves something, it's nearly double the dress in pink and it's dark red, at that. For no one speaks this way to the brick-maker's daughter, who has already overcome so much more than this sow's tooth of a woman.

'So!' she says, with an open *o*. And then to Marie: 'You're coming with me!' And to Hilde: 'Just try to stop me!' Gesche throws on her coat and leaves with the girl. On the street below, she opens the ample green coat as if it were a stable door, and carries Marie inside it to the train station.

For the whole train ride Gesche talks to herself. 'Oh, we'd like to see how far she'll get with that,' she says, 'not far at all, of course. It ends here!' Marie is silent and looks at the landscape and only tugs a bit at the green woollen cloth that Gesche still always wears around her shoulders.

'What will become of Friedjof?' asks Marie only once, tonelessly, and Aunt Gesche looks straight ahead sadly and presses Marie closer to her: 'He must stay there, so that you can come with me. She's not the same way with him as she is with you.'

Aunt Friedel, Lene's sixth sister, is waiting at the train station with the sleigh. The horse's breath has frozen around its mouth. As they travel across the bridge, the river groans beneath them.

At the wainwright's Gesche talks on and on to herself and pushes Marie through the rooms and finally tucks her into bed to go to sleep, but no sleep comes. The dark eyes remain staring, fixed on the child hands.

Day after day, Gesche pulls the curtains open and closed, lets air in and fires up the oven until it grows wide cracks, but nothing happens. Her eyes are always open when Gesche enters the room.

'Say something!' she begs and delicately fluffs the feather pillow, sets it at a steep angle, leans Marie against it and spreads a blanket over her thin legs and then over that her green coat. She comes and goes, fetching this or that. She often just stands in front of the bed and sighs: 'I should have never let you go to Kiel. It was obvious from the start that that Klemm woman has a heart of iron.' Then she turns and goes to fetch a glass of water. Marie only turns her head towards the window and looks out at the sparrows sitting and freezing in the hedge.

'What is wrong with you, child?' Gesche sets the water aside and sits down beside the bed. She combs her fingers through Marie's red hair. 'You're worrying me!'

Her white face is calm and serious. Her hands jut out from black sleeves. Marie reaches for Gesche with the left one. It is the day of Emerentia. The frost flowers on the windows are melting in the midday light.

'What shall we do?' Gesche asks and rubs Marie's hand, which is cold and translucent.

'Die,' she says. 'I'm dying now.' And she looks past Gesche, who moves next the headboard and tries to hold her.

'What are you saying?' asks Gesche quietly.

'The night is wrapping itself all around us, Aunt Gesche, no matter how colourfully we are dressed.'

'But it is daytime, child.' Gesche lowers her face so that Marie doesn't see her tears.

'We can't hold onto the night,' she says. 'Yes, we can grab it, but then we have nothing in our hands—it's as if our hands were made of glass.'

'Oh, stop,' says Gesche, 'stop it!' And bends down even lower. 'Why don't you want to live?'

'Because there is no one there any more. I've been dreaming, Aunt, even though I was awake. Of faces, the whole sky was full.'

This is a new kind of consumption, thinks Gesche. If the children want it, no penicillin will help.

They sit together for a long time, still and quiet. As quiet as the evening that glides through the window and into the room. Gesche thinks and thinks. If a child wants to leave, the world must make a great effort. 'Your father sings for an empty violin case,' she finally says, very softly, 'he cannot also sing for you, child. He simply cannot do it.' She receives no answer, and then Marie suddenly sleeps. A night, a day, and another night. She sleeps so that Ruven does not have to sing for her, too. Perhaps she sleeps simply out of love, which one still referred to as a gift with regard to Ruven. Perhaps those are just the two sides of the medal, either or, sometimes this way, sometimes that way.

In the meantime, Gesche tiptoes all around. She stands at the window or the door, she stands watch over Marie's sleep, and she writes to John, who is too broken for the war, to be sure, but because of it he must help in the factory in

Hamburg. In the wainwright's house, everything is quiet. Who can endure it? The whole house is like a clock stopped where there was once so much life, the work, the wheels, the barrels, the chicks, the stove. Only the dog whines, as if it were seeing premonitions of ghosts. And Gesche begins to find it so eerie that she takes the dog by the ears, as Mother Preuk once taught her to do, and she looks over his snout from behind him. But she only sees the kitchen floor, and no faces and no fire. What surprises her is that it is not her own that she sees. But she can't know that it is a Norwegian kitchen floor, in a Norwegian house, where someone has laid himself down to die today; for to see a little more than others is good and truthfully doesn't happen all that rarely, but what is the use when one doesn't know what belongs where.

'He is dead,' a man says in English, and then in German, with a strong accent, to the blond assistant. 'He's not breathing any more.'

For days, Ruven is left lying in the shot-up farmyard, just below the awning, somewhere in Styria. All he does is dream. Ruven dreams that the body can be stretched and billowed out like fabric. He is always after making it round again, like the earth, because that is its character, and also that of its inhabitants.

Ruven awakes below the awning with a blighty wound, at least. Well, the envy of everyone, he thinks, but where the right arm was—the bow arm!—is a single open wound. And the war and so-called homeland are lost, a blighty wound won't be necessary any more.

For days, Ruven gazes at mouths that meaninglessly open and close, until he realizes that they're speaking English. How did he get here? He feels across his blanket with his wrapped-up arm. He'd finally been bandaged. With his left hand, he covers an ear and looks, and then he shuts his eyes and listens. Sight and hearing have come apart, he thinks. I'm not seeing the sounds any more. They're without colour. Here this, there that. It's as if he's finally found his balance on a bicycle, but now the wheel won't spin any more. The old black eagle-wheel. Ruven feels homesick. For his old hearing and his old arm, too. And for the whole era. When one doesn't come across anything familiar any more. So much time has been lost and spoilt, so much time that one would have needed to make friends with the world and the things in it. One must be careful not to lose all contact. At the same time, he's already receiving mail, long letters from Kiel that have found their way through the chaos, as if Hilde's iron will went everywhere. They are letters that arrange and compose everything before Ruven understands what there is to be arranged or composed. Before he provides a sensible address. Hilde Klemm knows how it ought to go. And

Ruven reads. Marie must be sent to school, she's been spoilt by her aunt. Gesche Preuk simply took Marie in, this child is intractable, lazy, and after she does the chores for her uncle, she goes and riots all around the woods, and she needs governance, and in turn he, Herr Preuk, must have peace and quiet in Kiel in order to prepare himself, he was recommended for the Landesorchester by Professor So-and-so, even if it's also very tentative, the orchestra's only thinly staffed, and so on.

Ruven's eyes sink tiredly to the blanket and follow the flies that keep buzzing around the naked pear—around, and around— another joins and flies with them, in the same direction, all day long. Skin and bones stink from beside him. The head is swathed in bandages; it's impossible to know who is lying there. And Ruven himself: disassembled in hearing and sight. How is he supposed to play in the orchestra? Soon he receives the forms in the post, he just needs to sign them, and he writes: Ruven Preuk. With his left hand. With his left hand, he also assents to Marie, his little Marie, being sent to a home, for a better education. No more indulgence. Only so that there is quiet. And so that Marie can now become something in that place where the war was lost. Gesche makes a lot of useless noise. Ruven isn't listening any more.

The Americans send the prisoners home in late summer. In the event that home is still there. Ruven travels to Hamburg, although the train station itself doesn't know where it once stood. Somehow, it's all right. A person can simply step off the train and into the huge rubble heap. And he walks and walks, although the gorgeous old city doesn't exist any more, and the people all look different than before, and they plough, dig and pile as if they were expecting visitors, but no visitors come.

Who would want to come here, thinks Ruven. For whom are you all still curling your hair? For whom are you putting on lipstick? As if these things had to be a certain way. And as if scrubbing brushes, carpet beaters, hair rollers and dustpans were all that existed. Well, he has to ask the street and the toppled spires, the signposts whose paths have been lost. And then the rain falls, silent, as if it were falling on ploughed fields.

Ruven tilts his head back and for a moment too long he thinks that he's a nine-year-old boy, but he's in his late forties, nearly fifty! How that feels. How one loses coherence. As if one had good and important intentions in life, he thinks. As if all the devastation was just proof that we were on the right path. Like old Job, perhaps. He was so good that the Lord let the Devil loose upon him. And perhaps the hedges have been torn out around us, thinks Ruven, so that we might find out what we can endure. He stands still for a moment and looks at the women. It's more like we've uprooted them ourselves. And you women, he thinks, without the hedges, you women have lost your sweetness.

Ruven moves through the autumn, and then through a winter. A winter in which everyone huddles close. The wainwright's house is old and about to burst at the seams. All these people! 'Pomerania is all burnt down,' sing their children. They play again. They play 'trek to the gassing' and 'trip to Jerusalem' and as they do they laugh the way that children laugh.

There is no longer all that much to eat there. And what there is, Uncle John spreads it on bread and packs it up and takes it on his bicycle to Marie. One has a bicycle, at least. At night, one prays that the tires hold their air.

The home's administrators allow John to knock on the door very often. Uncle John is a thorn in the administrators' side, because they are hungry, too—but even more because it provokes a brutal soul, to see that someone comes from love.

'The girl is as thin as a riding crop,' says John when he returns. 'Hardly a hair on her head. She has an actual receding hairline.' John scrimps and saves more and more. He grows thinner and thinner. He even brings the last jar of honey to Marie.

'You must hide it well,' he says.

Marie nods. 'How much longer, Uncle John?'

'Not much longer. And then you'll be apprenticed. Then, at the latest.' He tries to put on a brave face.

'But I won't be able to take it here for much longer,' says Marie. 'I'm only still alive because Papa can't sing for me, too.'

John gives her a worried look. 'I'll see what I can do, my girl. You must batten down the hatches against each day and its dangers until I've figured out what to do. Only ever count from morning to evening, promise me that.' He turns and gets on his bike.

'Send my love to Papa.'

He nods to her. Then he grasps his heart. In the pocket above his heart there's a spoon. John pulls it out and gets off his bike again. He holds the spoon out to Marie. It's deformed, as if someone had tried to bend it.

'Directly in the heart, that's where the enemy wanted to shoot me,' says John and smiles. 'I flew two metres back from the blow, and a dark blue spot, like a plum, stayed on my skin for days. A Preuk doesn't give up his spoon so quickly.' He gets on his bike again. 'That's all in the past now, Marie, think about that.' He doesn't look at her again, and bikes away. A good hour-long bike ride. The air is so cold that one feels sympathy for it. And for oneself, too. With only one hand on the handlebar, the other inside the coat. The birds of prey on their wooden masts, they, too, are also very desperate. Perhaps not for life any more either, but instead frozen solid.

It is dark when Uncle John finally arrives at the wainwright's. The billeted all sit together in the kitchen and smoke. They talk about enormous farms and endless fields: 'Twenty men in a row to scythe, all at the same stroke! And barns as big as churches! And light! The Baltic light. Here, on the other hand, everything is dark as a swamp and tight as dirt on a grave,' they say.

'Ah,' Gesche says and puts the kettle on. 'Before you all came, there was more room here, too.' And then she snorts, just once, insulted. Ruven only sits among them. Once a day, he tends to the two violins and sings for the third.

'What is he doing?' Frau Zinowke, the old woman with three daughters, pulls back with a start and covers her mouth with her hands as if there were something contagious there. 'Where will we be,' she says in her broken German, 'if we are acting like that with all the things that have burnt? When are we eating and sleeping, eh, if we are all singing for the things that are lost? This means I should be singing for my sons, in three parts? And then for the instruments, too?' she asks. 'So, maybe the violins go. But the spinets and organs! And what organs they were, that were burning! How they are howling in the fire! All the pipes, all at the same time!'

Ruven plays violin without any inner stirring, without inner sound. It's only that his left hand is unable to forget its function. He only plays violin so that he doesn't disappear entirely. He could also talk about something. He could also visit Marie, but he does not do it because he just cannot. Because there is something like an impediment there, a thing that makes him grow angry when John suggests that he could so easily make the trip to see his child.

'That is none of your business!' Ruven says then, 'It wasn't meant to be this way! Everything was supposed to be different.' And perhaps he's also sensing that it might be over with the violin, if he doesn't throw all that he's got into it now. I can, he thinks, simply not cede anything else. And so, instead of making the trip to Marie, he travels to Kiel, to the state capitol, of which there is not much left, but nevertheless—the capitol, British, under Henderson.

Ruven looks at the apartment where Hilde Klemm and Friedjof live. 'Apartment' is an exaggeration; it's not much more than a landing atop a stairwell. Friedjof is already four years old and takes after no one, or if he does, then it's Hilde, only not so embittered. She, on the other hand, is anaemic and cross. Ruven, too, from now on. She wakes every morning, brushes his jacket and shoes, presses her lips together, and even takes her stomach tablets at such an early hour.

Ruven stays at the orchestra rehearsals as long as possible. He's doesn't mind that he's seated farthest back. The flutes of the two Nazis behind him nearly rob him of consciousness, but his right arm is too dead for a place farther up. They're playing Mendelssohn and David now, so that the denazification is audible. Thanks to the letters the leader sent to the occupying forces asking for the return of the orchestra's members, the orchestra is nearly back to its old size. They just have to silently replace their former Jewish colleagues.

After rehearsal, they go to the pub. Ruven sits in the corner and drinks one beer every evening. 'Strike that bill,' he says to the bartender, 'The evening's on me.' Then he nods to the others and goes home. He doesn't have the strength or the will or even the inclination for friendship any more.

He walks slowly down the street. One shouldn't return home faster than one should, he thinks, both here and there, there's no lingering. Hilde is already standing behind the door at home. They're not living on the landing any more, instead they're in the cheap concrete of a new construction, their breath drying the still-damp mortar. In there, they can live without speaking to one another.

Ruven paces through the apartment all evening, back and forth, and Klemm fears for the floorboards. He's let a beard grow. He pulls his hand through his hair and his beard and is silent, moves through the rooms possessed by an inner turmoil. The arrangement of the rooms disintegrates into yellow and brown and white. Ruven undoes the top buttons of his shirt and loosens his tie. His life, which had once tried to reach so far, is divided between these two places: the rehearsal hall and the apartment, as if there stood between them a stake and a chain that didn't reach any farther. A person is his own stake, thinks Ruven and stands on the balcony, he has a balcony now, and smokes.

He wears a heavy expression, but he's not thinking about it any more, he smokes a second cigarette: Just don't look back at Klemm, or farther still, into time. One doesn't go backwards, only forwards, or in the here and now. It's all right to stay in the here and now, after all that was. We act as though disturbance were a quality of man. We overlook it, look away from it, look forwards. Everything grows clearer and brighter and louder, so we'd like to think. There are more signs and street lamps, even one in front of the concrete house. Until eleven o'clock at night, it lights up the front room. More cars, too, the world is getting faster, but not necessarily better.

At the wainwright's they will soon be out of work, thinks Ruven. In his left hand rests the ashtray made of green glass. Agriculture, too, will become more and more motorized, he thinks. They will need rubber wheels. Barrels aren't made of wood any more, either. Everywhere, less and less is made of wood.

And in exchange there is more of everything else, more celebrations, for example. Everlasting celebrations, with paper hats and confetti. Dedications, anniversaries, birthdays, Kiel Week, Christmas, somehow perpetual Christmas, rockets, potato salad with sausage—look forwards! The months pass quickly now, potato salad yet again, sausage yet again, then the monetary reform, the German mark, cheers!, cheers!, like an earworm that comes over a person for a long time after rehearsals of Ravel's *Boléro*. Cheers! Cheers!

Ruven plays the violin for every occasion. They want him as a guarantor of recovered humanity. Culture, even when it's failed: humanity, risen again. Where was it, all those years? Why didn't it prevent those years? And him? And the school of hearts? He plays the violin. His heart is silent. His housekeeper breathes down his neck and she is always the first to clap, harsh and furious, as if she wanted to punish her hands for something. The sweet-corpse scent of 4711 wafts around her, the scent of the German economic miracle. And beer and sparkling wine. Cheers! It is inescapable, these days.

Ruven never asks after Marie. He can't. And Hilde Klemm knows to tell him just enough; she lets plaintive letters disappear. In her version, a fine young woman is growing up there in the capitol city. Here's to her health! Ruven sends money now and again. And sometimes he sits in the armchair for hours and just stares at the air in front of him and doesn't know exactly what's missing, only that something's missing, he is sure of it.

In the summer, he sits mutely in the allotment garden. They now have an arbour with a fence all around and a winding slate path. Hilde tends to their pennyroyal and their circle of acquaintances like a spouse. They hardly know any musicians. Hilde buys a cat and dwarves with a wheelbarrow or a doe, a better, softer world out of porcelain.

Friedjof swings on the seesaw in a pair of knit trousers. Soon he'll also be in a cowboy costume, Karl May, European Indian, the domesticated savage. He spits at the cat and has no head for music. Ruven doesn't pay any attention. He isn't present any more. Perhaps he's still leading a Druze-like life, who knows. He still seems to need to keep something inside, perhaps an ancient name, a heartbeat, which he can't forget but seems to want to forget, or to have to forget, because in an August or September, he seeks out shelter one last time and marries his housekeeper.

Marie stands at the window and waits for daylight. The dormitory is full of girls' breath. They lie in iron beds. Some have stripped off their blankets; others are sleeping on their stomachs, their hair descending into the empty space.

Marie doesn't look back at the other girls, not even at her only friend, her friend who still hugged her, pressing her soft and warm breasts against Marie's. They turned their aching backs towards the outside world, as if there were no traces.

Every children's game was interrupted in this place, everyone pitted against everyone else, the larger system recreated in microcosm, always alternating praise and humiliation until the curse took effect and everyone slandered and ratted on everyone else, lopping off stockings or entire braids in the night just to weaken enemies, until, as revenge, yellow, salty liquid was discovered in water jugs and soup bowls, or a child was found in the tool shed in the morning, naked and scratched and not saying a word. Even after she'd been beaten, she still stayed silent.

It is coming to an end. In just a few hours, Marie will leave for her apprenticeship. To learn how to make buttercream cake and aspic, she thinks, how to press tablecloths and bed sheets, how to plant potatoes and how to dress rabbits and chickens. Tomorrow she leaves; she is not yet completely broken. Lonely, but not completely broken. In her years here, she had often thought about Gesche's large green coat. She imagined this coat filled up with all the warmth of Gesche's body and heart; underneath it she found a bit of protection.

The next day, she is sitting on a bus. The dawn is clasping night to day. The home's director had simply given Marie a certificate to take with her and said, 'Don't stain the reputation of our house!' and offered a cold hand. Mute, Marie had turned away.

The bus sways from village to village. The teaching farm has a hundred and fifty hectares and a sweeping mansion. With a bath, even, but only for the farmers; the maids and the apprentices go outside to the pumps and into the muck.

The old farmer's wife leads Marie to her room, which is good for a year. The room can't be heated. Someone had pressed a floral pattern into the chalk walls with a rolling stamp. The farmer's wife spreads her arms wide and stands in the doorway: 'Rest until noon. After that, you won't walk around with empty hands again.'

Marie nods and sits on the bed. The damp laundry absorbs the mouldy air. Finally, she unpacks what few pieces of clothing she's brought with her, and puts Uncle John's spoon on the nightstand. At noon, she goes into the kitchen.

'What now, so red?' The young farmer Adolf Retwisch sits at the table and stares at her hair with blatant greed. He is Marie's age and already the head of the farm because the old farmer, along with his firstborn, was called up for the reserves and never returned, and the daughter, Ute, married Retwisch almost unseen, so that they wouldn't have to pay a farmhand, if they had even been able to find one. Ute is a head shorter than Marie, with greasy skin and a throat that is set too far forwards, she looks as though she were attempting to go under and through something.

For a hundred hectares, a woman could have a hunchback, they say. But when Ute inherited the farm after the war, the young men all shunned her and the farm and its hundred and fifty hectares. All except for Adolf Retwisch. He had taken hold and only said that they needed a maid to milk the cows, or at least an apprentice girl. Thus he'd imagined it.

In the kitchen it is so still for a moment that Marie can hear the old farmer's wife's digestion. Then Ute suddenly gets up and walks around Marie, as if she were a skinny cow or a maltreated horse and says, 'Freckles are a sign of a devil.' With that, she leaves Marie standing.

'Silence!' scolds the old farmer's wife from behind her. 'Are you trying to chase away our apprentice?!' The farmer's wife is almost embarrassed. She'd known Mother Preuk. They had even been related by marriage, and Retwisch says with a stupid grin: 'Red, in any case.'

The first six months pass quickly. First, digging, hoeing and sowing the garden is learnt, because it is spring and because in the spring, the farmer's wife is particularly meticulous with her beds and borders. As orderly as the military before it deploys. Neither the depth of the spade's cut nor the direction of the tossed earth is surrendered to chance. 'A sort of order that makes one feel unkempt to look after it,' says the pub's barmaid, whose wild beds are called a garden for the lazy by the villagers, 'Anyway, everything is back in order again now,' she says, 'the whole country. One must only cope with it. It is not funny. But we Germans sold our laughter, anyhow.'

Marie wakes up early, at five, and goes into the stables to the oil pump. She carries the cans full of oil into the house and heats it. Then she begins her chores. Everything has its procedure. On Saturday at four o'clock in the afternoon she's free, and may go into the village and seek out young people. She'd quickly sussed one out, a tall man with a gaze that goes through her and through her, and two rows of teeth that promise a long life. He drives the wagon standing up and carries two hundredweights on one shoulder and whistles, too, as he does all of it, and she already knows that his name is Gunnar Teede.

He stands one day at the farm gate and looks as though he is waiting for something. He says nothing, though, when Marie walks by, just looks down from his two metres and holds her gaze. Marie sticks her hands in her skirt pockets and walks faster than usual past him. Then she runs into her room, looks for a pencil and draws Gunnar Teede from memory. She crams the paper under her pillow and sits on the mattress, then stands up again, stands at the window and then at the door. She'd like to run all around and she is always inside and outside and also in the road in front of the farm.

'What do you keep looking for?' The farmer's wife doesn't look up from her work. 'What do you want out on the road? Do you want to leave? Or is someone supposed to be coming?'

'I don't know.' Marie turns red.

'Huh.' The farmer's wife is busy with the roulades, she's always in motion like this. Every day eventually has its meals, and the winter also asks what the summer has earned.

The farmer's wife wears a headscarf in the kitchen and an apron with buttons down the front. The apron is nearly worn out, the buttons come off and she sews on the next ones. 'Sunday is the marksmen's festival,' she says, 'you'll stay at the house until then.'

Marie waits for the festival. She pulls out the dandelions and thistles in the garden. On Sunday, she combs her hair and makes her neck long and straight and thinks about Gunnar Teede and turns her head a bit to the side and tries out a certain look.

At church, everyone slides around on the pews and seeks out the best view of whomever. The broad back, a solid fortress. Everyone in ceremonious black, the large hands folded. Amen. Everyone with a grip on themselves, the rights in the lefts, the right in the left, some kind of halfway middle under the eyes of the Allied High Commission, but of course there were more right-handed people in the Adenauer era. Amen. And afterwards to the shooting range, with glittering medals, the old men and the veterans as a closed group, closed off, among themselves and in the old hierarchy.

A white tent is set up beside the church. There is supposed to be rain, yet beautiful May is all that's shining. High in the sky, two hawks are circling, and there can be no talk of rain. In the tent, there are long tables with benches on each side, there are no windows. Soon there's not enough air to breathe. People breathe the beer. The long counter is polished, and soon everyone is tipsy, with red faces and stringy hair. But a tent belongs at the celebration; it had been declared in the rich farmer's plans for the party and signalled a large donation. The fact that this contribution ultimately failed to materialize because the rich farmer's frugality had once again occurred to him wasn't noticed by anyone, because everyone else gave so abundantly, if only to demonstrate that they were in no way inferior to the rich farmer. And now, too, they're all buying him drinks, so he's the first to topple back from the bench and onto the tarpaulin and then onto the planks of the floor, so that only his feet are visible.

The village daughters jostle each other on the edge of the dance floor. They're grating on each other's nerves. Marie, in her green dress, is the sole new addition. She stands alone at the entrance to the tent. She'd pinned up her red curls, but already half of them have fallen down again. There's a pleasant breeze at the entrance, and a good view.

Over by the shooting range, the young men stand around holding beer and cigarettes. Some even have mopeds. They haven't grown poorer since the war. They talk about HP and about the village daughters and keep glancing over.

Marie listens to the band. The volunteer fire brigade is also the volunteer village band, and their music has a little bit of the sousing along with the sirens. They screw and spin clarinets and flutes, until the baton-leader sharply raises his arm with the silver-wrapped pennant stick and then executes a snappy movement through the air, an elaborate and pointless signal, instead of simply counting out one, two, three, four and starting to play.

Ute and the other young women are standing next to the band. They look over at Marie and whisper to each other more than looks good on them. Ute stretches her head farther forwards than usual and pulls a piece of paper from her pocket. Marie observes closely. The paper travels from hand to hand. Then the last girl, a thin blond, brushes past Marie with the piece of paper and her chin held high, and walks outside and over to the shooting range. Marie watches the young people laugh. And then a short one with rickety legs approaches her. Hein Grull bows to Marie and says, 'I'd like to have such a striking drawing done of myself, too, if you'd be ever so kind.' Marie hears the blood rushing in her ears. She can see Gunnar Teede over Hein Grull's head, he's straightening up and looking over at them. Marie clasps her hands in front of her face and runs away from the party and into the little copse of firs, planted here for protection from the wind, and quickly emerges from the other side. There, the wheat is knee-high, not so easy to run through, so she walks along the border, where the camomile and delicate poppies grow. She could double over, her shame so weighs on her, heavy and persistent.

'What are you sneaking around here for?'

Marie spins around. Teede steps out of the darkness of the firs and laughs. His white teeth gleam bright in the dimness of the woods. He reaches to grasp her shoulder.

'I don't sneak around!' Marie splutters and shoves his hand away.

That was a cool manoeuvre, the young farmer Retwisch opines that evening. And then she played so hard-to-get. His wife crosses her arms at that, and complains that Marie thinks she's better than everyone else just because her father does something or other in the orchestra. Marie says nothing, only looks at Ute Retwisch and blinks back her tears.

From then on, Marie stays in her room on Saturdays and gazes out the window at the chickens, which bathe in the scattered ashes. They spread their legs and burble and babble and peer in two directions, as if they were doing something secret.

A summer passes in this way, and the trees slowly grow another year's ring. Marie is busy with many things: 'Eight elderberry flowers,' she says softly, 'two sliced lemons, eight litres of water, a half kilo of sugar, ten grams of yeast, wait ten days, then percolate and bottle.' Or: 'Shred heads of cabbage, layer in a wooden barrel, salting in-between, add caraway seeds, juniper berries, horse-radish, a cloth on top, a wooden plank, a rock, and give the whole thing four weeks.' In addition to all that, she has to spin the sour cream in the butter churn each day until the butter comes, drain off the buttermilk and then the water and shape a cube, then the butter stamp; in this case, it's a picture of a thistle.

Marie rarely takes any breaks. Only sometimes, to stretch her back while she sits at the loom, where she still weaves table runners and towels because it's cheaper than buying them. The loom has four harnesses, all she has to do is pull them and then everything goes faster, the warp jumps up and down, *tack-tack*, the shuttle flies back and forth, she hardly needs to look, and the beater tips forwards and back, while the fabric coils itself in the depth of the loom.

'You're good at that,' says Adolf Retwisch, standing alarmingly close to her. 'Hopefully, at other things, too.' Marie doesn't look at him. He stands in her room this evening, his shirt untucked and hanging open as if he'd been in a fight. He's drunk, nearly tipping over into the doorjamb. 'Good night to us all, the fox says when he's in the henhouse.' Marie startles back when she sees Retwisch's thick prick jump out from the constraints of his tight trousers as he undoes the button. She closes her eyes and tries to think about Gesche's coat.

'Red,' says Retwisch, 'Don't pretend you don't like it. All you reds want this. Who are you trying to save yourself for? For Teede? He won't take you. He doesn't have anything. Inherited nothing. And you?'

'Perhaps my father's violin,' says Marie and opens her eyes. She looks directly at Adolf's face.

'Close your eyes again,' he says.

'I won't do anything,' she says and straightens up. 'But you'll do something—go!'

And so there is a shift. Mother Preuk would have said it was old Joseph, from the beyond, having heard something about his violin. Perhaps Mother Preuk herself had given Retwisch a ghostly scare. Or perhaps it was only Marie. In any case, Adolf Retwisch has completely collapsed in on himself, and from now on, he gives Marie a wide berth.

Outside, the wine on the southern wall ripens. The farmer's wife tries a grape and spits it out again. Two storks clatter atop the roof for a whole afternoon. The farmer's wife wants to shoot them down because she believes that the pair, in conjunction with her son-in-law and the apprentice girl, will bring a calamity or two to the farm. But then the storks fly away, just when the farmer's wife has chambered a round in her gun. They fly over the empty fields in which hungry cats are searching for mice.

And then on the first Sunday in September, a large parade—with flags and coats of arms and brass players at the front and each one with a white jacket and lance, a deathly serious mien, as if this here were a state funeral and so unfolding in the requisite grandeur. The ring on the magnet is as large as a bull's nose ring, probably also really just a bull's ring, and at a full gallop they must skewer it with their lances and pitch it behind them, in a tall arc, it's all a bit elegant and knightly, it's a public event here, even the local press is invited. Everyone is in attendance, Adolf Retwisch, Hein Grull, Uwe Schlottmeyer and so on. And Gunnar Teede.

And while the geese above him peel off towards the southwest, Teede wins the tournament and must choose a queen to sit with him on the Holsteins and cross through the village to the pub. There, the bartender is already breathing on the glasses and polishing, while his wife, her head sweating, cleans the cellar and the kitchen.

Gunnar Teede rides along the row of young girls. Then he rides back again and then into the village, without a queen.

Marie sits at home at the window and gazes, like always, at the chickens, which are quite tired from the long summer. She's propped open the window and smokes secretly into the outside air. The ashes fall and remain on the bug-bitten leaves of the elderberry bush.

'So it is now,' Marie says softly, 'and it is nothing more.' In her left hand she holds Uncle John's spoon and rubs the hollow with her thumb. Then there are three knocks, and the farmer's wife sticks her head in.

'Go outside to the farm gate,' she says.

Marie looks at her, frightened, and thinks that it's her father coming by, or worse, Hilde Klemm. She cannot and does not want to speak with either of them today. There's just nothing to say.

'Hurry up,' says the farmer's wife, and gives her such a look that it's impossible to know what she means by it, and then she pulls the door shut again.

Marie runs across the barn floor to the farmyard. At the entrance to the farm someone is sitting on a horse, not stirring. It almost makes her want to turn away and go back, but Marie is too curious.

'What do you want?' She squints at Gunnar Teede.

'Just you,' he says, 'if that's what you want, too.'

She looks away quickly and says quietly, 'And if I can't?'

'Then I'll come back,' says Gunnar and laughs.

'Then come back,' she says, but it's hardly audible. And she looks down, avoiding seeing how Gunnar Teede is flushing red.

'Well,' he says, 'Then I'll ride alone now.'

Marie nods and goes back to the house, with an entirely different heart than the one she had before.

That was in autumn. Then came winter, and nothing happened. Gunnar Teede never came back. Frost blooms across the windows and people scatter ashes in front of their houses.

What is wrong with Teede, they ask. He never talks any more.

'He'll leave,' the bartender's wife says to Hein Grull at the pub. 'It will be better this way, otherwise there will be more misfortune. Where there are two steers and a red cape. And then there's crooked Ute, too, I'd watch out for that one.' The bartender's wife turns to the shelf on the wall behind her, and Grull tries to read something on her backside.

'And where will Teede go?' He asks.

'To the city, to study something.' The bartender's wife turns around so quickly that Grull doesn't have time to move his gaze back to the right place. 'What's down there?' She lets loose a throaty laugh. 'Oh, the red cape won't stay here for ever. An apprentice year goes quickly. She'll do the next one somewhere else, it's probably already been decided. But now you'll be on your way. It's too late!' And she pushes the tired Grull out the door and closes up for the day.

But decided or not, something happens in-between. Something like winter, only with five letters. Wails once again through the Lunten family. Sepsis, this time. Aunt

Meta, Gosche Lunten's fourth daughter, leaves two things behind—a small farmstead, because she'd been another widow, and a will and testament in a padded envelope, in which she declared that the farm and all its trappings should go to Marie Preuk.

'The only condition is that you start immediately,' says Aunt Friedel, who delivers the news in her usual brittle fashion.

Marie nods. She doesn't know yet if she should be happy. 'Right away, you said? I've only done a year, not even the whole year yet, and I can't till a field by myself.'

'Your grandfather will do that in the spring. All you'll have to do is help and keep an eye on things. And perhaps find someone who will pitch in.' Aunt Friedel offers a thin smile. She's suffered many years with her own husband. In that time, she'd had seven children and the corresponding body from bearing them.

Marie looks at her hands. 'Could you do me a favour, aunt? Can you speak with the farmer's wife? Her son-in-law . . . speak with him.'

Aunt Friedel walks, tall and stiff, into the kitchen. The long table stands stark and bare in the centre of the room. The farmer's wife is sitting at the end and tallying something up.

'What's this?' she asks.

'Resignation,' is all Aunt Friedel says. 'Marie must come with me, she's inherited a farmstead and she cannot put it off.'

'If she cannot put it off, what am I to do now?' The farmer's wife crumples the paper. 'She did good work, the girl, but her wages were for the full year.'

'But . . . ' Aunt Friedel rears her head back in indignation, pushing her chin into her neck.

'I won't have anything more to do with this!' The farmer's wife claps the booklet full of figures shut. 'She should go! I'm doing the math for my children. Ute won't stand in her way, that is clear. She should go!'

She doesn't have much to pack. Marie wears most of it. And then a frosty departure and a frosty walk through the village, past the Teede farm, but Marie doesn't say a word about Gunnar. Down the road, and then a bus, and later, once again on foot to the estate.

Mother Lunten is already at the side door of the steward's house. She's grown old. Her eyes are hardly visible, she's been crying so much, but she manages one brief smile: 'Yes, so it is. Death is more certain than life. Come here, my child. How did your parents give you that red hair?!'

Gosche, who is inside leaning with his back against the oven, lifts his hand to his head and grabs his sparse grey strands.

'There used to be a red tint here. All of you didn't want to believe it. Here,' he shoves his sleeves up and lifts an arm to the light: 'If you want to come look—red!'

'If you want to come look,' says Mother Lunten, 'and what if we don't?' Then she turns to Marie: 'What's your father doing now?'

Marie shrugs. 'We speak very little. And Hilde . . . '

Mother Lunten stops her with a wave of her hand. She cannot tolerate that Klemm woman. 'Time for sleep,' she says. 'We'll take a look around tomorrow. It's only two villages over, half a farm. The other half belongs to someone else. A cousin of a cousin, she's in her eighties but she's as crafty as a young racoon. Good night.' And she leaves the rest to the moon and the owls that are fluttering from branch to branch because of a shift in the weather.

The next day, they travel two villages over. The snow vanishes under their shoes into black footprints. The brick building is dark with moisture. The sows squeal from the barn, and the startled hens flutter into the lane. Marie walks down the row of cows, reaching her white fingers out to them. In the house, she sits on a chair and looks at the garden out the window. 'Here's a place to grow old,' she says, and thinks to herself that her father doesn't even know where she is. Perhaps he doesn't want to know. 'Oh, well,' she says aloud, 'then I'll just ride alone.' She pulls out her coat and takes the barn smock from its nail and goes and mucks out the sow bays, while Mother Lunten milks.

Then she pulls up turnips and spears them in four parts with the spade.

Luckily, the year goes by quickly. Everything there has its own momentum. Except for the cousin of the cousin next door, who suddenly takes to her bed and has no momentum at all any more. 'But I won't go to the hospital,' she says. 'The hospital is too far for me.'

Marie walks up the steps through the hedges each morning with coffee and buttered rolls for her, and also to heat the house and let in some air. Then she looks after the cattle. After milking, she goes to the dairy. At noon, she has soup at the cousin's, and so it goes, she is very busy, she becomes a stranger to herself and stops looking in the mirror and forgets her own face.

One Sunday, she knocks on the door of the house across the road to introduce herself. The neighbour, Frau Prigge, opens the door just a crack. 'What is it?' She scrutinizes Marie with one eye. Then she pushes the chain off and opens the door all the way. A very frugal appearance. She leads Marie to the unheated dining room, where her husband is sitting motionless at the table.

'A couple of years in Siberia,' she says quietly.

'Good afternoon,' says Marie, even making a little curtsy, but Herr Prigge only rears his head back mulishly. He's someone who loses badly. Behind him on the wall there still hangs the framed portrait of the Führer.

The farmer is silent. And then a quiet whisper: 'It's high time that the filth leaves this farm. Really, the whole farm should leave, the way it looks. Disgrace! A disgrace, that's what you've inherited over there!'

His wife nods. 'There was never any disgrace here. The British might want to pin that on us, but . . . '

'Silence!' The farmer slices his hand through the air. 'What do you know about the British? Let's see who allies themselves where, soon.'

'But . . . ' Marie looks at Herr Prigge.

'Let's see,' he says. 'Anything else?'

Marie steals another glance at the portrait, then looks again into Herr Prigge's grey face, and then she shakes her head.

Number three is one house down. The door stands open. The farmer Traude Möller is taking dragging steps across the floor. Her hip joints haven't worked for years.

'I've seen you over there. Don't make anything of it, that's just the way the Prigges are. They were already that way, too, before his Siberia. They're not right in the head. And cheap! Do you know what Frau Prigge served, when she had me over for supper? Oxtail soup, that's what she served! The farthest end of the ox! That's the kind of thing they serve in the city, and everyone thinks it must be something fancy. She's never served goulash. But at the same time, the Prigges have made money with something.

They've scraped together quite a lot. But what they've earned in reality . . . , you know . . . they've earned the cow's death!'

Marie still hasn't uttered a single sentence. The farmer goes to the front room and sits down in an old armchair. She gestures at the sofa, and then points to the window: 'Look at what a good view I have of your farm, Fräulein Preuk. If you only didn't let those hedges grow too tall, I love to watch what's happening. Ah, well . . . ' Traude Möller looks very reflective for a moment. 'I can tell you. There's not much to be desired in this story—the Uhde farm over there, that's still passable, you can even visit over there if you'd like, but next to them, the Eier-Klüvers, Herr Prigge ran over and killed their youngest child, and he wasn't even sad. But Frau Eier-Klüver was, of course! She just kept repeating: Why did I survive the war, then? And then she started with the drink—because, well, to be more precise it was the second child that Frau Eier-Klüver had been forced to part with. The first child was granted a much shorter lifetime. He was thrown against the wall by his wet nurse when he was three weeks old, and it wasn't because she hadn't loved him, but because the nurse was actually old Herr Eier-Klüver's maid, and she had nursed the baby since the young Frau Eier-Klüver had no milk. And so this poor maid had to spend the entirety of a long June day harvesting hay with the others, tossing the bales onto the conveyer belt, hour after hour, and she was only allowed to take breaks to nurse the baby. And this throwing motion haunted her even in her dreams at night, and so that's how it all came to an end for the little nurseling. It's hardly surprising that Frau Eier-Klüver can no longer cope with the world!' She's telling her all of this in confidence, Traude says. 'Not to hear it later on being gossiped about by someone else! But when Eier-Klüver invited me over the last time, she opened the door and just stood there with a stocking in her hand. So, I wouldn't go over there so quickly! And in number seven, by the reservoir,' Traude says quietly, 'the farmer Uhde still lives there with his sister. He won't open up for you at all. His wife hanged herself from the window frame with a clothesline. They said she was still half-alive when he found her. But because he knew from somewhere that her brain, well, he grabbed his wife and hung down from her, to finish the thing. He was acquitted, probably because of the costs that his wife surely would have incurred. In a sense, then, he did a service to the community, basically.' Traude lifts the pot and puts it back down. 'But what am I going on about. It's almost half past five!'

The village road has holes and gullies from the winter. The roadside is bare and colourless in the evening.

February grows sallow and still, then a howling March. The spring twists across the fields. The months and seasons bring out humanity's rhythm. The smallest green on the sunny side of a ditch, grape hyacinths and crocuses in its wake. For a whole week, Marie picks from the fields. On the hillsides there shimmers a veil of grass, first visible when it rains, when the earth is dark underneath. And it rains a lot.

Marie sweeps the water from her farm with a broom. She sweeps the muck from the stalls with a broom. She sweeps and sweeps and works and fails to see the spring.

One day, an aged man arrives at the entrance gate. He walks with slow steps in the direction of the farm-house and stops and stands there until Marie emerges from the stables. She crosses her arms when she lays eyes on the man, as if she had to keep something from her heart, while the man attempts a cautious smile.

'It's me,' says Ruven.

'Yes, it's you.' Marie doesn't move. 'You're here alone? And you came on foot from the train station?'

'Hilde didn't want to come with me. You know her.'

From a distance, one can see two figures on the farm, which was, at the end of the day, only half of a farm. They stand there and simply look at each other. It lasts far too long for the neighbours' liking.

But something can be read in Ruven's eyes. A mixture of delight and shame. In front of him, there's something that owes its existence to him and yet has had to pull through without him. Finally, Marie turns around, and Ruven follows her into the house. She serves him bread and butter.

'You don't have your violin with you?'

'Not today.'

'What do you mean, today? Are you coming more often nowadays?'

Ruven lets his hand with the bread fall to the table. 'Probably not,' he says quietly. The clock ticks above the kitchen door. 'Will you be able to do all the work here?' He looks at his daughter. His light eyes are still strong.

Marie looks away: 'Everyone asks that.'

'Who will tend the fields? Do you even have a horse and cart?' Here, Ruven pauses for a long moment. 'Can you ask your brother?'

'My brother? You mean Friedjof?' Marie laughs bitterly. 'Gosche has a horse and cart. And Friedjof won't come. Friedjof, no one has ever loved him. You never once held his origin against him; you didn't want to know anything about it. For you, he's never been told it. And he hardly knows me. How should he—let's just talk about something else, Papa.'

Ruven slides to the front edge of his chair. Easy, Marie, he thinks, don't treat me this way. You don't know the story.

The afternoon turns a dark yellow. Shadows grow in the corners of the kitchen. Marie switches on the light. The bulbs above the table flicker briefly. Marie sits down at the table again, across from Ruven. He suddenly reaches for her hand. At first, she has the urge to pull her hand away.

'Marie, I . . . ' Ruven collects himself, and then: 'How will things go with us, now . . . ?'

That is a difficult question.

'I don't know,' says Marie, and now she really does pull her hand back. How should it go?

That is the evening; then comes the night. She has to get up twice, perhaps it's her kidneys. The doctor had told her that they needed warmth. It's cold in her house. Marie cries in the corridor and is far too tired to move. Perhaps she shouldn't have left her father so alone. But to do more was impossible. How could he just come over like that? A person didn't just come over like that, not after so many years.

At five in the morning the alarm clock rings. The barn smock is damp, the pigs dig with their noses in the trough. They don't know how tired their farmer is. They squint with their eyes and clap their ears to their head. Marie tosses them straw in their stalls. The pigs crawl headfirst into the straw and sleep there until noon.

The glory-of-the-snow turns the lawns blue underneath the linden trees. Another Easter, the church is full, everyone's there. They are still hoping for a cleaner slate: *O Christ, our Lord, has drowned your sins in love's boundless ocean.*

Afterwards, they all go to one of the farms for coffee. Everyone's a bit strategic, too. Whenever a person is nearby, one is careful not to speak ill of him or her. The holiday would feel too long otherwise, and they look at the things left lying around in such a way that their fingers start itching to touch them. But hardly has one lifted a hand to work on a Sunday that someone else looks over, disapproving.

Everyone sees everything. It is as if the village were made from glass. If something isn't seen, it doesn't exist. Slowly, the Sunday elapses, loquacious and sated, and the men soon gather at the pub, where an advertisement made of tin hangs from the door: *Coca Cola.* The wakefulness of the market. Never had a country been rebuilt faster. Or uglier. The bartender slams the ashtray on the edge of the bucket and wipes it down with an old rag. It will be a sow's summer, Herr Eier-Klüver declares, because that's what's written in the hundred-year calendar. It won't matter to his chickens, says farmer Uhde, and drinks. His chickens won't see the summer. Herr Eier-Klüver is the first to own a modern feeder. His eggs are so cheap that the neighbours give away their own and purchase the cheap eggs from

Eier-Klüver. 'It will be a sow's summer anyway,' he says and finishes his drink and leaves. And Uhde thinks gloomily, sow's summer or not, it will be a summer in any case.

At home, Marie opens her windows. In the evening, her hair and the curtains smell like April. And then this month, too, is already over, and Aunt Gesche arrives for a visit with a bouquet of lilies-of-the-valley. In a chequered headscarf she rides in on a bicycle, the lilies-of-the-valley lying in the basket behind her.

'Such a fine scent,' says Marie, 'it doesn't suit me at all any more.' She places the bouquet in the living room, stands in front of it and gazes at the flowers, their lovely poison. 'Sometimes, I forget to look up for a whole day. All I do is look at the floor in front of me, where there's always something that's fallen, or something to sweep,' she calls into the kitchen. And then in the doorway, she says very quietly, 'I also forget to breathe properly. And then I lie in my bed at night and take a breath for the first time all day.'

Gesche makes a worried face. 'How long do you want to keep doing this alone?' she asks. 'Aunt Meta at least had her old farmhand. He's not around any more, of course, but there must be others.'

'Not very many,' says Marie, 'And most of them are missing an arm or a leg.'

'And marriage?' Aunt Gesche asks and purses her innocent lips.

'Marriage?!'

Aunt Gesche points to the lilies-of-the-valley in the living room: 'Every year, I watch how they wither. That's when they become poisonous, when they start to wither. You can kill bulls with them.'

'What do you mean by that?'

'Just that without a man, a woman also becomes poisonous.' 'Oh, Aunt!' Marie pulls her apron off the hook. 'Such nonsense!'

'But someone must come here,' Gesche says, 'otherwise there will be no grandchild.' Then she goes home. Then she comes back. Then she brings John with her and soon Gosche, too. They pitch in everywhere.

'What is this, then? Is this my farm or yours?' Marie runs here and there and never gets an answer.

Gosche installs new windowpanes in the stable. Down below to the right, and up above in the middle. He smooths the putty with a single movement of his thumbs. Uncle John builds a veranda with a large double door to the garden. In the evening, the sun shines through it, and two steps lead down to the lawn. 'It should really have had three,' he says, 'a bit grand, you know, but you don't live so loftily yet, my girl. Just don't jump towards me over the two. One, two. That's how you do it.' He demonstrates, slowly. 'And the third one, you imagine.' He nods, examines the latch on the door and bobs up and down on the floorboards. 'Tongue and groove,' he says, 'that holds.' And then he simply stands there for a long time.

Outside, the sun shines flat across the hedges. Aunt Gesche kneels on a gunnysack in the garden bed until it's dark. 'Now all we need is a dovecote for pigeons,' Uncle John says into the darkness, 'tomorrow, in the middle of the farm.' He puts his tool away and thinks of the past, of the nights and days in the wainwright's, when his little brother Ruven still had pigeons.

'But this is enough, now!' Herr Prigge stands at the window across the street and counts. When he gets to eight, he sticks his thumbnail between his teeth and tears off a piece of the nail: 'She has pigeons already, now!' His wife doesn't answer. She only sits on the couch.

On the tenth of June, Gosche sweeps out the barn floor and mounts to the ceiling a light with a tin shade.

'She can never get enough,' hisses Herr Prigge as he bites down on his sore cuticle. 'She wants everything!' But no one hears him, because at that moment there is such a racket in the street that even the pigs in their stalls startle out from under the straw.

Aunt Gesche presses a hand over Marie's eyes.

'What is that?' Marie cries and sees only loud black spots, because Gosche was pressing so hard in her excitement.

'A dieselross tractor!' Gosche shouts. The geese run up to it, the gander in the lead, making himself as big as he can and nearly going under the wheels, he hadn't reckoned with those. Indignant, he drops back to his women and wins their support. In the farmyard, the green tractor stops, a loading platform in front, and on top of that a mower and a plough.

'That'll be installed at the front of the tractor,' says Gosche, 'because of the distribution of force.'

'Naturally,' says Marie, 'and brand new!'

The men gather around the new contraption and talk shop until five o'clock in the afternoon. At some point, Herr Eier-Klüver and Herr Uhde arrive, too. The gander is hoarse and waddles, perturbed, back and forth. The women sit on the porch.

'But now I've lost the point of all this,' says Marie. 'What are they preening themselves for, and making faces like they're plotting something?'

'Eh,' says Gosche, who is leaning in the doorway now, 'It's something like a helping hand. You'll of course have to do the hunting yourself. But sometimes you must bait the boars.'

'How you talk!' Aunt Gesche is indignant. 'As if the girl weren't bait enough already! We also discussed something completely different. It was more about . . . well, I have the old cane there . . . I got that from your Grandmother Preuk, it was always in the back of the wardrobe. And then suddenly it just, without anyone touching it, tipped out of the wardrobe, and then I thought, what does it want now, and picked it up and brought it to the kitchen . . . ' At that, everyone begins to interrupt her and soon the conversation has three voices. Everyone makes plans over each other, and then a bit of rum in the coffee, and it's also quite warm out today.

The baiting has results. Soon there is an invitation to the next birthday party. One of the young farmers on the other end of the village road; she hasn't ventured so far yet. A huge feast and special built-in bar in the room where the maids once slept. The maids have since been replaced by machines, and now one only dreams of the maids and drinks a beer alone.

'I don't know which blond is better,' says Max-from-the-bend and puts his beer glass down. He's combed his hair back with milking grease. His sister has rolled curls and even pantyhose from the little factory in the region, and they cling to her calves like dusty cobwebs. Marie wears the same cardigan she always wears, and the same dress, too. She smokes three Marlboros, until Max-from-the-bend invites her to dance. They dance for three rounds, and then she returns Max to the edge of the dance floor.

'No, you don't really want to do that,' he says.

'What do I really want, then?' Marie looks at him defiantly.

'To please men, for example.'

'I don't see a man here.' Marie hears laughing from behind her as she departs so hastily that some stare after her. On the road, she begins to run. She runs up to the farm gate and then she slows down again, so that the cousin or Traude Möller doesn't also try to ask her anything.

At home, she grows very quiet. I am just the way I am, she thinks. Through the window comes the fresh scent of hay. She sits on the floor and is as quiet as a stone. The only thing she can't do is stand up. How heavy a body can be, like an illness. And yet she is still so young. But she is a woman with a body and a body with an age, in which its history comes to light, in which its hardships come to light.

And in August, the cousin's end comes to light in her old body. She can't really stand up any more, and doesn't want to eat anything any more. Marie goes to the cousin's house to bathe her. When a person rots, and in summer, at that. Marie arranges flowers, vanilla flowers, they don't make it better and they wrap and unwrap around the bare calf.

'My child,' murmurs the cousin, 'as if you didn't have too much work already with your half of a farm. The other half should be willed to you outright, too.'

'Spare me!' Marie says. 'I'm making you coffee now, and then you'll stand up again and we'll go outside. It's such a beautiful August.'

Marie and the cousin make one round around the house. The old body is very light and thin. Like an abandoned wasp's nest, thinks Marie, I could almost carry her.

'Should we go inside?' She asks quietly.

'No, no.' The cousin straightens up a bit, 'I just had such a good idea, I need to take a couple more steps.' Marie must bring a pen and paper out to her, as she has to change something in her will.

When she's finally lying down again, the cousin is very relieved, also by the way that Marie tucks the blanket in around her.

'It's good this way. Here, at least, a person can feel where she ends, and where the world begins,' she chuckles and closes her eyes. 'Yes, yes, the world does indeed begin at the blanket.'

'Sleep now.' Marie strokes her white hair and then tip-toes out of the room.

Heavy and damp, autumn moves into the garden. The lamps in the house have a halo of mist, as does the moon. A great glow in the evening sky, the hoots and howls of the cranes, day after day, until they're all gathered for their autumn flight and then they're gone. Marie watches. She picks the last apples and stores them in a bed of straw. Then she writes to Gosche, who still doesn't have a telephone, to ask if he'll come for the butchering. And he does. With leather apron and whetstone.

Early in the morning, Marie puts water out. The sow gets her last meal, and Gosche already has her by the hind leg and pulls her out of the bay and along the corridor to the washroom. The heavy ladder leans on the wall, the sow should be on it, head over heels, but she doesn't want that. She runs, once towards Marie, once towards Gosche, raging all wild and mean and she absolutely does not want to die. Marie and Gosche are forced with alarm onto the table, so that the sow doesn't bite off one of their legs. She circles the washroom and bawls and brays so much that Marie covers her ears and Gosche stares, the knife in his hand, as he kneels on the tabletop.

'She doesn't want to,' cries Gosche, 'What a catastrophe! She just doesn't want to!'

'Then leave her.' Marie sat down. 'Then she should go back in her stall.'

The whole room smells of mortal fear. The light-coloured hooves skid away around the curves. Gosche has to jump onto the stove and push the door to the corridor open from there, so that the sow finally clears away.

'Well, you can get down off the table now,' he says and takes a seat on a chair and tries to catch his breath. 'If anyone had been looking in the window,' he says, 'he would have gone straight to fetch the doctor, to bring us to the asylum. Good heavens!' Then he looks at Marie. 'Well, and you? There's no real farmer's wife hiding inside of you. A bit too many notes heard in the cradle, that makes an impression.'

'Then I'll just overwinter without sausage. Or bring the pig to the butcher.'

'Of course you'll be bringing the pig to the butcher!' Gosche stands up again. 'We won't be jerked around! I'll get the meat hook and we'll go! But not this sow. She's too intelligent. You'll be able to breed her. Grab the stag, the spotted one, he'll have to be taken out of the stall anyhow.'

But he should be brought farther away, not to the neighbouring village, argues Marie. The butcher in the neighbouring village is always coming around and asking after bull calves for knackwurst. The calves should be damp still, and shouldn't have had a single drop of milk yet. And then he was to shove the damp calves into a sack—horrible!

'Well, then we'll take your stag farther away,' says Gosche, 'it doesn't make a difference to me.'

The trailer returns in the afternoon with three tubs full of pork. The bacon soon follows, it will be smoked in the yard. Marie cooks the liverwurst until midnight, the rest goes in the barrel of brine with a bit of saltpetre, salt and sugar, and at some point it's done, too, and Marie relaxes. Until Christmas, she hardly works at all.

On the first day of Advent, the cousin waves her over and says, 'Bathe me carefully today, Marie. I'll be exiting the stage.' This soon becomes a corpse washing, however, because the cousin can't wait any longer and exits while Marie is boiling the water in the kitchen and it sounds like applause under her headscarf. And so she washes the dead body, for as long as it is still warm, combs the thin white hair, binds the chin and stays overnight. When it grows too uncomfortable for her, she talks loudly into the silence. She speaks with the cousin as if she still lived, and opens the window at three in the morning and lets out what wants out.

There is a modest funeral, and even the wake is not particularly lavish. The sisters of Herr Uhde and Frau Eier-Klüver go home early. Marie isn't invited, and she has also inherited nothing.

They hadn't received a single napkin ring, the Uhde sister complained on the way home. And she'd cared for the cousin completely for free. Frau Eier-Klüver doesn't answer. She has to concentrate very hard on the path because it's always trying to veer away from her.

Marie sits at Traude's, who also wasn't invited, and Traude knows the whole story. 'You see, here comes the oldest sister.' She points at one of the women, who is walking up to the entrance in a black coat. 'She did nothing for the cousin! But her second son is apparently inheriting the other half of your farm. Unseen. He apparently lives in the city.' Traude squeezes her eyes shut. 'But I only see a couple of old women. He must be too busy in his city. Hopefully it won't be uncomfortable, when he's our neighbour.'

There's a clamour that night. The noises move through the darkness alone. Then headlights streak over the farm. Marie smokes at the window and watches. 'The heir is beautifully motorized,' she says softly.

The following day, the first snow finally falls. Marie shovels the path to the barn. She doesn't look once at the house next door and is soon back in the kitchen, settling into her needlework. But then she stands up again and walks to the mirror for the first time in a long time. She combs her hair and pins it up neatly. She presses her skirt smooth and paces back and forth, far too unsettled to sit still. She even carefully puts on her single earring, before taking it back out again. Why must I make myself beautiful? Is he making himself beautiful? Probably not, thinks Marie, and yet today, she often finds herself unnecessarily in the entryway which offers the best view of the house next door. Then she goes back in the kitchen. She nearly misses the knocking. She smooths her dress again and goes to the door. She waits a moment, so that her breath doesn't betray her, and then opens it.

There he stands, the heir. He looks at her, disbelieving, and forgets everything he'd been preparing to say on his walk through the hedge. Such a thing.

'But now I'm shocked,' Marie says quietly.

The man at the door averts his gaze and blinks at the barn, as if there were something to read on the weathered boards. 'As am I,' he says. Then he turns back to look at her again. 'But I did say that I would come back.'

Marie moves to the side and nearly steps into the umbrella stand. 'Then come in, Gunnar Teede, you'll find the kitchen down the corridor.' And gazes after the giant man, who fills out the space from floor to ceiling. One knows where the world begins, she thinks. What could one say? She gestures towards one of the chairs. Gunnar remains standing and self-consciously rubs the back of his neck with one hand. One of Marie's feet is cold, the other hot. 'Do you hear the cows?' she asks. 'Two of them belong to you, now,' she says, 'and eight to me.' She grins.

Marie milks Gunnar's cows first so that he can take them away soon. When she's finished, she waits. She hears his steps in the farmyard, his cough. She presses her face into the round belly of a cow. It is entirely quiet. It sounds as though two people are waiting. She turns around and Gunnar is a shadow in the door, but then he turns away and leaves and she strokes the smooth hide of the black pied cow for a long time.

Later, she sits in the kitchen and counts the week's money. She miscounts three times. The pencil snaps. She can't count any more. She listens to the noises in the stables. She hears the way Gunnar talks to the cows. He hasn't yet driven the animals over to his property.

Marie doesn't look up when he comes into the kitchen. He needs fewer steps than she does to go from the door to the table, and then he's standing behind her. She nervously adds up the items. It was an expensive week. Gunnar lays his hands on the back of her chair. Then he bends over her and props himself on the table and reads the numbers. 'That one can miscount so beautifully,' he wonders.

At night, Marie leans on the windowsill and gazes across the farm. She waits until all the lights in the village have been extinguished. Then she pulls on her coat and quietly leaves the house. The soft snow absorbs the sound of her feet. The door across the way is not closed, it creaks as it opens, but they both act as though it was completely silent. Marie feels her way across the dark floor. She hears Gunnar locking the door behind her, and the night on the floor is enormous.

They are married in the early summer of 1955. Marie totters around in the calf-length sugarloaf of a dress, with swan feathers from the estate pond on her head and a tightly bound bouquet in her hand. The night before, the neighbourhood smashed cups and plates in front of their door, and everyone was a little drunk from that point onward, except for Marie. Not on her wedding day, either. Instead, she's almost pale. Pale, too, is her father, who sits mutely next to his wife at the long table until he finally stands up in order to very carefully play the violin. But it doesn't go as smoothly as it should. Too many old and happy weddings come into Ruven's mind, and he feels a melancholy that he hasn't felt for a long time. But at least he feels something. Finally, he puts the violin away and stands for a moment behind his chair. Then he quietly says, 'You know, everything has changed so much. Perhaps I don't need violins any more. I almost hear the music better without the violins. These gowns made of wood on which music only breaks, like the ocean on the shore. But I don't want to let go of one thing, that is, what happens to the violinist? What happens, when, confronted with loud music, he has forgotten to love? A man who has acquired fame, one forgives him for such a thing. One says, he had to dedicate himself entirely to his subject. But if a musician never amounts to much. What was his life, then? This is what I ask myself.' Here, he sits and doesn't say anything more for the rest of this day, until Hilde insists that it's time to leave and extends an icy hand to Marie.

It's only once the two of them are gone that it turns into a cheerful wedding. With polonaise and spinning and a lot of light and many shadows, for the establishment of a new wedding party and a new marriage.

As a gift, Marie receives the inherited cane from Aunt Gesche. 'It doesn't work any more, I admit,' she says, because the cane had predicted for her an entirely different development, 'but in spite of that it can't be burnt or destroyed.'

That would be the practical thing to do with such canes, says Gosche. No one, though, dared do something like that to such a bone.

The first child arrives in November. 'Well,' whispers Traude, 'This doesn't really look like a premature birth. Not altogether marital, but what does that matter.'

'Yes, what does that matter,' Marie says and gazes into the cradle. 'You know, Traude, Gunnar and I, that had basically been decided and pronounced, just not by the pastor.'

Traude nods. 'And not by the cane, either.'

'No, not by the cane, either.' Marie traces the tiny hand with a finger. 'This one is a lovechild,' she says.

Herr Prigge develops a heart problem from all that his wife has to report to him. He can't look at all any more, himself. For the protection of his heart, he sits in the kitchen and only stares out back at his pasture, while his wife goes here and there and sometimes also glances out of the skylight, in order to contain this impertinent bliss.

'They stand there, in the middle of her yard in the morning sun, their faces on each other as though they'd been knitted together! And then they go back inside, hand in hand, and hand in hand they come back out again later!' Frau Prigge is all out of breath. And then in the evening, the two of them had sat down in that attached arbour, at which point she'd moved a bit onto the street in order really see things, and that's when, in their Russian hut, which was really already such a disgrace, they put a flask of liquor on the table and Gunnar Teed lay an arm on his wife's shoulder, without pulling the curtains closed! Herr Prigge stands with white foam in his pursed lips as she makes this report. She sees the veins bulge in her husband's throat. But her husband is silent. He stares with an empty gaze out the window and is silent and only lays a hand on his heart and breathes out four times with a gasp. Ah. Ah. Ah. Ah.

Three more children are born. At each birth, Ruven sends his greetings, nothing more. He lacks the strength for more. Marie also doesn't expect more from him. She doesn't know him at all any more.

Soon, she's taking all four children with her into the field, setting them in the shade at the edge of the field in the afternoon. Humming, they push little rocks back and forth, as if they were taking care of endless fields, while Marie thins the turnips.

It is the year that Armin Hary is the first person to run the hundred metres in 10.0 seconds. They hear it on the radio, and Marie lights a Marlboro and says, 'The world celebrates speed.' She sucks in the smoke and looks at her husband. 'And I always only see you, too, in double-time.' Gunnar nods and doesn't answer and soon goes back out to the fields.

Every year now, he buys another paddock. He enlarges the stalls, the passages between them, and the windows. Soon they have twenty cows and eighty pigs. The pig stall receives four ventilation propellers in the wall. Gunnar builds a dry well, a new dairy, and a hay barn. He digs a new and deeper well and leaves the little swamps and marsh blisters to dry in the meadow. In 1965, Gunnar sells the horses, burns the tackle behind the stable and buys a small combine harvester. He sits on it with a sunshade and pulls the barley, the rapeseed and the wheat under and through. And when the village road gets slick and black pavement, he borrows the paving machine and drives it across the farm, so that from now on, the geese's feet grow hot as they walk in the summer.

Why does he struggle so, Marie asks one day.

'Oh, I'm struggling for you. I do all of this for you,' says Gunnar.

But at that, Marie is standing in front of him, and she says, 'If you want to do something for me, then leave everything that you're doing for me now.'

'Not yet,' says Gunnar. 'But soon. When everything is finished.'

'Everything,' says Marie, 'will never be finished.'

Holy, holy, holy is the Lord. The music comes from an audiotape. The light falls through the coloured squares of the chapel window. The window depicts nothing, the colours have been arbitrarily arranged. They are reminiscent of nothing. Festivity is neutral as death. The pastor's speech is very boring and doesn't have anything at all to do with Hilde. Friedjof didn't come. *Holy, holy, holy is the lord.*

After the funeral, Ruven takes a grey bag and puts everything in it, shoes, clothes, pill dispenser. Then he takes a second grey bag and then another. In the evening, he piles the bags in the garage.

Ruven also throws the small rug protector away. He doesn't take off his shoes any more. He walks in his shoes across the white carpet. He sets a second and a third ashtray on the balcony beside the birdhouse, and night after night, he sits there wrapped in a blanket and sings and lures the pigeons.

The pigeons drink from a cup without handles. They suck the water without falling off. The male pigeon makes his throat fat and walks in a circle on the wide concrete ledge. Then he sticks one of the female pigeons with his beak and walks in a second small circle. Then they fly into the evening. '*Holy, holy, holy is the Lord,*' sings Ruven quietly. And images fly around in his field of vision again.

Yes, faced with the force of life and his love he had saved himself once again and made a Preuk out of a Klemm. One last attempt to forget Rahel, whose whereabouts he never managed to ascertain, despite many inquiries. She had disappeared from all traceable documentation.

For a short time, the circumstance of marriage had generated an easy warmth in Hilde, and between her furies of washing and cleaning she even sometimes had the urge to laugh, usually somewhat shrilly. She bought herself new dresses, and then some evenings she took them off in front of Ruven with alarming slowness. He had sympathy for her in such moments. Suddenly she seemed vulnerable, and he took her head in his hands and asked: 'Who are you, then?' Then she cried and closed herself off.

After sixteen years of marriage, Hilde finally died of the cancer in her stomach, and into the hole that she tore open and which also wouldn't stay open for long, suddenly Ruven's memory poured—at first, like shapes from a dream the images emerged the more he wanted to shove them away, but they were also like wraithlike targets in a carnival shooting gallery, which after every mental shot suddenly popped up again, with eyes and distinct features. They looked serious and concentrated, three graces of a spring, Emma, Lene and Rahel, over whom an empire had rolled its deaths in the course of just a few years, deaths that would have been enough for a thousand years. Holy, holy, holy is the Lord. And yet in his holiness he permits everything, everything, thinks Ruven and falls asleep on the sofa.

In the morning, he also eats breakfast on the sofa. The three violin cases lie atop the table in the kitchen. The kitchen has the best acoustics. Ruven sings in the kitchen, or he imagines singing. Whatever cannot or must not be lived is transferred inside.

He puts potatoes in the oven to bake and goes onto the balcony, to the pigeons. His ears are very tired. From the city, Ruven only makes out the fourth of the fire brigade. The rest is noise.

Thus it grows quieter and quieter around him. Year by year, people decrease. But he lives. For the bit of music that he still makes. Sometimes he even plays, still, as if he were at a celebration of something, duets with a former colleague from the orchestra.

He has the feeling, Ruven tells Gesche on the telephone one day, that things belong very close together, the pigeons, the water, the acoustics and the isolation, and that time is, in fact, slowly suspending itself. 'Aha,' says Gesche. 'But are you all right, then?' Then she quickly gets off the phone and calls Marie. She should concern herself. And Marie concerns herself. Every week a trip to Kiel, they hardly speak, but Marie tidies the apartment and prepares meals.

'We should bring my father here,' she finally says and shakes the tablecloth out in front of the veranda door. 'You should see how he's living! He's getting worse and worse. He doesn't hear the doorbell or the water boiling. He only hears when he wants to, but he never really wants to. He only ever just wants to think, and forget about the fact that he had been intending cook, until at some point he discovers the red-hot pot on the stove.' Marie stands in the veranda door with the tablecloth. 'We have the guest room,' she says finally.

'I'll have to think about it,' says Gunnar. 'It's not such a simple matter. Living together with your father under one roof. We should live at least far enough from each other that we can put on a jacket and shoes for a visit.' But at that, Gunnar gives Marie a look that tells her something will be figured out.

It is a warm afternoon in the year 1970 when Ruven steps out of his son-in-law's Opel. Marie takes two of the violin cases from him. He carries the empty one himself. With shy steps, he follows his daughter into the cousin's old house. She'd planned it this way. This way, they will have the farmyard between them. Marie shows him the two rooms and the kitchen. She stands a bit bowed over in front of him, although she's in the prime of her life. But she has to summon up love for him again. Before she leaves him alone, she says, 'What was, is not to be changed.' Then she leaves, before he can answer.

Most of the time, Ruven sits in his room plucking the strings of the violin. Sometimes he also sits in front of the house and looks out at the farmyard or at the road. The road is now two metres wider than it had been in the past hundred years. In front of the bridge over the tiny drainage ditch, there are four anti-tank barriers that can be raised up sinking into the asphalt. Who knows how to work the mechanism for these anti-tank barriers, Ruven once asked old Herr Eier-Klüver, but Herr Eier-Klüver only shrugged.

The automobiles now drive so fast on the road that they try to keep the grandchildren away with stories of torn-off heads. The farmers' automobiles are new each year. Well-dressed gentlemen carry the contracts with Mercedes and Opel in briefcases through the villages. Every year a new car in the garage, and every five years, a new stove and countertop. Such clean gentlemen also carry around descriptions of the newest poisons and nitrogen compounds. Everyone becomes a good poison brewer. Gunnar is the sole exception. And there is no new Opel in the front of his house either, instead he keeps the old one between rusted machines and meat hooks, and there is no kitchen for Marie, just an oven, cupboards, table, that's enough.

An enormous and beautiful chaos reigns on the farm. What Gunnar spent nearly fifteen years establishing grows over again, because he has suddenly changed direction.

One morning he was, like every day, in a big rush to leave to do the threshing and hadn't begrudged himself a break until the afternoon. The light-brown rapeseed plants had kept winding themselves around the cutting spool. He'd had to hack at the stems with a hatchet, a storm to the west, and finally he was back in the seat and moving on, but without looking closely at where he was going, until suddenly antlers emerged from all the shrubbery, then there were eyes rolled back, a death-jerk, and when Gunnar was out of his seat and down again and in front, there was a contorted animal on the ground, between rapeseed and mower, missing all four of its hooves.

He had threshed up a young stag. He had immediately killed it with a blow, to be sure, but the image was now in his head. 'Life is finite!' The animal seemed to shout in its death. 'Life rolls, and when it's all rolled out, then you'll lie there and not take a single step again, you'll only have what you've become!' Then he went back to the house, sat in the kitchen and drank schnapps, four, five, back-to-back, until the threshed-up stag swam in his vision. On that day he'd sworn never again to hurry, and instead to simply live.

Since then, once the necessary stable chores are done, he sits on the veranda and has visitors, and having visitors means talking. When there are no visitors, Gunnar raises golden pheasants and partridges and then, at some point, rabbits, and tells his stories to them. And when everyone is fed and taken care of, Gunnar walks across the farm looking for Marie, who hurries more now than she used to. He usually finds her in the laundry room next to the kitchen, and then he clasps her in his giant arms and lifts her up and says, 'There is nothing more delightful in the world than a Marie like this one!' And then Marie fights him off, growing red, and says, 'Let me down, Teede, I have to work.'

Ruven rarely sits over there with the children. His old reticence makes him bad company. Sometimes he plays them something, but the grandchildren aren't interested in his playing and it only makes Marie sad, and so he prefers to sit at home and converse with the air and the three graces, and more and more often with Fritz too, the old otter.

Gunnar had told him that Fritz Dordel had supposedly moved back to the heath farm after the death of his mother. But no one has set eyes on him. They say he's deathly ill, and so surely not very sociable. Ruven had listened to this and then circled the kitchen table the following night, first anti-clockwise, then clockwise. That Dordel got away with it. Anti-clockwise. That all those Dordels got away with it. Clockwise. But with what else was one supposed to have occupied the country. Ruven saw his reflection in the kitchen window. One day he'd visit Fritz. He wasn't yet at that point, but he thought about it. And then the next day, he walked in that direction, but it was a far distance to the heath, and after half an hour, he turned around on the path, because something occurred to him, something that he had to think about more. And then he assembled the parts of his life and put the images next to each other and suddenly he saw the tripling of a disquieting visage. Next to every grace was this face, and while he couldn't quite distinguish it yet, it always had the same name, Fritz. He headed out and over the farm.

Across the way, he knocked on Gunnar and Marie's door. When no one answered, he went around the house and through the side door into the laundry room, where the freezer and the washing machine were. Marie could most often be found here. She preferred sitting here to the garden. She had no more strength for the garden any more. Its life and its colours now gave her occasional anxiety.

When Marie noticed him, she startled: 'What's wrong with you?' The heating system started up, chugging. 'You look terrible!'

'I have to clean house, Marie,' Ruven says quietly. 'I've forgotten so much.' He smiles weakly. 'I don't know at all where to begin.'

'Let's not speak of these things.' Marie says quickly. 'I have too much to do.'

For months, Ruven searches for the stories. The Klunkenhöker woman emerges, Joseph, Sofie and the badger. How they all parade out. Ruven stands in the populated kitchen. The white table, the floor with grey tile, and in front of them, the smoke shapes that are growing more and more colourful as the sounds and the colours return home.

Ruven walks to the cupboard and takes out a paper sack filled with sliced bread. Every Monday, he climbs the three steps into the sweet-smelling car interior of the traveling shop and buys a sack like the one he's holding. The shopkeeper, Rindmöller, is so fat that he can barely find space behind his steering wheel. Once he's blared his three-note chord, he simply turns sideways in his seat and immediately has the counter and register in front of him, and with every sharp push on the brakes, the little scouring pads and rubber bands fall down onto it from where Frau Rindmöller had hidden them.

Ruven puts his sack of bread, butter, and often potatoes on the counter in front of Herr Rindmöller and has his counted-up, warmed-up money ready in his trouser pocket. Old Traude is already standing behind him with sherbet sweets, yellow and orange. They're for the grandchildren, she always says, and then asks after the violins.

'They sing,' says Ruven and: 'Come on over, hear them for yourself!'

'No,' says Traude then, 'I'm really too old for things like that, Herr Preuk.' And then she laughs, embarrassed.

Now Ruven puts a slice of bread on a plate and sits neatly at the table and eats. His temporarily liberated way of moving has become almost petty. Everything must be in its place. Everything now serves his orientation. He must be precise, distinguish the real things from the smoke shapes. For the dreams, too, are no longer certain to end when the night does. Today, well, today I'll to go the heath, he thinks, and sweeps the crumbs from the table onto the plate held beneath, washes up everything very slowly, the cup, the knife. Then he pulls on his Sunday jacket, puts his hat on, grabs the walking stick and sets off.

The heath farm isn't exactly where Ruven had it in his memory. Since way back when he'd left here with the elder Dordel, the house hadn't changed a bit. Even the straw is still here on the roof. It would burn very well. It would create a backdraft that would pull up the leaves of brittle plum trees in front of the house. Ruven stands still in front of the garden gate. He's been walking for over an hour and feels his bones.

He had taken the detour through his old village and over the church steps, in order to arrive at the farm from behind, over the juniper heath. A feeling, that he had to take the old path one more time and then digress from it at the end, had propelled him. Now his left hand holds onto the fence, he supports himself with the right on his walking stick and he has such dullness in his ears that he fears he has gone deaf. He knocks with his stick against the gate. Nothing. Perhaps he'd lost all of his hearing on his last walk to Fritz's. Just now, where he wants to hear the truth.

Ruven looks incredulously at the mute movements of his stick on the gate. He closes his eyes and takes a deep breath. He waits. Further, he says to himself, just a bit further, and opens his eyes again and hits the fence once more, this time much harder. He hears a dull clang, well, it was the effort, his blood pressure, perhaps also a bit of agitation. Ruven lifts the latch and walks slowly on the cobbled path around the western corner of this cottage. He breathes in deeply one more time, before he presses the white doorbell.

Through the ribbed glass of the house door, he sees a shadowy shape approaching. But that's a woman, he thinks. What kind of wife could the otter have, he thinks, no woman ever liked him.

When the door opens, there is a young, eager woman in a light blue smock standing before him. Ruven only sees the movement of her lips. He wants to visit Fritz Dordel, he murmurs. 'Tell him that the prodigal son is at the door.' The prodigal son, the lost son—lost, he thinks, yes, that is true. But it wasn't another person who lost me.

The woman at the door looks at him quizzically. Ruven nods. 'Tell him that Ruven Preuk wishes to speak with him.'

'You shouldn't have gone to such trouble, Herr Dordel is not very talkative.'

'And you, miss, may I ask who you are?'

She's his caregiver, the woman answers. She only comes by once a day to make sure everything is in order. And Herr Dordel's son never comes by.

'He has a son?'

The woman nods and shows Ruven to a room. It's the room where Ruven learnt the violin. Now Fritz is lying there in a large bed. His face is very grey, with a dark spot on his forehead. Two wizened hands rest on the blanket.

When he sees Ruven, Fritz squints myopically. Then he struggles to prop himself up on his elbows, raising his upper body halfway. His mouth forms a downward crescent, until he suddenly—and to Ruven's surprise—begins to laugh, clasping the spot on his forehead with a shaking hand.

Ruven stands mutely at a distance. Fritz quits laughing, looks up from his lower position and breathes laboriously. Ruven stares at him for a while.

'You shouldn't be more than ashamed yet,' he finally says.

Fritz looks confused. Then he begins to laugh again.

'That's good! Preuk, that's good! Come, sit!' Fritz points to a chair by the window. Ruven takes the seat without leaning back. He places both his hands in front of him on the knob of his walking stick and looks calmly at Fritz. They wait.

'We could also discuss the hunt first,' Ruven says finally, 'How is the big game, Fritz?'

Fritz gives a dismissive wave. It no longer interests him. Hunters today aren't interesting company, he says. They know neither how to sit patiently nor how to handle a gun. They are totally helpless, overwhelmed by the smallest thing. Fritz grows very talkative. One of these hobbyist hunters ran over a boar last fall, he was close by and drove over straight away because such an animal would ultimately really be worth something. 'And then he sits in his car and doesn't move! He should get off the boar, I said, but the man didn't react at all! I had to tear him out of his car and get it off the boar myself!' Fritz sits up on the edge of the bed: 'They call that hunting!'

The whole time, Ruven is looking calmly into his face. Once, he sticks his hand into his pocket and fingers something.

'But you, you've always been a good hunter, right?'

Fritz looks at him with distrust. 'Well, I can shoot.'

'And how are you with the dead?' Ruven asks, 'One has to master that, of course, one isn't permitted to be squeamish there.' He feels a bit dramatic, the way he's talking about the dead, but now he's already struck this tone.

'Who out of all of us is squeamish? I wasn't raised for squeamishness. No one was ever squeamish around me. But you're trying to get at something,' says Fritz, who smells a rat but just can't sort it out yet.

'Not necessarily,' says Ruven. 'I also just enjoy talking about the woods with you. They say, you know, that the woods have grown safer.'

'I didn't know when the German woods were unsafe. During the Thirty Years' War, perhaps, but since then?' Fritz lies back down again. His breath is loud and laboured. He touches his forehead again. 'What do you want, Preuk? Say it already.'

'I want to know what happened back then in the woods.'

'You mean the story with that Red?'

'Emma.'

'The old story? You're still on that old story? Unbeliev-able.' Fritz closes his eyes until he speaks again: 'That wasn't us, Preuk. You know we were on the wild boar hunt. The woman was only the connection. And the wild boars, they quite possibly ate their best sow themselves. They stopped that nurse, two of them. It looked like she knew them. She greeted them, even. Then they held something out to her, and when she shook her head, then they held something else out to her. Something like a book. But the woman only loudly said No. Then they dragged her into a house and then out again, and threw her into a ditch. She didn't move an inch after that.' Fritz thinks back. 'Then they pulled her out again, as if they'd thought of a new plan, and they laid her crosswise across the carriage seat and singed the horses' muzzle hair. None of you saw that, eh? And that's when the horses ran off.'

Ruven hasn't yet moved. 'You've not changed at all, Fritz. The way you tell that story. I almost wonder if I should stay any longer.'

'Stay,' says Fritz quietly. It almost sounds like begging. 'It's rare that someone visits. And how is this old story supposed to concern me? Should I be sadder?'

'I heard that you have a son. Why doesn't he visit?'

At that, Fritz laughs until he's out of breath.

'You get better and better, Preuk! Yes. I have a son. That's right. But he doesn't visit.' He turns a light blue. He seems to be trying to concentrate. His breath rattles. 'I'm at the end, Preuk. And now, of all times, you come here and want to hear my confession! Unbelievable.'

'I don't know whether I'm hearing your confession, Fritz. That's a matter for the pastor. Old stories are just coming to mind again, a story about my knife, for example, and a boy who didn't tell the truth about this knife for a long time.'

Fritz grows quiet. He blinks his tired eyes. 'You still remember that?' He glazes at the blanket. 'My old man broke my collarbone for that. Yes, Preuk, you were a bad person long before I was. Now we finally have it. And a coward, even.'

'Perhaps. But all I ever really wanted was to play music. I couldn't do anything else. But what did you want? You can say it now. We both didn't become anything. I'm not a soloist, and you're not an SS officer. Although we were both very gifted. But for me, the beginning of the war interrupted things. And for you, it was the war's end. We were disappointed. Someone once told me that the world is sick. I didn't understand it at the time. But now I understand. It was sick with trump cards, with enormous promises. With the jack of clubs. The small man who intended to grapple with the big answers had gotten lost and didn't know any more what he was supposed to do in the world. Myself, I always believed that without music, without all of the great music, I couldn't exist. I gave away everything for it. But perhaps I should have simply lived, like the others did. Just like the others. But what did you want? And what did you want from me?'

Fritz doesn't answer. Perhaps he's asleep, he's closed his eyes. Then he moves his lips. Ruven can't understand him. For a long time, he looks at the sick man. The light had grown so dim and dusky that Fritz was hardly visible in the bed. A heavy silence spreads itself across in the room. Then Fritz opens his eyes and stares directly at Ruven. As he does, he clasps his forehead again, as if it were reminding him of something, some kind of monumental story.

'You know so little,' he finally says. 'In fact, you know nothing. How the others actually lived. And they lived, yes, and they even loved you, but you know nothing about them. I, on the other hand, know everything. But me, they didn't love me.' He is already laughing again. 'Isn't that funny?'

Ruven stands up, with some trouble. For a couple of seconds he stands helplessly in front of the chair. There's a rushing in his ears. He makes a gesture with one hand, an utterly lost gesture. He opens his mouth, two, three times. Then he goes to the door and leaves and walks to the garden. There, lupines grow in the un-mown grass. There is a knife in Ruven's pocket. It's an old knife, and an old story.

'You can't do anything besides fiddle,' Fritz Dordel had announced triumphantly to anyone listening back then, perhaps six decades ago by now, because Ruven couldn't throw this knife in such a way that it stayed stuck in the bark of the village oak. It was a very bad knife with a bent blade that couldn't find a hold anywhere. But to tell that to the others—back then, Ruven was too proud for that.

What is wrong with you, his father had asked, when Ruven wouldn't eat anything at the table that evening. The boy was still so overwhelmed with humiliation, and he said, without thinking, because it just came so easily off his tongue, that Fritz Dordel had stolen his knife.

'Stolen,' said Nils Preuk with contempt, and then again: 'Stolen!?' And Ruven had only nodded, his face burning. 'He won't get away with that!' cried Nils, and after the meal he was taut with anticipation, even though it was nearly dark.

He had cursed on the same trip to the heath, and it was good that Ruven wouldn't be going there for his violin playing any more, and Old Dordel was no great musician anyhow. Up there, he'd knocked on the door so violently that Ruven felt as if he, too, were being struck. And when the door opened and old Dordel stood there, without any clue and smiling, Ruven nearly fainted.

'Your son steals,' Nils said coldly. And Dordel scowled at them indignantly, but then he said quietly, that's just like him, the devil, but the devil is different than Ruven. Then he'd turned around and shouted into the house: 'Fritz!' And when Fritz was at the door, the old man had hit him in the neck and said, 'There's another complaint already!'

Fritz looked confused and only said that he had nothing to do with anything. Then Ruven would help him remember, snarled old Dordel, and Ruven looked Fritz in the eye, himself quaking with fear, as he said, 'You stole my knife.'

'I didn't,' said Fritz, and his cracking voice ran through all possible notes in indignation.

'Did he? Or did he not?!' Nils Preuk was still red in the face.

'He did,' Ruven said again, because he couldn't go back now and because Fritz had started it with the enmity, anyway.

Before old Dordel slammed the door shut in order to thrash his son just behind it, Ruven tried to steal a second glace at Fritz, but his eyes refused to do it. Later that night, Ruven was out of the house with the knife, running to the church on foot, and he stuck the knife in a hole under the steps.

Now he had it in his pocket. But it is bad and dull, he thinks, no one can get up to any mischief with it now, and he turns to the house again, goes back into the stinking room and stands in front of Fritz's bed. He looks down at him for a few moments, then pulls the knife out of his pocket and places it on the small bedside table.

'I'll be coming more often, now' he says. 'Even if I were to take your life, it wouldn't bother you. What do you have to lose? You haven't anything to lose. But you can receive something. I'll bring my violins with me. If I shouldn't know, then at least you should know.'

'How often do you want to come?'

'For every violin, or for every woman, one time. So, three days. Three days are not too many.'

Ruven turns around, exhausted, and observes out of the corner of his eye how the whole body of the terminally ill man begins to shake, until he convulses and one last ringing laugh breaks out. While the door shuts, he hears Fritz shout: 'Yes, there is something, Preuk! There is quite a lot! I have a son! A son, Ruven! He'll inherit this here, and then you'll be neighbours! But there is even more! Come again tomorrow, with your violin! Bye, bye! Bye, bye!'

On the first day, Ruven comes with the little violin from Joseph. And he plays, and at first it's nothing, but then. Fritz had let himself be seated in the armchair. His furtive gaze. He had a good grip on himself for a while. But then, bye bye. He can't bear it. It is as though Emma were laughing loudly in the violin music, so much so that he has the urge to look around for her. The light grows heavy. Ruven, too, must conserve his strength, in order to endure this. Bye, bye, both of them vanish, they have no more strength.

On the next day, Ruven comes with the Linde'sche. Lene next to the juniper tree. Lene in the white house on the Elbe, her light hair, the blue skirt and the knitting. Fritz is lying down and stares at the blanket. His eyes fill with tears.

'And now,' asks Fritz, 'What will tomorrow be?'

'Tomorrow I'll come for the last time,' says Ruven. And he comes, with the empty case. Rahel. The heath outside, silent and barren. Ruven sings. His aged voice quavers. He sings Grieg, *taa-da-daa-dee da-dee-da-da* . . . Fritz remains silent, only keeps rubbing the spot on his forehead, feeling the grey skin with his fingers.

Fritz Dordel shot himself in the head last night, Marie says the next day, when Ruven seeks her out in the laundry room. Cleanly, through the forehead.

'He didn't really want to suffer, of course. Hunters always have the nerve not to suffer like normal people,' she says, 'A hunting licence is not a licence to avoid fate.'

'Perhaps he just didn't want to betray the name of his son,' says Ruven, watching Marie through the open door.

'But I think I finally know it.' He thinks he sees Marie briefly wince, and when she lays a hand on his arm for the first time since her childhood, he begins to tremble.

'Yes,' says Marie, 'Perhaps he didn't want to spill anything. But despite that, he left a message behind for you, a note with a number and a name. Herr Eier-Klüver brought it by. You should call it.' Then Marie lets go of Ruven's arm, walks slowly into the kitchen and returns with a piece of paper.

'Gertrud Meidner.'

Never heard of her, Ruven thinks and takes the note.

There is no reason for conjecture. But a certain notion still rises within him.

'You wish to speak to Frau Meidner?' 'Yes,' Ruven says quietly into the telephone, then still more quietly, 'Perhaps also Rahel.' His tired hand can barely keep the grey plastic of the receiver to his ear.

'Oh, but this is very unfortunate,' says the woman's voice on the other end, 'Frau Meidner died three days ago. You're calling three days too late. Were you acquainted?'

The washing machine shudders on the polished concrete. Foam in its eyes. The refrigerator is full of meat. They rest on top of light green roof batten, in case the rain doesn't end and everything here is underwater in the winter. The fridge hums with a tired pulse. Ruven stands in the middle of the room and hums quietly along with it.

Then silence.

A deep futility settles among the household appliances. No home. No place. Only absence. In the artificial honey, a fly perishes atop the twisted golden Jacob's ladder. Another keeps flying around and does its daily work. Already another summer. Or soon, autumn. They say that in the autumn, the birds sing for no reason at all.